THE RED KING

A Soldier With Richard the Lionheart, Part II

Richard and the Master of St. John.

ROBERT BROOMALL

A Bluestone Media Publication

Books by Robert Broomall

California Kingdoms
Texas Kingdoms
The Lawmen
The Bank Robber
Dead Man's Crossing (Jake Moran 1)
Dead Man's Town (Jake Moran 2)
Dead Man's Canyon (Jake Moran 3)
Death's Head, A Soldier With Richard the Lionheart
K Company (K Company 1)
Conroy's First Command (K Company 2)
The Dispatch Rider (K Company 3)
Murder in the Seventh Cavalry
Scalp Hunters (Cole Taggart 1)
Paradise Mountain (Cole Taggart 2)
Wild Bill and the Dinosaur Hunters

For James, Heather, Diane

and

Claire

PROLOGUE

ABU FLATH LED the horse toward the castle.

The castle was small and nondescript—shabby almost, if a castle could be called shabby. It was formidable, though. It sat at the top of a steep mountain with a sheer drop behind it, and the pine trees all around had been freshly cut down so that an enemy could not advance upon it unawares.

The horse was a big Frankish war beast with a high-backed saddle. Across the saddle lay a suit of Frankish armor, the mail gleaming in the summer sun. A Frankish longsword and conical helmet were tied to the saddle's pommel.

As Abu Flath neared the castle gate, he was challenged by a guard on the wall. "What do you want?"

Abu Flath, who in another life had been called Tarik, cried, "I bring a gift for the emir." With a sweep of his hand, he indicated the horse and armor.

"Leave it," the guard told him.

"I wish to offer it to the emir personally. I wish to join your company."

The guard conferred briefly with one of his fellows, then disappeared. Abu Flath waited a long time in the sun, then the castle gate creaked open and the Emir Sanjar al-Imani appeared, flanked by a pair of heavily armed guards. Sanjar approached Abu Flath while the guards ran behind them and took positions facing down the mountain, as though expecting an attack.

Sanjar was a mean-looking fellow with a greasy face and bad teeth. His oily moustache twisted upward at the ends. He wore a robe of expensive red silk, though, trimmed in gold thread, and the sword at his side was of the finest Damascus steel.

Sanjar stared at Abu Flath with hard eyes. "You have something for me?"

Abu Flath indicated the horse and armor.

Sanjar walked around the horse, looking it over, patting its rump and neck. He examined the armor, tested its weight. He took the sword from its scabbard, swung it a few times. "It is a good horse," he said. "The armor is of no use to us, but it is well made and we can sell it back to the feringhees for a good price. The sword I may keep for myself. How came you by this?"

Abu Flath said, "A feringhee warrior, lord. I found him asleep at a well, and I killed him."

Sanjar considered. "He must have been lost, or maybe running from a fight with our people. A scout would not be so heavily armored. How did you kill him?"

Abu Flath drew a thumb across his throat. "I left his head by the well as a warning to the infidels."

"Good work." Sanjar nodded in appreciation. "This armor belonged to a big man. You must be very strong for one so young."

Abu Flath said nothing.

"And you wish to join us?"

"I do, lord, if it pleases you."

"Tell me why I should not take this gift and send you on your way, or—better yet—kill you?"

Abu Flath gave a half-shrug and smiled. "Because if you do that, my long journey here was for naught."

Sanjar grinned at this audacious young man. "You are fortunate. It happens we have need of a man. You may join us."

"Thank you, lord."

"Where do you come from? Homs or thereabouts, from your accent."

"Yes, lord. I was left on my own at an early age, and I have been living by my wits ever since. I wish to make my way in the world, but I have found I cannot do it by myself. I had heard of you, and I was on my way here to offer you my services when Allah sent me the feringhee so that I might demonstrate my skills."

Sanjar stared down the mountain in the direction the guards were facing. "Tell me, have you seen any soldiers about?"

"Feringhees? No, this is the only—"

"Our people, these would be. Nizari fanatics."

"Nizaris, lord?"

"A religious sect. Foul creatures who demand I pay them tribute, even though they have no authority over me. Others have given in to them, but by the beard of the Prophet, I shall not."

Abu Flath shook his head. "I have seen no one, lord."

"You're certain? No one who could have been a spy, perhaps?"

"No, lord."

Sanjar seemed to relax. "Good, good." He beckoned Abu Flath. "Come."

Sanjar led Abu Flath through the castle gate, the two guards following, walking backwards, still facing down the mountain. The first thing Abu Flath saw in the castle yard was a post to which a man was chained. At least it seemed to be a man—he was so starved and burned by the sun it was difficult to tell. His clothes were in tatters; his blistered, blackened flesh hung off him in strips, the newly exposed skin beneath bubbling in the sun. He was so covered with flies and maggots that he seemed to be moving in some kind of eerie dance. A guard gave him a sip of water—just enough to keep him alive and prolong his agony.

"This is the man you are replacing," Sanjar told Abu Flath. "He disobeyed an order." Sanjar smiled. "You won't disobey me, will you?"

Sanjar took Abu Flath to a guest room for the night, as a reward for killing the feringhee. In the morning they would find him a permanent billet.

If the outside of the castle was nondescript, the inside was anything but. The room Sanjar gave Abu Flath was small but well furnished, which was to be expected since Sanjar and his men made their living by brigandage. Sanjar himself had begun as a roadside thief and murderer near Aleppo. He had formed a gang and eventually they had taken this castle from its owner and claimed it as their own. That was years ago. They raided caravans, travelers, villages—anyone or anyplace where money or items of value might be found.

Sanjar was adept at following the political winds, and he had always stayed in good stead with those in authority, paying them well, which was why he had never been hunted down and punished.

Abu Flath was provided with new clothes, food and drink. "Would you like a woman?" Sanjar asked. In deference to Abu Flath's youth, he added, "You have had a woman before?"

Abu Flath didn't want a woman, not tonight, but he said, "I have, lord, and, yes, that would be most excellent."

They sent him a slave girl who couldn't have been more than fifteen. She offered to stay the night, but Abu Flath sent her on her way when he was finished with her, claiming weariness. After that, he lay on his bed, waiting.

It was late. Quiet.

Abu Flath rose. He left the guest room and made his way through the castle. He moved silently, as he had practiced a hundred times in the Old Man's castle, passing the few guards and servants who were awake without their seeing him, as though he were invisible. He left the hall and went to the mews, where Sanjar kept the falcons which he loved more than life itself, or so it was said. He stayed there for a few minutes and left, carrying a sack. He then went to the stables, where he procured a long coil of rope.

He slung the rope over his shoulder and crossed the castle yard to the steps leading up to the catwalk. He searched for the nearest guard, found him. The man was stationary on the catwalk, gazing over the darkened mountain side.

Silently Abu Flath mounted the steps. He watched the guard, matched the man's breathing, became one with him. He crept up behind him, cupped a hand over the man's mouth and slit his throat in one smooth, practiced motion— not like his fumbling efforts the first time he had killed a man, in training.

He lowered the dead guard to the catwalk and moved further down the walk so that he would not slip in the guard's blood. He tied one end of the rope over a merlon and lowered the rest of the rope over the side.

He waited, watching for more guards, but none came. There was a tug on the dangling rope and it tightened. Sounds of scraping. A black-clad figure appeared on the rope and climbed over the parapet. It was Abu Flath's trainer, Harun al-Asad, the lower end of his black keffiyah pulled across his face. He was followed up the rope by a dozen other men.

Wordlesslly Abu Flath led the party to Sanjar's house. They killed the dozing guard at the door and hid the body.

They entered Sanjar's chambers, which were as lavishly furnished as those of a sultan, and followed the sound of snoring to Sanjar's bed. The emir lay with two naked women, one on either side of him.

One of the women seemed to sense their presence. She opened her eyes to see Abu Flath, who placed a finger to his lips for silence. Terrified, the woman nodded. Asad gently laid a hand over the other woman's mouth and woke her.

Her eyes went wide in the semi-darkness but she knew enough not to struggle. The dagger in Asad's hand was inducement for that. The women were quietly assisted from the bed, and two of Asad's men ushered them from the chamber, still naked.

Abu Flath took the sack he had brought from the mews. He stuck his dagger inside and drew it back out, with Sanjar's prize gyrfalcon, Jabalea, impaled on its tip. The bird's head hung loose where Abu Flath had snapped its neck.

Abu Flath held the dead falcon under Sanjar's nose, letting the feathers tickle him. Sanjar snorted and shook his head. Abu Flath tickled him with the feathers again. Again. Sanjar sniffed, shook his head harder, and woke to see the dead bird in his face.

Sanjar gave a shout and scrambled backwards on the bed. He looked around at the men standing there. He was naked; his greasy hair tumbled over his forehead and face. Recovering his wits, he grabbed for his dagger but it was not there. Asad had taken it.

Asad nodded to Abu Flath, who tossed the dead gyrfalcon in Sanjar's lap. Sanjar stared at his prize possession.

"You owe tribute to the Master Sinan," Asad told Sanjar. "We have killed the falcon because you are late. You will pay what you owe now, or you will die."

Sanjar was finally able to take his eyes off the bird. "I will pay," he said hurriedly. "I will pay."

"One thing more. Your tribute is now double. See that it is paid on time from now on. We will not be so friendly when next we visit you."

"Yes, yes," Sanjar burbled. "I will." His eyes darted between these black-clad men and his dead falcon. His eyes met those of Abu Flath, but Abu Flath showed no emotion.

~

"It is time," Asad said.

Abu Flath's training was complete.

He had learned riding and climbing. He had learned the use of sword, knife and strangling wire. He had learned how to employ poisons and how to move as silently as a shadow. He had learned to go long periods without food or shelter, with only the word of Allah to sustain him.

He had been punished when he did badly, deprived of food and warmth, and he had been rewarded when he did well, with hashish and alcohol and women. He was told the women were virgins but suspected they were whores or slaves. He didn't care. The true virgins would be his when he reached Paradise.

Asad wore a black robe and turban, as always, and for this occasion Abu Flath dressed in the same fashion, as Asad led him into the great hall of Masyaf and the presence of Sinan, the Old Man of the Mountains.

Originally from Persia, Sinan had been master of the small Nizari sect for more years than anyone in the hall could remember. The Nizaris had formerly been among the most fundamentalist of Muslims, but under Sinan's direction they abjured the strictest tenets of their faith, especially concerning the use of alcohol. Their headquarters was the mountain fastness of Masyaf, from where they demanded tribute from lords as far away as Damascus. Those who did not pay were assassinated by Sinan's men—indeed, the Nizaris were sometimes called the Assassins—and as a result, treasure flowed in. No man, however well protected, was beyond their reach. Even the great Sultan Yusef, Salah-ad-Din, feared the Nizaris and had made peace with them.

The hall was large and ornately decorated. From his seat the Old Man watched the two men approach. For all his wealth, Sinan dressed plainly and his grey beard grew long down his chest. It was said that he had once ordered one of his disciples to leap off the mountain top to his death in order to impress a visitor with his men's loyalty, but Abu Flath did not know if this was true.

Asad knelt before Sinan, head down. Abu Flath did the same. At last Sinan said, "Rise."

The Old Man studied Abu Flath with cold, hard eyes. It was said that the Old Man had the power to read minds, so Abu Flath tried to keep his own mind blank. To Asad, Sinan said, "He has passed all his tests?"

Asad said, "He has, lord."

"Good." To Abu Flath, Sinan said, "You are now ready for the task which has brought you to us, the task that will gain you entrance to Paradise."

The Old Man beckoned a waiting servant, who advanced, bowed and presented Abu Flath with a dagger.

So it was to be a stabbing. Traditionally the Old Man presented his assassins with the weapon to be used in their mission. The dagger looked plain, but the blade was sharp as a razor's and the balance was perfect. It was a weapon of beauty.

The Old Man beckoned another servant, who handed Abu Flath a white robe.

"Put it on," the Old Man ordered.

Abu Flath unfolded the robe. It was of an unfamiliar cut, with a deep hood attached. It was made from heavy, coarse wool, the kind that rubbed the skin raw. Forgetting himself, Abu Flath showed his distaste for the garment. "What is this, lord? What is my mission?"

At another time, the Old Man might have erupted in deadly rage—he did not tolerate being questioned. Now he merely chuckled and said, "You are to become a feringhee holy man."

PART I

Chapter 1

ROGER RECOGNIZED HIS assailant's voice—he'd heard it hundreds of times in the last year—but it was difficult to reply with the dagger's blade pressed against his throat. "The ring is mine," he croaked. "My father gave it to me."

The blade pressed harder; Roger felt blood trickle down his neck. "You lie," the voice said.

"I'm telling the truth! My father left me at an abbey as a babe, along with this ring and a bag of silver for my upbringing."

The blade's pressure eased a fraction. "Which abbey?"

"Huntley. In England. Trentshire."

"Who was your father?"

"I don't know. He never gave the abbot his name."

The blade was removed from his throat. Roger drew a deep breath, gulping in air, and turned to face one-eyed Henry of Deraa. Henry was still in his armor and covered with dried blood.

The two men stared at each other for a long moment. Henry's good eye gave away nothing, but realization sank in on Roger. He could scarce believe it, but it had to be true. There could be no other reason for Henry's reaction. He had recognized the ring, and he could only have recognized it if -
-

15

Henry fetched Roger a blow on the jaw that laid him on his back.

Roger lay on the floor of the church turned stable, blinking and trying to recover his senses.

"You damned fool!" Henry said. "You imbecile!" He went to kick Roger in the side and only with effort held himself back. "I left you at Huntley so you'd have a secure life, so you'd never have to endure hardship like this, and the first chance you get, you run off and become a damn soldier. You addle-pated pile of camel dung." Then he did kick Roger in the side. "Why did you throw it all away?"

Roger knew enough not to tell Henry how he had longed for adventure and to see the world, how he'd hated life in the cloister. So he told him about Ailith and how he had saved her from being tortured as a witch, and how he'd killed Auberie in the process and had to flee for his life.

Henry growled, thinking that over. "A witch, eh? Hmph, I guess it couldn't be helped." He kicked Roger in the stomach again. "For an idiot, you've done well for yourself. A knight already, and commanding of a company of footmen, though I'd be sight happier were you still in the cloister."

Roger started to say something but Henry beat him to it. "Why are you lying on the ground? It's not bed time. Get up."

Roger climbed to his feet, and Henry indicated his sliced cheek. "You'll have a nice scar there."

"At least I still have both my eyes," Roger shot back.

To Roger's surprise, Henry laughed at that. "Observant little bastard, aren't you? Well, you're here and there's bugger all to be done about it. You've a lot to learn about being a knight, but I'll train you."

"Maybe I don't want you to train me."

Henry kicked him in the knee.

"Ow!" Roger said, bending over.

Henry said, "Maybe I don't care what you want. You'll do what you're told. The first thing a knight has to learn is how to follow orders."

Roger straightened and winced from the pain in his knee. "If you've finished hitting me and kicking me, perhaps you'll be good enough to answer the question that's bothered me for as long as I can remember."

"What's that?"

"Who was my mother? And why did you leave her?"

Henry looked down. Outside, the sound of celebration continued unabated. Here it was quiet and cool. After a moment Henry said, "Her name was Aethelflaed, and I've tried to bury her memory for over twenty years."

"Why?" Roger demanded.

"Because I killed her."

Chapter 2

HENRY TOOK A turn around the small building. "I've never talked of this before, but I guess you have the right to know. Your mother was beautiful, but she wasn't built for hard work or child bearing. Because of that, and because she was devout, she had originally planned to enter the Church, but I persuaded her to marry me instead.

"She was the daughter of a freeman, and I was a young knight, eager to make my way in the world. We met by chance and fell in love. It was the kind of love these damned troubadors sing about, the kind you don't think exists in the real world. But with us, it did. We came from different levels of society. Plus, I was French and she was English. We were outcasts, but none of that matters when you're in love.

"I had a small holding in south Trentshire—I'd won it in a tournament—and there we lived, happy and well away from the world. In due time Aethelflaed became pregnant, but she had a miscarriage. Her mother and the older women advised her not to attempt to have more children, but I . . . I wanted sons and I persuaded her to try again. I persuaded her that it would be all right."

His one good eye stared into the past. "She died in childbirth. It was long and painful and very . . . " His voice tailed off.

Roger felt his stomach twist.

After a moment Henry went on. "I blamed you for her death. You took her from me, and I hated you. I wanted to kill you. I almost did, too—my dagger was drawn, but I was restrained at the last moment by a priest. I knew that every time I looked at you it would remind me of her, and I couldn't live with that, but I also knew that Aethelflaed would want no harm to befall you. So I gave you up. Huntley Abbey has a good reputation. You could have had a good life there, the kind of life your mother would have had if it wasn't for me."

"Do you still hate me?" Roger asked.

There was a pause, then Henry said, "No. I killed her, not you."

"And the ring?" Roger said.

"The ring belonged to your mother's great-grandfather—Aelwulf, she said his name was. He was an ealdorman or something like that, and he came from the ruling family of a kingdom called Mercia, part of which I gather included Trentshire."

Roger had never heard of Mercia, but he bet Fauston would know what it was.

Henry went on. "The ring had been passed down through the generations. Aethelflaed was the last of her line. Now you're the last. The ring means nothing to me, and I thought . . . I thought you should have it."

Roger said, "So after you abandoned me, you came here to atone for your sin?"

"If that's what you want to call it."

"And you never remarried?"

"Does it look like I remarried?" he snapped. "No, I never remarried. I never looked at another woman and I never will." He straightened and gazed at Roger as if seeing him for the first time. He gestured with his hand. "You look like her, you know. She'd have been proud of you."

One part of Roger wanted to embrace this man, while another part wanted to kill him, and a third part was too stunned to have any reaction at all.

At that moment both men became aware of a commotion on the city walls, coming from the direction of the Accursed Tower.

Chapter 3

"AMAZING!" RICHARD SAID, looking around in boyish wonder. He had never been in an Eastern city before. "The architecture, the layout—it's far grander than Toulouse or Montpellier." With a grin he added, "It's certainly better than London. God's breath, a drearier place I've never seen."

Beside him, his good friend Alart of Vouzin laughed. The two men were riding down the Rue de St. Andrew, still clad in armor. It was near sundown; they had entered the city not long before. They'd had to wait most of the day for the Saracen garrison to be marched off into captivity. The crowd pouring into the city eddied around them—soldiers, either drunk or looking for drink, camp followers, knights and clerics and merchants seeking quarters. Flutes and viols played; drums pounded. There was laughter and shouting, a feeling of overwhelming joy. Men made way for Richard, cheering him, and he smiled and acknowledged them with waves of his hand.

The city was a mess. Bodies and destroyed buildings were everywhere. Rocks from mangonels and boulders from trebuchets littered the streets and made them impassable in places.

"Think how it will look when it's cleaned up," Richard went on. "Thank God they surrendered and didn't make us destroy it."

Alart said, "Plus, we received excellent terms. My compliments, sire."

21

To ransom the city's garrison, Saladin had promised to pay 200,000 gold bezants, release 1600 Christian prisoners, and return the True Cross captured at Hattin. Payment of the money and prisoners was to be made in three equal installments, with the Saracen prisoners to be released accordingly.

Richard shook his head. "Two and a half years these fellows sat before these walls, and they got nowhere. I was here for a month and I took the place. I would have taken it sooner had I not been so ill."

Alart raised his dark brows. "Do you think Saladin will keep his word about the ransom? Conrad of Montferrat says he's just playing for time."

"Conrad?" Richard said. "What does that blowhard know about anything? Saladin is an honorable man. He will keep his word." Then he added, "Geoffrey of Trent has already approached me with the name of a prisoner he wants released. Some woman who was captured by our friend Qaymaz when Saladin attacked the camp."

"Does she come from a wealthy family?" Alart asked. He was thinking of an additional ransom they might get for the woman's release.

"That's just it," Richard said, "she's a commoner."

Alart raised his brows again. "A whore?"

"That's my guess. Trent didn't say."

"My God. What did you tell him?"

"What do you think? There are enough men—and women—of noble blood being held by the Saracens. We've no time to waste with whores or mistresses, or whatever this creature was to Lord Geoffrey."

Richard reined in, waving to the men who cheered him and clapped his horse's rump in appreciation. From this position they had a view of the Accursed Tower's crumbled battlements, where Richard's red banner with three lions was being unfurled. A moment later, the banner of Philip of France, blue with gold *fleur-de-lis*, was unfurled beside it.

This display let anyone approaching the city know who was in command. It would remain like this for a full day, then the banners of the army's lesser nobles would be hung from the outside walls, adjusted by height according to the rank of their owners. There were so many great nobles here, the walls would be a riot of color and heraldic device, like some kind of fantastic market day display, and Richard looked forward to riding out and seeing it.

Richard smiled, pleased because his flag had been unfurled first—he enjoyed beating Philip at anything. He was about to ride on, when Alart tugged his sleeve. "Sire—?"

Next to the first two banners, a third had been lowered. This flag featured three horizontal bars, two of red and one of white.

"What the Devil?" Richard said. "Whose flag is that?"

"Never seen it before," Alart said. "I've no idea who it belongs to."

"We'll soon find out."

Richard spurred his horse through the mob, ignoring their cheers now, followed by Alart and his bodyguards.

At the Accursed Tower Richard dismounted and climbed the steps to the battlements, angry because the effort left him short of breath. *Damn this illness.*

He reached the top and came upon a knot of men arguing. Among them were shaven-headed Conrad of Montferrat and his cousin, Archduke Leopold of Austria. Except for his face, which had been wiped fairly clean, Leopold was still covered from head to foot in dried blood, as though he did not want to let people forget how active he had been in the final fight. The tower guards' captain was pleading with the two men but stopped when he saw Richard approach.

"I might have known you'd be involved in this," Richard told Conrad. The big German smirked and Richard continued, "Whose banner is this?"

"Mine," Leopold said proudly. His people had worked all day sewing it, and had just gotten it finished in time to hang it here.

Alart of Vouzin frowned. "With all respect, my lord duke, your banner is gold with a black eagle."

"I have a new banner," Leopold said. "I designed it myself in honor of the siege. I got the idea when—"

Richard drew himself up. "By what right do you hang your banner here? Philip and I are kings, you are a duke. My memory may be slipping, but I do not believe a duke to be the equal of a king."

Richard didn't trust Leopold. Was the Austrian trying to grab all the glory for himself, was he trying to act like he was the hero of the crusade? Even worse, with Conrad's conniving, was he trying to cause division in the crusade's leadership?

"As you so ably point out, I myself am not a king," Leopold replied, "but I represent the German emperor."

"Perhaps, but you are not the emperor, and that is not his flag. As a practical matter, the German contingent of this crusade no longer exists. You command little more than a company of men, and while your men are undoubtedly valiant, your presence makes no difference to our success. Now I suggest you remove your banner from this spot and place it on the lower walls tomorrow."

Leopold stood straight. "My banner has as much right to be here as yours. The late emperor Frederick was the first crowned head to take the cross and the acknowledged leader of this crusade."

"Not by me, he wasn't," Richard said. He drew his dagger and cut the cords holding Leopold's banner to the merlons, letting the new banner flutter from the battlements into the stinking ditch below.

"That is a more suitable spot for your flag."

Leopold's suntanned face turned dark red. His hand went to his sword and for a moment Richard thought he would draw it, which made Richard happy because he enjoyed a good fight.

Alart interposed himself between Richard and Leopold. He raised a hand to Richard and in a calm voice said, "Sire." Then he turned and addressed the other men. "This is not the time for acrimony, my lords. Not on this joyous day. Let remember what binds us together and forget our differences."

Conrad held Leopold by the arm and said something to him that Richard couldn't hear. Leopold relaxed somewhat. He came to a form of attention and bowed stiffly to Richard.

"Thank you for the lesson in heraldry, sire. I hope I may one day return the favor."

Conrad said, "Brilliant move, Richard. As always."

"You will address me as 'sire,' " Richard told him.

"I am king of Jerusalem, and I will address you as an equal," Conrad said.

Conrad led Leopold off, Leopold not breaking eye contact with Richard until he had departed the tower battlements.

Chest rising and falling in anger, Richard watched them go. Gradually he calmed down and he turned to Alart. "Well?"

Alart cleared his throat diplomatically. "By the rules of etiquette, you were right, of course. Still, you might have been a bit more tactful. I fear you've made an enemy for life."

"So what?" Richard said. "England is a long way from Austria. What harm can Leopold ever do me?" He looked sideways at Alart. "I suppose Philip will wet himself because of this?"

"That does seem to be his usual reaction," Alart said.

At that Richard laughed and clapped his friend on the shoulder. "Then something good will have come of all this. Come, let us find our quarters and get settled."

Chapter 4

WITH A SMOOTH motion, Roger drew the dagger from his belt and sailed it blade first toward the straw target. It hit the target and bounced off.

"You still can't do that?" Fauston marveled as he came up from behind.

"I've made it a few times," Roger replied defensively.

Fauston wore a wide-brimmed wool hat, one side of which was pinned up by a tin badge in the shape of a sea scallop shell. It was the mark of a pilgrimage to the shrine of St. James of Compostela, Christendom's second most popular pilgrimage destination after Rome.

"Why the getup?" Roger asked him, retrieving the dagger.

"I've taken a job guiding pilgrims around the city and the battlefield. Now that the siege is ended, they're coming to Acre by the boatload."

"A guide? I thought you more likely to be picking their pockets."

"I'm an honest man now," Fauston reminded him, "I don't do that anymore. Well, maybe a bit, just to keep my hand in. Not sure what I'm going to show these fellows, but I'll make something up." He canted the hat rakishly. "I thought this would make me look more authentic."

Roger cleaned the dagger and returned it to its sheath. "You haven't been to Compostela, have you?"

"Of course not. I got this from a Portugese pilgrim. Traded him a Saracen helmet for it."

27

"When do you start?"

"Today. I'm on my way to the pilgrims' inn now. With luck, this job will provide me enough money to leave Acre."

Roger swatted at a fly buzzing in his ear. "You're still determined to go?"

"I am."

"You're welcome to join the Death's Heads, you know."

"Thanks, but I'll let you be the hero."

"You're Brock the Badger, you're far more of a hero to these fellows than I am. Why do you want to leave the Holy Land, anyway? With Otho dead, no one is interested in chasing you."

Fauston shook his head. "I just want to get away and start over. I've had my fill of the Holy Land—though I admit it was fun being part of the earl's entourage."

"Did you know that the earl is trying to have Ailith freed as part of the prisoner exchange?"

"No, I didn't know that. Please God he'll be successful."

"Please God she's still alive," Roger said. His brow clouded. "I pray every day that I'll get to see Dirk again. If I do, I'll make that bastard pay for taking her, even if it kills me."

Roger faced the straw target again. He braced himself, drew the dagger and let it fly.

This time the dagger stuck in the target. "Ha!" Roger said.

Then it fell out. "Damn!"

Fauston laughed merrily. As Roger once more retrieved the dagger, Fauston said, "They say Richard is eager to march on Jerusalem."

Roger snorted. "Do these men look like they're ready to march anywhere?"

Fauston gazed around the nearly deserted camp. The army—those who had not found quarters in the city—had been moved to a new camp several miles from Acre, to get away from the pestilential old camp. The few men visible were either sleeping or passed out drunk. "What men?"

"That's my point. The army's in no condition for a campaign. Most think we'll remain here till spring."

Fauston said, "Be that as it may, I'd best get into the city and attend to my flock."

Roger sheathed the dagger. "I'll walk with you."

They started toward the city, its siege-battered walls looming on the horizon. It was a hot day, lassitude hung in the salt air. Traffic increased as they got nearer the city, mostly soldiers going into town to get drunk and look for whores, or men who had already done that and were returning to sleep it off. They were quiet for a bit, then Roger said, "What do you know about Mercia?"

"Mercia!" Fauston stopped in surprise. "Why do you want to know about Mercia?"

Roger thought about revealing how he'd learned that Henry of Deraa was his father, then thought better of it. He still wasn't sure he believed it himself. "Oh, I heard someone mention it. Apparently it was a kingdom in England?"

They started walking again, and Fauston said, "It was. Took up more or less the center of the country. The richest lands, the fattest sheep—the prettiest girls. Trentshire was part of it. At one time it was wealthy and powerful, then the northern section was conquered by the Danes, and because the kingdom was thus weakened, the other part fell in thrall to Wessex. Men dreamed of returning Mercia to its former glory, then you French came along and that was the end of that." Fauston's eyes narrowed shrewdly. "Does this have something to do with your ring?"

Roger looked at the ring. "Yes. I was told it was of Mercian design."

"You may be right," Fauston said. "I know it's English, but I couldn't say more than that. I'm a highwayman, not a jeweler."

St. Andrew's Gate was visible now, busy with traffic. "I'll leave you here," Roger said.

"Where are you going?"

"The old camp."

Fauston stared at him. "Why would anyone with half his wits about him want to go to the old camp?"

"There's something I need to get."

Chapter 5

𝕿HE ABANDONED CAMP lay baking on the plain, like an unwanted memory. Tattered rags flapped in the sea breeze. Everything had been left as it was when the army had moved to the new camp, the old tents and other equipment being deemed too pestilential for further use. Garbage was everywhere. Here and there men picked through the ruins. Crying seagulls wheeled overhead, while others scurried along the ground searching for something edible.

To Roger's left was the Toron, the hill where the great lords—lay and ecclesiastical—had lived, and at whose foot Roger and the Death's Heads had turned the tide of battle during Saladin's assault. For two and a half years the Toron had been the center of camp life. It was no great stretch to say that it had been the center of Christendom for that same period. Now it was nothing. Most of the parti-colored pavilions were gone, though a few still stood and a few others were being taken down by servants, baggage packed away to be moved into the city. This was where Ailith had lived. Roger wondered where Ailith was now, and if she was still alive, and he blamed himself for her fate.

Moving along the Toron High Road, Roger came to the Concourse, heart of the camp's business and financial activity. A week ago the Concourse had teemed with life. Now it was empty. The merchants' well-stocked tents, like the merchants themselves, were gone. The more permanent structures had been looted or burned during the Saracen attack.

Not far past the Concourse, at the intersection of the Toron High Road and Chartres Road, were the square and the wooden stage where Roger and Helvise had listened to music on Sunday afternoons and where Coelred had strutted while performing in Roger's play, *The Common Soldier of Acre*—Coelred, who later died in agony when his leg was sawed off at the hip. It was all eerily silent now, empty, the open space around it waiting for an audience that would never come.

Roger turned down Resurrection Road. How many times in the last ten months had he made this same turn? He knew every dip, every bend in this road by heart. It was like returning to a past that was already distant, like coming back from a future time, even though he'd only been gone for a week. He came to the area where the strange people called the Bugars had once camped. The Bugars had disappeared—dead, most of them, the rest gone who knew where—to be replaced by the Irish, whose survivors now pitched their tents far south of the city.

He reached the old English camp. Unlike large swathes of the crusader lines, this section had not been ransacked or burned during the Saracen attack; they had passed it by. The streets were still laid out in orderly fashion, their corners marked with white-painted rocks. Roger saw the tent where he'd joined up, signed in by James of St. Claire, who was killed a few days later on the city walls.

Here was the Death's Heads' camp. And here was his old section tent, his home for almost a year. He fingered its canvas sides, the patched fabric rotting from rain and sun and salt air. In places the stitching had popped apart. One of the ground ropes had come free from its peg. Automatically he bent to fix it, then realized there was no reason.

He went inside, surprised by how small it seemed. He remembered his fight with Dirk here, Bald Matthew's stew, the Great Louse Race. He seemed to be surrounded by ghosts and laughter—Cole and Grandad, Black Jack and Slowfoot and Egwulf. And Will. Will, his best friend, wasted away to nothing by disease and starvation.

He left the section tent and went to the company commander's tent, the one he had shared with Helvise. His stomach tightened as he neared it. He steeled himself and ducked inside. Nothing had changed. It was like she was still there, like she would come through the tent flap at any moment, back from a turn fighting at the city walls, or bubbling with happiness because she'd learned to read a new word. He could still smell her. He could almost feel her next to him, her breath soft on his cheek. He remembered her naked body on the cot in the warm afternoon light, remembered the roundness of her buttocks. Remembered the musical sound of her laughter, her German accent.

Her wooden chest was there, with the green dress inside. He pulled out the dress, felt the smooth fabric, held it to his face and could almost pretend she was still in it. His eyes misted, and he put the dress back.

In one corner of the tent was Helvise's crossbow, its dark wood ornamented with the carved dragon tiller. This was what he had come for. He took it, along with her sheaf of iron bolts.

He stepped outside and looked around, committing the sight to memory. The plan was for the camp to be burned and the land returned to agricultural use, if that was possible.

He started back through the camp, lost in thought.

"Death's Head!"

He looked up and saw a man on horseback at the head of a large retinue and baggage train. It was Leopold, archduke of Austria.

Leopold spurred his horse over. "Death's Head—I am glad to see you! I had planned to visit you before I left." He dismounted and pumped Roger's hand. The last time Roger had seen Leopold, he'd been wearing armor and covered with blood as if he'd bathed in it. Now he was clean and wore a surcoat of red and white—he'd said he would make those his new colors.

Roger squinted. "Before you *left?*"

"Before I left the Holy Hand."

Roger didn't understand. "Why are you leaving?" Roger was entitled to be on familiar terms with this powerful lord. They had fought side by side and shared food and water on the field of battle, and that conferred rights far beyond those that normally bound society.

"I had a, shall we say, disagreement with your King Richard. You must have heard about it."

"I did, my lord." Roger doubted there was a soul in the army who didn't know how Richard had thrown Leopold's banner in the ditch.

Leopold went on. "It was an insult not to be borne, and in good conscience I can no longer serve alongside that man.

So . . ." Leopold gestured with his hands. He was one of their best men, and they were losing him to a mindless act of pig headedness. It did not auger well for the future.

Then Leopold said, "But what are you doing here?"

Roger held up the crossbow. "I came to retrieve Lady Helvise's crossbow."

"Ah, yes. A valuable weapon. A shame to let it rot. But I'm sure its value to you is more sentimental than military."

Roger was tight lipped. "It is." He added, "I shall be sorry to see you go, my lord."

"Don't be. Richard doesn't want me here, he has made that clear. I shall return home, where I have pressing duties. I will also go to Halsbach and have a memorial erected to Margravina Helvise and her husband in the church there."

"That is good of you."

"She deserves that much. She was one of our true heroes out here." Leopold paused. "I know you were planning to join her in Halsbach."

Roger felt his eyes misting again. "Yes."

"I'm sorry," Leopold said. He placed a friendly hand on Roger's shoulder. "If you are ever in Austria, come and see me. We will go hunting together."

"I would like that, my lord. I would like it very much. Have a safe trip home. It's been an honor serving with you."

"And with you. I wish I could stay, but things do not always go as we wish them to."

He mounted and rode back to his entourage. He looked over his shoulder once and waved. "Goodbye, Death's Head!"

Chapter 6

LEOPOLD OF AUSTRIA wasn't the only great lord leaving the Holy Land.

King Richard accompanied Philip of France along the mole to his waiting ship. Richard wore his red surcoat with the three lions of England, Philip wore blue with the gold *fleur de lis* of the House of Capet. Around them a great crowd had gathered. Banners flew from the ships and from the towers surrounding the harbor. Trumpets blew; choirs of priests and other clerics sang *Te Deums*. The smells of salt water and dead fish mingled with the clinking of censers and the aroma of incense.

The two made an incongruous pair—the huge Richard and the slightly built king of France. They walked arm in arm, Richard mindful of the grease stains on Philip's shoulders, left there by his stringy hair. "I wish you weren't leaving, brother," Richard lied. "Are you sure you won't reconsider?"

"You have made that impossible," Philip told him smoothly. "You negotiated with Saladin behind the council's back. You negotiated behind *my* back, and I am supposed to be the army's co-commander. That is an insult I cannot ignore."

"I'm sorry, but Saladin said he would deal only with me. I had to act quickly to preserve the city and save further bloodshed. I wanted to inform you, but there wasn't time."

Philip said, "I accept your apology, but I am still leaving. Now that Acre has fallen, I consider my crusading vow to be fulfilled. The Pope forced me to come here, and I have done my duty. I'm leaving most of my army with you, though. The duke of Burgundy will be in charge of them."

Richard winced inwardly. Hugh of Burgundy was a sour old prune who held no great regard for Richard. "Excellent!" Richard said.

They reached the ramp that led up to Philip's galley, and Richard removed his arm from Philip's. "You *will* remember your promise?"

Philip nodded solemnly. "I swear not to interfere with your French possessions for a period of three years, beginning from this day."

"Thank you, brother," Richard said. The little weasel would probably start trying to undermine Richard's authority the moment he landed in France.

Philip said, "Good luck, brother. May you be in Jerusalem soon."

"I anticipate little trouble on that account. We shall take Jerusalem by Christmas."

Now it was Philip's turn to lie. "I pray you are right."

Richard said, "I will say a prayer on your behalf at the Holy Sepulcher."

"Thank you," Philip said. "Oh, and a word of advice? Get yourself an heir. That is your first duty as a king. If you don't have one, you'll have no end of trouble later on."

Richard felt himself blush and that made him all the angrier, but he clenched his jaw and tried to smile. "I'll work on it, I assure you."

Philip turned away. Richard watched him climb the ramp to his ship, wishing he could run after him and chuck him into the harbor. Alart of Vouzin eased up beside Richard. "You've gotten rid of Philip, you've gotten rid of Leopold. All that remains is Conrad, though he may prove a tougher nut to crack."

Richard was still smarting from Philip's remark about getting himself an heir. "I'll deal with Conrad tonight," he said.

Once Conrad was gone, Richard would have what he wanted, what he needed to have if he was to be successful — full control of the army. He couldn't have shared command with a glory hound like Leopold or an old woman like Philip, much less with a living corpse like Barbarossa, who had done everyone a favor when he died on his way here. The army needed one firm hand in charge. And that hand would be Richard's.

He had what he wanted all right, but from this day forward he would be forced to keep one eye on France.

He needed to end this crusade quickly.

Chapter 7

"𝕬 FORTNIGHT!" CRIED the bishop of Beauvais. The usually warlike bishop was installed in a fine house with a pretty young mistress, and he was in no hurry to take the field.

Balian of Ibelin, leader of the native barons, added. "The men are exhausted from the siege, sire. They'll never be ready to march in a fortnight." Balian was gaunt, his face lined, with a lot more grey in his smoothed-back dark hair and beard than there had been two years earlier.

"I agree," said the earl of Trent. Trent was pale and drawn from illness. He stood with the big Fleming, James of Avesnes. James had been here almost since the start of the siege and had lost most of his teeth to malnutrition. "Normally I would vote to advance, but under these circumstances I think it's better to rest here till spring, then march south."

"No," Richard said. "we're not waiting."

They were in the hall of the Templars House, where Richard had taken up quarters. All the great barons of the crusade were present. Richard stood at the high table, his commanding presence dominating the hall. "We need to strike quickly, my lords, while we have Saladin off balance. My men are fresh and eager for battle. Those of you who want to come with us are welcome to do so, the rest may do as they will."

This pronouncement set off another round of cries and complaints. The barons needed new men and horses. They needed supplies. They needed time to reorganize.

"Then I suggest you get busy," Richard told them.

"What about the prisoners?" Beauvais asked. "We can't leave three thousand Saracens sitting at our base of operations."

"I have a plan for the prisoners," Richard said.

Henry of Champagne, the young count who had been the army's commander during its darkest hours, spoke up. "The ransom hasn't been paid yet. War is expensive, and that money would come in handy."

"Saladin is an honorable man," Richard replied confidently. "He will pay." He looked down the high table to where the duke of Burgundy sat. "You've been quiet, my lord Burgundy. What will the French do?"

Grumpy old Hugh acted like the question surprised him. "Why, we're ready to march when you are, sire."

This reply startled Richard. If, as Richard suspected, Burgundy had been charged by King Philip with keeping Richard away from Jerusalem for as long as possible, why did he support an advance? What treachery was this? It nearly made Richard re-think his plan.

Henry of Deraa made his voice heard above the tumult. Henry was plainly—almost shabbily—dressed, as always, as he stood by a bench in the lower part of the hall. Some of the barons hated him and some loved him, but most all respected him. "The king of England has the right of it," he said, praising Richard for the only time Richard could remember. "We came here to take Jerusalem, so let's do it. A bold move now, before Old Sidesaddle has time to reorganize his army, might break him."

Richard clapped his hands. "Good, it's settled. Now—"

"There is one more thing," intoned Conrad of Montferrat, who sat just down the high table to Richard's right. Conrad rose slowly, like some great beast surfacing from the ocean depths, his fresh-shaven square head gleaming in the torchlight.

Richard smiled. He had known this was coming. He had counted on it.

Conrad went on. "Before we march anywhere, I intend to assume the crown of Jerusalem. We've put this off long enough."

Handsome Guy of Lusignan, who still wore the gold circlet, replied smoothly. "There is nothing for you to assume. Your perseverance in this matter was once admirable from a certain point of view, but it has grown wearisome. The barons of this land have sworn their fealty to me."

Henry of Deraa said, "I never swore you fealty, and I never will. I'll not bend my knee to a pimp."

Guy's languid demeanor turned to hatred. "You'll rue those words."

"You always say that, yet I'm still here."

Before Guy could reply, the old arguments broke out again, as they had for the last two and a half years. Conrad's claim to the throne appeared clear cut—he was married to the last king's surviving child, Isabelle, but by the complicated politics of the kingdom, the kings of France, Germany and England were partly responsible for

41

disposition of Jerusalem's crown if there were no male heirs. Frederick of Germany was dead, and Philip of France had departed the Holy Land. That left Richard of England as the only one of the three guarantors present, and Richard was irrevocably in favor of Guy.

Richard wasn't that fond of Guy, but he was bound to support him, not only because Guy was a kinsman but because Guy was a vassal, and a lord was obligated to his vassals in the same way they were obligated to him. Also—and more importantly—Guy would do what Richard told him to do.

Conrad, on the other hand, opposed Richard's leadership. His presence in the field could lead to a rebellious faction of barons coalescing around him, and that in turn could lead to disaster. Conrad might have done well in the defense of Tyre, but this was Richard's war now, his to win or lose, and if Conrad did not understand that, he would learn it soon enough.

The wrangling went on until Richard brokered a compromise, the same compromise he had intended from the start. Guy would hold the crown of Jerusalem for his lifetime, after which Conrad and his heirs would succeed to the title. Since Conrad was older than Guy, there was no doubt whose victory this was. If by some chance Guy died first and left the kingdom to a potential son, Conrad could only take the throne by war, and he was almost certain to be blocked by the Papal courts.

Many of the barons were against this compromise, but save for a few like Henry of Deraa, none wished to go against the great king of England, hero of the age. Conrad had been outmaneuvered by Richard and he knew it. His dark eyes smoldered, and he jabbed a finger in Richard's direction, a sign of disrespect that went unnoticed by no one. "This isn't over. You'll beg me to be king one day."

Richard grinned. "I rather doubt that, my lord."

Conrad stalked from the hall, motioning his supporters to follow him. "We leave for Tyre."

Richard watched them go. "That's the end of Conrad," he told Guy. "All he has left is Tyre, and if you're wise, you'll take that from him, as well."

"I'll take Isabelle, too," Guy said. "A prize like that is wasted on an old goat like Conrad. I'll make her—"

"Yes, yes," Richard interrupted in a dismissive tone. "No doubt."

Richard caught Alart's eye, and Alart nodded in appreciation. Richard had everything he needed now. Immortality was his for the taking. He turned to face the rest of the council. "Two weeks, my lords. Then we march."

Chapter 8

"𝔄 FORTNIGHT!" CRIED Tatwine. "We can't be ready to march in a fortnight."

"The king says we can, so we have to be," Roger told him. "The earl isn't going to miss the capture of Jerusalem. He's been through too much for that."

Roger had made the reformed criminal Tatwine his squire. He'd wanted to make him commander of the axe men, but Tatwine didn't like authority—obeying it or wielding it. So Roger had put him where he could be the most use, as sort of his unofficial second in command.

Tatwine attempted to bolster his argument. "What's left of the company can't be found most days, and the new men need to be trained."

"King Richard is closing the taverns and brothels in the city, so the old timers will be back. We'll have to do the best we can with the new men."

Roger had returned from visiting the wounded in the sick tent. A few of them would be available for duty before the army marched, but not many. Ralph the Red, who had been opened up like a gutted deer, was by some miracle still alive, though he wasn't expected to live long.

Nearby, Short Peter marched a group of recruits across a patch of hilly ground, yelling at them to maintain their column of fours. Short Peter, who was in reality well over six feet tall, was the only one of Roger's company commanders to survive the last battle. He was in charge of the spearmen, and the former poacher Slowfoot had been given command of the axe men. There had once been five hundred men in the earl's force, but even with the reinforcements there were only enough left for two companies of spearmen and a company of axe men, and it was a stretch to call the axe men a company.

Tatwine watched the new men struggle up a low rise. "God help us if we get in a fight."

The recruits came not only from England but from other places as well—France, Italy, places in Eastern Europe whose names Roger couldn't even pronounce. They'd been outfitted with jacks and helmets and weapons taken from dead men. They carried the cut-down spears that had been used for the final assault on the city because new, regulation length spears had yet to be found. All the helmets had the red Death's Head painted on them, though—Tatwine had made sure of that. Tatwine had somebody else do the painting these days—a Spanish *morisco* who'd gotten his start painting the walls of the parish church in his spare time. Many of the recruits had taken the earl's silver specifically so they could wear the painted helmets and march under the Death's Head banner, which Tatwine had studiously repaired. He'd fashioned Roger a white surcoat with the same emblem, though Roger had yet to wear it.

Roger said, "We'll get in a fight, all right, you can count on that."

Suddenly Short Peter cried, "Horsemen right! Prepare to repel!"

On uneven ground the men had to switch from a column of fours into a two-deep line, facing right, spears leveled. The men stumbled around, looking lost. One fellow turned the wrong way, leveling his spear as he did and nearly impaling the man behind him.

Tatwine said, "What the—"

Short Peter went after the culprit but Roger beat him to it, grabbing the boy by the collar of his jack and shaking him like a master shakes a recalcitrant puppy. "What do you think you're doing? If your spear had been the proper length, you'd have killed that man."

The boy stared wide eyed at this fierce apparition with the newly sewn scar on his cheek.

"Don't you know your right from your left?" Roger demanded.

The boy shook his head. "No, my lord."

"You'd better damn well learn then. Maybe if I cut your left arm off you'll remember the other one is your right."

"Yes, my lord."

"And stop calling me 'my lord.' I'm nobody's lord." Roger remembered how Payen wanted to be called that, and it infuriated him. "You address me as 'Captain.'"

"Yes, my—yes, Captain."

Roger took the spear from the boy's hand and shoved—almost threw—him into line facing the right direction, then handed him the spear so hard that the boy stumbled and almost fell on his butt.

To Short Peter, Roger said, "Keep them at it, centenar. If they ever learn to march, we'll start weapons training."

Biting back a smile, Short Peter touched the brim of his helmet with his forefinger. "Right, Captain."

Roger stalked back to where Tatwine waited. Unlike Peter, Tatwine could not hold back his grin. "Did you see how scared that lad was?"

Roger sighed. "We've got our work cut out for us, Tatty." Then he started away. "I'll be back in a bit."

Tatwine was surprised. "Where are you going?"

"I promised someone I'd pay them a visit, and I can't put it off any longer."

Chapter 9

ᴴENRY OF DERAA'S tents lay on the southern outskirts of the sprawling new Christian camp. As one of Outremer's chief barons, Henry could have taken quarters in Acre, but he chose to remain out here with his men. Unlike the city and the rest of the camp, which had become beehives of activity after King Richard's surprise announcement, Henry's camp was relaxed and confident. These men looked like they were always ready to march at a fortnight's notice, Roger thought, and they probably were.

Henry's men resembled highwaymen or pirates more than they did knights. They wore raffish clothes; some had rings in their ears. Henry had knighted most of them himself, and he cared little about their backgrounds. A few were native born but most, like Henry himself, had come to the Holy Land from elsewhere, to escape the law or their wives, to find adventure or loot, or to serve God by punishing the Saracens.

Henry sat in a camp chair by a makeshift table, playing chess with a bearded thug, as Roger approached. Everyone stopped watching the chess match and stared at Roger. Henry followed their gaze, then rose. "Well, well, the long lost son."

"I'm still not certain I believe that," Roger cautioned.

Henry paid the remark no mind. "Are your men ready to march?"

"They will be."

Henry rubbed his hands together, grinning at his men, who watched in amused anticipation. "So, are you ready for some training?"

"Look, I only came here because I said I would. I've been in battle before, I don't need any—"

"Do you have a horse?"

Roger shook his head. "No."

"A knight must have a horse. I'll have a couple sent round for you to choose from. You don't plan on wearing that old footman's jack of yours in battle, do you?"

The jack had been pretty much hacked to pieces in the final assault on Acre. "No, I'll have to draw a new one from—"

"A knight requires a proper hauberk." Henry had his men fetch some suits of mail, and Roger reluctantly tried them on till he found one that fit. It was an older style, with sleeves that only came halfway down his arm, but that type would be more comfortable in the searing heat of the Holy Land than a newer one with long sleeves and gauntlets. Someone gave him a leather cap and someone else pulled the hauberk's mail coif over his head.

"Comfy?" Henry said.

"No," Roger told him.

There were leggings to go with the hauberk, and a conical helmet that fit over the coif. The helmet had a long, uncomfortable nosepiece. Henry laced the hauberk's aventail across the lower part of Roger's face, then stepped back, admiring. "There, now you look like a knight. You'll need a sword as well."

"No, I won't," Roger said. "I use an axe."

"Use what you like, but you're not truly a knight until you have a sword."

A grinning rogue handed Henry a sword. Henry tossed the sword to Roger, who caught it by its studded, leather-wrapped hilt. The sword was old, but well made.

Henry said, "You'll need to give it a name. Every knight's sword has a name."

"All right, I'll think of something," Roger promised. He had no intention of naming the sword. "Are we finished? Because I need to get back to—"

"Not yet." Henry planted his legs wide, fists on his hips. "Hit me."

"What?"

"Hit me. With the sword."

"Why?"

"You need to learn how to use it. Hit me."

"You've no armor, no shield. I'll kill you."

"What's wrong, sonny—afraid you can't do it? Go on, try."

Roger rolled his eyes and hefted the sword to get a feel of it. Feeling awkward in the suit of mail and the strange helmet, he took a half-hearted swing at his father, but when the blade reached its destination Henry was no longer there. He'd stepped away from the blow as nimbly as a minstrel might step to one side in a dance. Around them, Henry's men laughed.

Roger gripped the sword more tightly. He swung again, harder this time, backhanded, and again Henry seemed to vanish, to more laughter from those watching.

"Damn you," Roger said.

Roger circled Henry. He didn't like being made a fool of, and he was determined to teach the old goat a lesson. He feinted a lunge, then bent and took an arcing swing at Henry's ankles—if the stupid ass wanted his feet chopped off, that was his problem—but Henry effortlessly hopped above the slicing blade.

"Christ's sandals," Henry roared, "is that how kings of Mercia fight? No wonder the place doesn't exist anymore."

He put back his head to laugh, and, as he did, Roger dropped the sword and rushed him. Roger's mailed shoulder caught Henry in the gut, knocking the wind out of him as he put the older man on the ground. Roger slammed his forearm into Henry's nose, stunning him and drawing a grunt of pain. Roger raised his fist to strike Henry in the face, but the wrist was taken hold of and he was drawn off by one of Henry's men. "That's enough, young sir."

To his surprise, Henry, once he recovered his breath, started laughing. "Good work," he said, "I wasn't expecting that. By Heaven, we'll make a knight of you yet."

Henry's squire Thierry—everyone called him Teary—offered to help Henry to his feet, but Henry shook him off and rose on his own, brushing dust from his old surcoat. His nose was bleeding and he touched it gingerly, wincing. "Not broken, I think." He looked around and said, "Thirsty work."

At that prompt Teary offered him an oversized cup—it was more like a small bucket—of wine. Henry took an overly long drink, then poured the rest of the wine over his head, shaking his hair like a wet dog. "Ha! That feels better."

He handed Roger a huge wooden sword. It weighed maybe twice as much as a regular sword. "Practice with this every day. Swing it until your arm tires and you can swing it no longer. Then swing it some more. And when you can no longer raise your right hand, switch to your left. You have a lot of work to do before you take the field."

He took the wooden sword back and tossed Roger the real one again. This time he took a shield. "Now come on. Hit me."

Chapter 10

IF THEY HADN'T already tried to poison her, the knife attack would have been successful.

Ailith was alone on the grounds of the *harim*, in the little garden set aside for the concubines. She walked in the lush grass near the pool with its burbling fountain, inhaling the sweet scent from the orange and lemon trees. The light footstep behind her would normally have gone unremarked, but because of the poisoning attempt she was alert for trouble and she spun to see the African girl, Lamiya, lunge at her with a knife. Ailith had grown up in a hard world; she knew how to fight. She sidestepped the blow and kicked the taller girl in the stomach. As the girl bent over, Ailith grabbed her knife arm and kicked her in the stomach again, doubling her up and knocking the breath out of her.

She wrenched the knife away from the girl, dragged her to the tiled pool by her hair, and shoved her head under. The girl struggled, her feet beating a frantic rhythm as she tried to escape Ailith's strong grip. Spray from the fountain splashed Ailith's face and clothes.

"Stop!" cried a man's voice. "Stop!"

Ailith didn't stop. She pressed Lamiya's head under, feeling her struggles weaken. A hand gripped Ailith's arm. "Kill her, and the emir will flay the hide off you. He'll have no choice—the other women will demand it. The emir won't be so enamored of you with half your skin missing."

Ailith's heavy breathing slowed. She relaxed her grip on Lamiya's hair and pulled her, gasping for breath, from the pool. The African girl lay on her side, sobbing and retching. Ailith straightened, conscious of the other concubines watching her from various points around the park.

The attack hadn't been Lamiya's idea, Ailith was sure of that. The African girl couldn't have been more than seventeen or eighteen. Prior to Ailith's arrival, she had been the universal object of the *harim's* scorn because of her skin color. She was probably just glad that everyone had found a new person to hate. She'd probably been grateful they had volunteered her for this job so she could prove herself to them.

So who *was* behind it? Aysun was the obvious choice. Aysun was the Preferred One, but she was in her 40s now, and though she had borne the emir three children, she had put on weight and she feared for her place. Perhaps she saw Ailith as a threat. Or it could have been Qawaya, next oldest of the concubines. She was reputed to be a skilled lover, and she wanted the top spot, but she had to act quickly because she was in her mid-30s. Or it could have been the beautiful Kurd, Dilara, or saucy Rasha. Both of them made it plain that their goal was to become the Preferred One. It could even have been the chief eunuch, Narcissus. Narcissus thought *he* ruled the *harim*, and he schemed with as much relish as the women. The *harim's* other two women, Zafina and Jasara, were battlefield trophies who had no design on the top spot. They disliked Ailith but they probably wouldn't try to kill her.

Ailith kicked Lamiya in the side. "Get up. Get out of here." The girl complied, staggering, still coughing and retching. Ailith smoothed her wet hair and picked up the knife. It displayed fine workmanship, with a carved ivory handle. Ailith smirked at Aysun and the watching concubines, then flipped the expensive knife into the pool.

She turned to the man who had stopped her from killing Lamiya. He was of medium height, roundish, with a trim chin beard. "Who are you?" she demanded in what little Arabic she had picked up since being here.

To her surprise, the man responded in French, salaaming. "You may call me Hassan. I am the new doctor, come to see your companion's leg."

"Margaret's in the latrine," Ailith told him. Margaret had contracted a severe case of diarrhea. The would-be killer or killers had used her illness to get Ailith alone without Margaret to protect her. Once Ailith was dead, they would have had Margaret killed or—more likely—sold as a field slave, a fate worse than death.

"Your French is excellent," Ailith told Hassan.

Again he bowed. "I learned it from your people. In the camp before Akko."

Ailith stared. "You were in the camp?"

"For two years."

"Why?"

He shrugged. "They needed doctors. I needed money."

She studied him. Then—"I think I remember seeing you there. Yes. People were talking about you because you saved the life of the duke of Berry."

"I did."

"Why did you leave? You were becoming quite wealthy as I recall, and God knows there was no shortage of business."

He chuckled. "Your Christian brethren were embarrassed because I saved a certain German noblewoman whom they deemed beyond hope. For that, they planned to kill me. I was spirited from the camp by the lady in question and an English soldier."

"An English soldier?" A strange feeling came over Ailith. "What was his name?"

"The name escapes me, but he wore a helmet with a red skull painted—"

"Roger," she breathed. She could scarce believe it, and yet she could believe it all too well. The German woman must have been Roger's lover, Helvise.

Hassan's face brightened. "Yes, Roger—that was it. Do you know of him?"

"Roger is one of my dearest friends. He saved my life back in England."

"Did he? Well, Roger's friend is my friend as well." Hassan placed his hand over his heart. "You may count upon me for anything."

"Thank you." She was about to say more when Margaret returned.

Margaret was wan; she had lost a deal of weight during her captivity. She hobbled on her right leg, using a crutch. She saw some of the other women comforting the drenched Layima, saw Ailith's wet hair and robe, and sensed the tension in the air. "What happened?" she asked Ailith.

"Our 'friends' tried to kill me. Again."

"Again?" Hassan said.

Ailith nodded. "The last time it was poison. We had a stew, or whatever you Muslims call it, for dinner. A servant brought bowls of it to our quarters—Margaret and I don't eat with the other women. While we were waiting for the stew to cool, one of the cats that wander loose around here got up on the table and started lapping the liquid from my bowl. Margaret saw the cat and shooed it away. Margaret and I washed our hands, said grace and prepared to eat. I was raising the spoon to my mouth when Margaret knocked it from my hand. I thought she had gone mad, but she pointed to the cat. It lay on the floor, writhing and vomiting blood."

"Weren't for that cat, Ailith would have been dead," Margaret said. "We both would. We have the servant what brings us the food taste it first now, to make sure they don't try that trick again."

"A bad business, truly," Hassan said. "I am glad you are safe."

Margaret sat on one of the garden benches and Hassan examined her ankle. The ankle had been broken in a fall from a horse during Saladin's attack on the Christian camp. It had been set with a plaster cast a day after their capture, but only after Margaret had walked a considerable distance on it. Hassan examined the skin around the cast carefully. He sniffed it. Then he pressed here and there along Margaret's ankle and lower leg, watching her reaction. She winced but the pain didn't seem severe. At last Hassan nodded. "It appears to be healing well. You will probably have a slight limp the rest of your life because it took so long to get this treated, but other than that you should be fine."

Margaret greeted the news without emotion. "I can live with a limp. Ain't like we spend all our time dancin' around here."

Hassan smiled. "I will call on you again in a few days. In the meantime, take care to protect yourselves. The *harim* is a source of more intrigue and plotting than the sultan's court—Dilaria against Rasha; both of them against Qaymaya; Aysun and Narcissus against everyone."

"I'll take your advice," Ailith told him. He started away and she called after him. "Hassan?"

He turned.

She hesitated; she felt funny talking about this with a man. In a low voice she said, "Can you get me something—a potion or something—to keep me from . . . from getting pregnant?"

Hassan's brow knit. "Are you sure? Most women of the *harim* consider it a great honor to bear the emir's children. It helps ensure their place in the household when they get older and are no longer attractive, or at least gets them settled in their own house, with a pension. The alternatives are slavery or being turned out of the *harim* penniless."

"I don't care about any of that," Ailith said. "I just don't want to have that monster's children."

Hassan considered. "There is something I can give you. I will bring it with me on my next visit."

"Thank you."

Since Ailith had joined the *harim*, Qaymaz had sent for her more than he had all his other women combined, which—along with her Christian religion—no doubt accounted for much of the *harim's* animosity toward her. As brutal as Qaymaz was on the battlefield, he was surprisingly tender in his love making, his ministrations far more skilled than poor Geoffrey's. Against her will, Ailith found herself giving in and enjoying it, and thus hated it more every time. Ailith shuddered at the thought of Qaymaz's touch; he revolted her. She shuddered at the thought of any man's touch except . . .

Roger.

Roger had loved her and she had loved him, and yet she had turned him away. Instead, she had prostituted herself—for that's what it had been—to Geoffrey of Trent to acquire material things. She had forsaken real love, and this was what it had gotten her. She deserved her fate. Maybe it would have been better for all if Lamiya had killed her just now.

Better for all but Margaret. Margaret was only in this mess because she was Ailith's friend. Ailith no longer cared about herself, but she did care about Margaret.

When Hassan was gone, Ailith turned to her friend. "We're getting out of here, Margaret. I don't know when and I don't know how, but we're getting out. I promise you."

Chapter 11

IT WAS MID-AUGUST, and in the sweltering heat, Acre bustled. Meeting King Richard's departure schedule called for a great deal of work. There was grain to buy, repairs and purchases of weapons to be accomplished. There were wagons and casks to fix, animals to attend to, and a hundred major and minor nuisances that arose each day. The armorers' hammers could be heard well past curfew, horns and trumpets blew, animals brayed, sweating men unloaded supplies from the ships jammed in the harbor.

Above it all towered Richard of England. His health was returning, and whether practicing with weapons in the morning, inspecting soldiers in the afternoon, or singing to his friends in the evening, his dash and eagerness inspired the army. Even those who had been most adamant about remaining in Acre until spring were caught up in his enthusiasm.

That enthusiasm did not, unfortunately, extend to Geoffrey of Trent. Geoffrey was sick in bed in his house on the Rue de St. Jean, diagnosed with tertian fever. Bouts of fever alternated with periods of freezing cold, and each one left Geoffrey weaker. He was unable to go with the army, so Richard had named him governor of the city. He was at times semi-delirious, but at this moment he was lucid, and was being visited by Balian of Ibelin, James of Avesnes and Henry of Champagne.

"I like the house," Balian said, looking around, his greying hair slicked back, ring in one ear. The house was built in the Roman style—maybe it had once *been* Roman— two floors, with everything laid out around a peristyled pool with fluted columns. There were mosaics on the floors; parts of these mosaics had featured human figures, and those figures had been gouged out by the Saracens for religious reasons. The walls, which had been painted with scenes from mythology, had been whitewashed for the same reason. "The goldfish in the pool are a nice touch," Balian added.

"Big fat ones," said toothless James of Avesnes. "Surprised nobody ate them during the siege."

"They did," Geoffrey said in a weak voice. His bed had been set near the window, where the sea breeze could reach him. "Fellow I'm renting the house from re-stocked them from Tyre."

Balian grinned. "Nothing too good for the governor of the city, eh?"

Young Henry of Champagne said, "We're off for Jerusalem in two days, Geoffrey. We'll miss you."

"We'll try not to have too much fun without you," James added. "Maybe I can grow some new teeth while we're gone—I'm hoping for a miracle when we get to the Church of the Holy Sepulcher."

Henry grew serious. "Saladin's finally paid the first installment of the ransom, but he didn't pay the full amount, and he didn't release all of our prisoners who were on the list."

"Did you manage to get Lady Ailith on the list?" Balian asked Geoffrey.

"No," Geoffrey said. "Richard dismissed my plea out of hand because she is not of noble blood."

"That's too bad. I liked Ailith."

Henry went on. "Richard declared that Saladin has defaulted on his promise about the ransom and prisoner release. In response, he refuses to hand over any of the Muslim prisoners."

"What's he going to do with them?" Geoffrey wondered.

"He claims to have a plan for them, but nobody knows what it is."

"If he leaves them here, they'll be in your charge as governor," Balian told Geoffrey.

Geoffrey groaned. "I'm too sick to worry about prisoners right now." He kept thinking about Ailith and how—

From downstairs came a racket, followed by a woman's strident voice. "Why is everyone standing around? You call this working? Well, it's not. Don't stand there gawking, you ape. Fetch my trunk."

The three guests looked at each other, then at Geoffrey, who seemed to have sunk deeper into his bed.

Suddenly the door was flung open and a woman burst into the room. "There you are!" she cried to Geoffrey. "And, look, here are the Three Wise Men—Balthazar, Melchior and No Teeth."

James, Balian and Henry of Champagne bowed deeply. "Greetings, Lady Bonjute."

Geoffrey tried to look happy. "What are you doing here, dear? I thought—"

"You thought you were rid of me, didn't you? You thought I'd gone home. Well, I haven't. Our ship was caught in a storm and sank. Lost half those on board. We were picked up by a Genoese vessel whose captain turned out to be a pirate. He planned to hold us for ransom, but I soon put a stop to that."

"I imagine you did," Geoffrey mumbled.

"What?"

"Nothing, dear. Nothing."

"Queen Berengria came back with me. She's off to pester King Richard about giving her a child. Bet he'll love that."

"Why do you say that?" Geoffrey asked.

"Oh, Geoffrey. You're so naïve."

Henry of Champagne cleared his throat. "We'd best be going, Geoffrey. We've lots of preparations before we march."

"I'm glad someone's making preparations," Bonjute said with a telling glance at her husband. After the three guests had bowed again and departed, she rounded on Geoffrey. "What's the matter with you?"

"I'm ill. Tertian—"

"My God, Geoffrey, this is so typical of you. You sit out on that stinking plain for a year, getting more than half your men killed and accomplishing nothing, and now that the real fighting is ready to start, you're too sick to take part in it."

Geoffrey attempted to say something, but she kept going. "How are you going to win glory this way? How are you going to draw the king's notice?"

"Perhaps you should go in my place," Geoffrey suggested.

"I'd probably do a better job. You're going to let that ass Leicester get ahead of you in the race to become the next justiciar. Do you know he's vowed to be the first man into Jerusalem?"

Geoffrey said, "I—"

"I know, I know—you vowed it too, but you can't very well do it from your bed."

Bonjute looked around. "Where is Otho? At prayer?" Otho was the pompous priest she'd talked Geoffrey into making his chaplain.

"Dead," Geoffrey said. "Killed in Saladin's attack on our camp."

"Pity. I shall have a church built in his honor when I get home."

"He would have liked that." *The swine.*

"I'm going to go and get this house in order. My first task will be to root out your whores and send them packing." She pointed at her husband. "And don't think you're going to spend the rest of this crusade in bed."

"No, dear," Geoffrey replied. He sighed and added, "I believe I'm feeling better already."

Chapter 12

THE PILGRIMAGE TRADE was booming. It seemed that at least one shipload of pilgrims arrived at Acre every day, which kept Fauston busy in his new role as a guide.

Fauston's latest tour group was composed mainly of Hollanders and Flemings, well-fed burgesses on a once in a lifetime trip. These trips had been planned—and paid for—well in advance, before Jerusalem and the other holy sites had been lost. There were few places of religious significance in Acre—no famous shrines, no sites where miracles had been performed. Fauston had to take his company somewhere, though, so wearing his rakish hat from St. James of Compostela, he started this tour, as he started all of them, with what religious attractions there were. They went first to the once-impressive Cathedral of the Holy Cross—badly defaced because it had been turned into a mosque during the Saracen occupation—then to the Accursed Tower, where legend said that Judas of Iscariot's thirty pieces of silver had been minted.

"Can we get some of those silver pieces?" one of the Hollanders asked.

Fauston had heard this question over and over again, and he replied patiently. "The Last Supper was over a thousand years ago. Likely those silver pieces have been melted down and re-minted a hundred times since then, if they haven't disappeared entirely."

The questioner and a few of the other pilgrims didn't like that answer, but there was nothing Fauston could do about it. They visited three other churches, one of which had been used as a stable during the siege, and a couple minor shrines, then Fauston led them to the old siege lines and the battlefields. Here he had to embellish, since most of the siege had consisted of men standing around starving or dying from disease. So he made up stories about deeds of glory performed by famous nobles. Here the count of Bar, God rest his soul, had made his famous last stand. Here the bishop of Beauvais, no man was holier, slew a Saracen giant in single combat. Here the late Philip of Flanders had saved the life of the king of France; and here Richard of England had single handedly turned back Saladin's great assault on the Christian camp, wounding the sultan and making him flee for his life.

As always, Fauston concluded his tour by taking his charges to the beach. He ignored the off-duty soldiers skylarking in the water and led the pilgrims to a small area of the beach that had been set off by colored ribbons attached to stakes. There was a slight depression in the center of the area.

"What's this?" asked one of the pilgrims.

Fauston doffed his hat respectfully. "This, gentlemen, is the exact spot where King Richard of England first set foot in the Holy Land."

"Lionheart!" someone cried in a heavy accent, and the pilgrims raced under the ribbons and started digging at the beach with their hands, packing the sand into little bottles.

Fauston had happened upon this *finalé* to his tour by accident. His very first group had asked to see the place where the English king had come ashore. Fauston had no idea where that was, so he chose a likely spot and took the group there. To his amazement, that group—like these Hollanders—had started digging the sand, taking it away like the spot was a shrine and the sand was some sort of relic. Fauston had fenced off the area after that, and almost every group since then had behaved the same way. Other tour guides now took their charges to this spot, as well.

When the tour was finished and the pilgrims pronounced themselves satisfied, Fauston led them to the Golden Keys, a tavern popular with clerics. Here the pilgrims had less chance of being knifed or robbed than they did in other taverns, and the girls—should the pilgrims desire feminine companionship—were less likely to drug them and steal their possessions or have them carted off unconscious by ships' captains looking to fill out their crews.

While the pilgrims sat at tables and quaffed cups of arrack, Fauston leaned back in a chair, enjoying his drink and counting the time till he could take them back to their rooms. In the street outside the tavern, a regiment of Turcopoles was marching out of the city to the new camp. Turcopoles were lightly armed native cavalry with turbans and flowing, parti-colored robes. It was a colorful sight— kettle drums boomed, accoutrements jingled, horses' hoofs clattered on the stone paving.

Fauston became aware that one of the pilgrims was talking to him. It was Ekkehard, the shrewd, heavyset wool merchant who seemed to be the group leader. "What?" Fauston said.

Ekkehard spoke louder, repeating himself. "Do you know where we can obtain relics?"

Fauston gave the man his most ingratiating smile. "As it happens, I have a connection in that trade. Are you looking for anything in particular?"

"St. John the Baptist—we need something to do with the Baptist."

"Is that the only thing that will do?"

"Yes," Ekkehard said, "it is for our parish back in Breda—the Church of St. John the Baptist. We promised we would bring them something."

Fauston stroked his chin. "How much would you be willing to pay?"

Ekkehard inclined his head toward Fauston and lowered his voice. "The parish has authorized us to spend two hundred bezants, perhaps a little more."

Fauston's attention pricked up. This was getting interesting.

A gloomy fellow named Steen said, "It may prove a difficult task. The Baptist's relics were burned by the Romans, and no one knows what happened to them after that."

Ekkehard said, "We have to have the—what do you call it?—the *certificate*, too. To prove the relic's authenticity."

"Yes," Steen said, "there can be no sale without a certificate. We have been tricked before." He slapped a painter called Hieronymus on the back of the head, leading

Fauston to suppose that Hieronymus was the one who had been tricked.

"It's a tall order, but I'll see what I can do," Fauston said. "No promises, mind."

When they were done drinking—it took a while; the Hollanders swilled liquor like bishops at an investiture—Fauston led the pilgrims back to their rooms. "I'll be in touch," he told the bleary eyed parishioners from Breda.

Ekkehard pounded Fauston on the back, slurring his words. "You must hurry. We leave here for Tyre in two days." Acre, Tyre and Antioch were currently the only cities in the Holy Land that were open to pilgrims. Most elected to begin their tour at Acre because there were even fewer religious sites in Tyre—although Alexander the Great had once captured the city in a famous siege.

Hieronymus, the painter who had been tricked, swayed precariously with one finger raised. "Remember the certificate. There must be a certificate."

Fauston assured them that the certificate would be no problem and hurried off in search of Gregory the Greek. Gregory had procured a splinter from St. Peter's boat for Fauston during the siege, and Fauston hoped he could find something belonging to John the Baptist.

Fauston looked all over the city but he couldn't find Gregory. He searched the growing suburb of Montmusard—populated by Christian refugees from Saladin's conquest of the Holy Land—but Gregory wasn't there, either.

"Bloody Greek. Never around when you need him."

Gregory could be in Tyre, he could be in Constantinople—he could be dead, for all Fauston knew.

And Fauston had only two days to find something belonging to the Baptist—and the two hundred bezants that went with it.

Fauston swore in frustration. He was about to give up when an idea occurred to him. The idea was risky, but the more he thought about it, the better he liked it. Besides, it wasn't like he had another choice.

The next morning, he rose early, made the sign of the cross and left the city.

Chapter 13

𝕵AUSTON PASSED THROUGH the old camp and headed for the graveyards beyond.

For two and a half years, Acre had been the charnel house of the world. The graveyards were so vast it was difficult to comprehend them. They were like cities, cities of the dead. Most of the graves were shallow and many, especially the older ones, had seen their lightly packed soil washed away by the winter rains, leaving the bones exposed to animals and the elements.

The smell, both from the graveyards and from the carcasses of thousands of horses that had been left to rot, was indescribable, even after all this time. Fauston pressed his sleeve to his nose. Around him, crows and seagulls fluttered and swooped and pecked; hordes of rats scampered unhindered.

Fauston knew he was about to commit a grievous sin, but he was able to rationalize it. After all, he told himself, one bone was much like another. Why should he deny the pilgrims their bit of satisfaction? They had come all this way for a relic, it would be sinful to send them home empty handed. In the end, he was making them happy, and that was a good thing.

He made his way to a section of the graveyards where jumbled bones lay piled in the sun, tossed there by flood waters, and appeared to have been that way for some time.

That exposure helped give them a weathered appearance, which was necessary because the bone Fauston was looking for was supposed to be over a thousand years old.

He sifted through the bones, trying to ignore the smell. The bones' hard, scratchy feel was repulsive at first but he got used to it. The long siege had inured him to worse. He needed a bone with no sinew or scraps of flesh remaining on it. That part wasn't difficult, but a more daunting task was finding one without small teeth marks showing where it had been gnawed upon. Rats would not chew a saint's bone—God would not permit such a thing.

It took him a while to find a bone that hadn't been visited by rats or gulls or wild dogs, but he finally found one—a forearm. He didn't know whether it was a right forearm or a left one, but he would tell the pilgrims it was the right—the right arm that had baptized the infant Jesus. That should add a few bezants to the price.

He wondered who the arm had belonged to and how the poor fellow had died—and whether he had been Christian or Saracen—but there was no time to speculate on that. He put the arm in a sack and took it back to the Death's Head's camp, where he found Tatwine and some other men sitting around a cook fire, yarning and polishing their armor while they waited for the stew to boil. Fauston took the arm bone from the sack and laid it on the edge of the fire.

"Here!" cried Tatwine. "What you doing, Brocky?" As a former criminal, Tatwine knew Fauston by his outlaw name of Brock the Badger.

Fauston, who still wore his hat from St. James of Compostela, winked. "Official Church business, old son."

Tatwine gave him a sideways look. "Thought you'd gone straight?"

"I have, but this is an emergency." Fauston was lucky that Steen had mentioned John the Baptist's relics being burned. Otherwise Fauston might have found himself in trouble with the religious authorities, who took a dim view on the selling of false relics.

When the bone was sufficiently charred, Fauston took it to the beach, where he threw it repeatedly against the rocks, chipping it—passersby staring at him like he was mad. Next he immersed it in seawater, hoping the salt water would give the bone an even more weathered look. He took the bone from the water and rubbed it on the pebbly beach, scouring it with sand to make the color more yellow.

When the bone looked old enough, Fauston took it to a jeweler's shop in in the city and purchased a box for it. The box was expensive, but a relic this important needed a commensurate reliquary. It was custom-made olive wood, lined with red velvet, with a chased brass clasp—Fauston had to pay extra to have the job done right away. It was costing him a lot of money, but he thought of it as an investment. Besides, it was still cheaper than paying Gregory would have been.

When the box was finished and the "relic" laid on its velvet cushion, Fauston looked over the finished product and nodded, satisfied.

Now came the hardest part, getting the certificate of authenticity.

Fauston couldn't read or write, so he couldn't make a certificate himself.

But he knew someone who could . . . .

Chapter 14

"**N**O!" ROGER SAID. "Absolutely not!"

Roger was wearing full armor and swinging a heavy wooden sword, his face pouring sweat. There was a large bruise on his left cheek. Fauston was tempted to ask what he was doing, but he looked angry enough already. On his left arm Roger carried a long triangular shield with the red Death's Head painted on it.

Fauston started to say something else, but Roger cut him off. "No! It's against the law. It's against God's Law."

Fauston tried to be reasonable. "There's no one else I can go to, Roger. The pilgrims leave tomorrow."

"You'd better learn to read and write pretty damned quick then." Roger paused, tired and short of breath from swinging the sword. "It's a sin, Fauston. Don't you see that?"

Fauston carried a pilgrim's leather bag, or scrip, over his shoulder. He still wore the hat from St. James of Compostela. He had gotten fond of the hat—he thought it gave him a rakish look, plus it kept the glaring sun off his face. "I've only come to you because there's no other choice. My usual relics supplier is nowhere to be found."

Roger put down the shield and switched the wooden sword to his left hand. "No. No. No."

Fauston took a deep breath. "I'll give a third of the money I make to your men, for supplies."

Roger raised the sword, then lowered it. "It's that important to you?"

Fauston shrugged. "I want these people to go home happy. They've come a long way."

"Give my men half."

"Oh, come on—"

"Half."

Fauston stared. In a resigned voice, he said, "Done."

Roger unlaced his helmet and took it off. Tatwine hurried up and helped him remove his short-sleeved hauberk and the leather haubergon that went beneath it. Roger wiped himself with a towel and gulped a huge cup of water. Then he glared at Fauston. "Come on."

"What happened to your cheek?" Fauston asked him as they walked.

"Some bastard hit it with a shield."

They repaired to Roger's tent, where there was a small table and a camp chair. Roger took the chair. "What am I to use for paper? And pens? And ink?"

Fauston cleared his throat and reached into his scrip. He pulled out a sheet of vellum, along with two sharpened quills and two small pots of ink, one black and one red. "I took the liberty . . ."

Roger stopped him with a look. "What shall I write?"

Fauston tried to recall what had been on the certificate from St. Peter's boat. "Say that you, by God's grace archbishop of Tyre, affirm that this holy relic of St. John the Baptist is genuine. Given by your hand on whatever date you wish to use."

"What is the archbishop of Tyre's name?"

"Josicus."

"Josicus? What kind of name is that?"

"I don't know. I didn't name him."

Grumbling, Roger began to write. Fauston knew Roger didn't want to do this, but once he got started he showed meticulous pride in his craftsmanship, like the former abbey copyist that he was. He used red for the capital letters, printing his words carefully so that they looked like something an archbishop's clerical staff might prepare. Better, even.

Fauston beamed as Roger worked. "Like old times, isn't it?"

Roger shot him another look. "Except this time might end up with us in the ecclesiastical dungeons. Or in Hell. Hell of a certainty."

"Oh, well, we were going there anyway," Fauston said.

"Yes, but I don't feel like being tortured by a Church inquisition on the way."

When the words were printed, Roger signed the bottom of the sheet with a flourish. He blew on the ink to dry it and held it up for inspection. "You realize this needs the archbishop's seal to make it authentic."

Fauston reached into his scrip again. "I took the—ah— liberty of having one made."

He handed Roger a gold ribbon, a ball of red wax and a copy of the archbishop's seal made for a hefty fee by a forger in the city—there wasn't much profit left in this relic, but Fauston felt that he owed it to the Hollanders.

Roger placed a piece of the ribbon at an angle beneath his signature. He melted a blob of wax with the candle and let it drip onto the ribbon, then pressed the seal into the wax, holding it there to make a good impression.

He put the "certificate" on the table to let it dry. "This is the last time I do this, Fauston. I mean it, don't ever—"

Somewhere a trumpet sounded, followed by more, then more, until it seemed like all the trumpets in the Holy Land were blowing. There was distant shouting, then shouting all around them.

At that moment, Tatwine ducked his head into the tent. "Roger! King Richard has commanded the army to assemble!"

Chapter 15

THE ARMY WAS drawn up in a vast square whose sides were a half-mile long, with the ranks facing inward. Banners and flags of all sizes and designs fluttered over the host. Roger and his Death's Heads were with the English contingent, which was led by the earl of Leicester, the earl of Trent being too ill to attend.

They were near the Mahomerie, a little mosque outside the city. They had marched here, some singing hymns or war songs, and Richard's heralds had steered them to their assigned places. It was quiet now. The sun beat down. Horses stamped, harness jingled, men shuffled their feet. Spectators from the city filled the gaps between the units, some on horseback, some sitting expectantly in the sand.

Roger sat his horse in front of his men. Tatwine stood beside him, along with a man carrying the Death's Head banner. Roger wore his new Death's Head surcoat over his hauberk. Across the square, he made out his father Henry of Deraa's red lion banner.

"What are we doing?" Tatwine said in a low voice.

"I've no idea," Roger replied. "Maybe there's to be a Mass or something before we march south."

He wondered if he would ever get the money Fauston had promised him to buy supplies for his men. They'd probably leave Acre before Fauston could get it to him. That was a pity because there was no place to buy supplies where they were going—anything they wanted would have to be purchased before they left Acre. Oh, well, there was nothing to be done about—

A blast of horns.

One corner of the square opened, and King Richard rode his great bay horse Fauvel into the square's center, accompanied by his heralds and standard bearer. Behind them were Hugh of Burgundy, Alart of Vouzin, Andrew of Chauvigny, Guy of Lusignan and the rest of the army's commanders. Richard wore his red surcoat with the three gold lions. His armor was polished so that it shone like silver. He absorbed the cheers of the army and of the onlookers, then, after a minute, he raised a hand and the cheering died away.

Richard straightened in the saddle, and his commanding voice carried over the assemblage. "*Messieurs!* It is more than a month since Acre was taken, yet the sultan of Damascus has failed to pay the full ransom installment as he promised. Therefore . . ." he let the word linger on the hot air, "let it be known that all agreements contracted between the sultan and the council of barons are null and void."

That started a lot of talking. Another blast of horns was followed by an excited roar from the spectators at the rear. Men craned their necks to see what was happening.

"Eyes front, there!" commanded the vintenars.

A company of Turcos opened a lane in another corner of the square, and the Muslim prisoners of the Acre garrison were herded in, hands tied behind them.

There were nearly three thousand of them, along with some women and children. The men were bearded and filthy. They were scared, but they tried to maintain some kind of discipline and formation. They were Saladin's best troops, and they were proud of that.

"What the Devil?" Tatwine said.

Roger had a sudden inkling what might happen, but he dismissed it. Something like that could never happen here, especially with King Richard in command.

Under the leveled spears of Templar footmen, the prisoners were marched into the huge square and formed up, the women and children being pushed to one side.

Robert de Sable, Grandmaster of the Templars, walked his horse next to Richard. He beckoned, and three of his men, wearing white surcoats with red crosses, approached the square, carrying long executioner's swords.

"Christ . . ," murmured Short Peter.

The executioners faced the king, genuflected and crossed themselves, then turned and started down the lines of prisoners. They worked in teams of three, a swordsman and two helpers. As they approached each prisoner, the prisoner was made to kneel by the first helper, the second helper pulled down his head by the hair, and the head was struck off by the swordsman. Some of the prisoners complied pridefully, showing disdain for their killers; others yelled insults at their killers, and these had to be forced to the ground and restrained by extra helpers.

There was the repetitive *thwack* of the swords, the smells of blood and of men voiding themselves. Prisoners cried out—why was this happening? Women and children wailed and screamed. A few of the watching Christians fainted— whether from the sight or the heat, none could say.

Roger stared helplessly. This wasn't happening, it couldn't be. King Richard would never permit it. Yet here it was, and Richard was observing the spectacle impassively.

"Don't watch," Roger growled to his men. "Keep your eyes on the back of the man in front of you or stare at the ground." As leader of the company, the man out front, he was forced to watch, though, forced to keep his roiling stomach from erupting. Of all the things he had seen since he had arrived in the Holy land, this might have been the worst.

A number of men in the army's ranks—knights and footmen—vomited. Others grew restive. "Silence, there," ordered the vintenars.

Across the square, James of Avesnes stared in amazement. "He's going to kill them all."

Henry of Champagne curbed his nervous horse. "Is this the act of a Christian gentleman?"

Balian of Ibelin said, "He said he had a plan for the prisoners, but I never thought it would be this."

Out on the plain mounted Saracen patrols saw what was happening, and they rode as close to the Christian army as they dared, blowing horns to show their solidarity with the prisoners.

The executioners soon wearied. It sometimes took them several blows to sever a victim's head now. One fellow missed his stroke completely and took off the fingers of a soldier holding one of the prisoners down. While the howling soldier was carried off, the executioners were replaced by fresh men and the killing started again.

"This is taking too long," Richard snapped. "At this rate we won't be done till Michaelmas. We need help—and will someone shut those damned women up! Heralds, summon the council."

While men vainly attempted to quiet the prisoners' wives and children, heralds blew the call for the council.

The great lords walked their horses forward and assembled around the English king. He looked them over and found the man he wanted. "Henry of Deraa. You and your fellows assist the Templars in their work."

"No," said Henry.

The air around the king grew quiet. In a low voice Richard said, "I beg your pardon?"

The one-eyed baron sat straight in the saddle. "I said no, sire. My men and I will not be part of this."

"I am told that you hate Saracens more than any man in the army. Was I told wrong?"

"You were told correctly," Henry replied. "Had it been up to me, we'd have offered no quarter and killed every man jack of the bastards when we took the city. But we gave our word to their surrender, and as a Christian I do not go back on my word."

Guy of Lusignan said, "What's wrong, Deraa? No stomach for the job?"

Henry spoke to Guy but kept his eyes on Richard. "What's wrong, is that, unlike you, I am a man of honor. When I give my word, I keep it."

"We can't leave these fellows here," Richard explained. "If they get free, they can cut our supply lines, maybe even retake the city."

"You should have thought of that before you took them prisoner. I did."

Richard glared at him. "I'll deal with you later, sir."

Richard was furious at being spurned by a man like Deraa, a man of no breeding. He was about to call for volunteers when his eye caught a banner across the square, among Leicester's men. There was a stout fellow who would gladly do Richard's bidding.

He beckoned a herald and pointed. "Roger of Huntley. Bring him to me."

Chapter 16

ROGER HAD SEEN his father, Henry, arguing with King Richard, so he had an idea why he was being summoned. He was so tense that he could hardly breathe.

"Ah, Roger." King Richard greeted Roger warmly, then indicated the Saracen prisoners in the square. "Take your Deaths Heads and help the Templars clean up that bunch, would you?"

Why had Richard picked him for this? It was Tatwine's flag, Roger thought. It must have caught Richard's eye. The damned thing made Roger and his men look like a bunch of crazed killers.

Roger straightened, aware that he could be signing his death warrant. He felt his father's gaze on him but took pains not to meet it. "I'm sorry, sire, but that is something I cannot do."

Richard's look grew cold. "That wasn't a request, Huntley, it was an order."

"Then it is an order I must respectfully refuse, sire."

There was an intake of breath around the council. It was one thing for a renegade like Henry of Deraa to defy the king—he had done it before—but for a newly made knight like this to do it was unheard of.

Roger went on. "Believe me, sire, refusing your order is not something I do with pleasure. You made me a knight, and for that I am eternally grateful. But knighthood confers responsibilities, as does being a Christian. And one of those responsibilities is faithfulness to one's word. We gave our word to let those men live, and a man's word is an oath to God and as such may not be broken."

"We wouldn't have to do this if Saladin hadn't broken his word to us," Richard pointed out.

"I know, sire, but these are men, soldiers who fought us honorably. This seems like—I don't know, it seems like murder."

"War is murder," Richard said.

"Prisoners are executed all the time," the sour-faced earl of Leicester told Roger impatiently. "Besides, these fellows are infidels."

"They're still people," Roger protested.

Leicester snorted. "That's debatable."

Geoffrey of Lusignan chimed in. "We saved Meshtub and the fellows worth ransoming. Who cares about the rest?"

To Roger, King Richard said, "You know I could have you executed for failing to obey an order?"

"I do, sire," Roger replied.

"Yet you still refuse to obey?"

Roger stiffened in the saddle. "I don't—I don't see that I have any choice, sire. I just can't do it, and I can't tell my men to do something I won't do myself."

In a kindly tone, the count of Vouzin said, "Maybe you were around my son and his monks at Huntley too much, eh?"

Was the count offering him a way out? If so, Roger jumped at it. "That's possible, my lord."

Richard considered that. Then he said, "I'm not having you executed. You fought bravely during the siege. I know you're no coward. I don't like killing these men, either, but it's a military necessity. We march tomorrow, and we can't have a mob of enemy soldiers in our rear—and we can't weaken our force by leaving men to guard them. They'll free themselves if they can—it's their duty—and if they do that, there's no end of mischief they can cause. They might even be able to keep us from taking Jerusalem—since all of our supplies come through Acre. Are three thousand lives worth the loss of Jerusalem? Is keeping an oath to God worth the loss of our goal?"

Roger hadn't thought about that; he didn't know how to reply. It was fine for him to stand on a principle; he was one man. What about Richard, who had all of Christendom to answer to? Was standing up for a principle worth the failure of the crusade? That was the decision Richard had to make. Where did one draw the line? *How* did one draw the line?

The earl of Leicester, of all people, came to Roger's rescue. "Bah! This fellow is Trent's pet. Trent would have complained about killing them, too. Let's not waste any more time—I'll get my men to finish them off."

Richard looked at Roger—sadly, it seemed to Roger—then said, "Very well."

Leicester wheeled his horse and rode off, shouting orders. King Richard turned to Roger and Henry of Deraa, and whatever sadness had been in his eyes before was gone. "You two, and your men, will march with the rear guard. You will eat the army's dust until we reach Jerusalem. Then I will decide what to do with you. I wish to see no more of you until that time."

Roger and Henry shared a look, then bowed to the king and returned to their units.

When they were gone, Richard shook his head and said to the council. "Saladin executes our men after Hattin, simply because they are Christians, and everyone pretends he's a model of virtue. I execute these men for sound military reasons, and people act like I'm in league with the Devil. If Saladin valued these men's lives so much, he should have paid their ransom as he promised to. I won't let them keep us from our goal. As commander of this force, I would be derelict if I did. Let's get this over with."

Many of Leicester's soldiers were reluctant, but they were terrified of their commander, whom they called the Gravedigger—and they arranged the prisoners in lines of a hundred men. Then other soldiers moved down the lines, cutting off the prisoners' heads. There were no sounds under the azure Mediterranean sky but the methodical *thunk* of swords, the pitiful pleas of the victims, and the wailing of the prisoners' wives and children, who were held back by guards. The surcoats of the Templars and Leicester's men were splashed and dripping with blood. Heads and bodies and pools of blood lay in neat lines. One step ahead of the executioners, Leicester's priests went down the lines, as well, making the sign of the cross and condemning the victims' souls to Hell. When the footmen got tired of chopping off heads, they turned to slitting throats, or driving a dagger through the eye and into the brain. At that point, a number of the prisoners struggled to their feet and, with hands tied behind their backs, tried to run. A few of the Christians laughed as these men, trapped in the square, were chased around and killed by Templar horsemen, as if in some macabre travesty of hunting.

When the last Saracen was dead, the Templars and Leicester's men doffed their blood-soaked surcoats and burned them in a pile. The army marched back to camp in silence, and the stunned spectators returned to the city. When the Saracen carcasses had been stripped by the souvenir hunters and vendors of curios, wives and children were allowed to reclaim their family members. The rest were left in the sun for the buzzards and dogs and rats, who were only too appreciative of the gift.

Chapter 17

"**I**'LL GIVE THE bugger his due," Henry of Deraa remarked, "it's a clever setup."

He and Roger stood on a slight rise, observing the army as it prepared to march. King Richard had studied the disaster at Hattin and was determined not to have it repeated. He had devised a marching formation of three parallel columns. Closest to the sea were the baggage and spare animals. Next came the knights and men-at-arms. The third column, facing potential attackers from the hills, was made up of spearmen and archers. They would shield the other two columns from the Saracens' mounted archers. This way the Saracens couldn't kill the knights' horses or get at the baggage train. The Genoese and Pisan fleets stood out to sea, affording protection from that flank. They would also bring water casks to shore periodically, assuring that men and animals would not break down from thirst as they had at Hattin.

The army was so vast that, from Roger and Henry's position with the rearguard, the van was lost to view. "A brave sight," said Garnier of Naplouse, Grand Master of the Hospital, who stood with them, along with his marshal, William Borrel.

"It is indeed," Henry replied. Garnier commanded the rearguard. The Templars traditionally rode in the van, the place of greatest glory, while the Hospitallers traditionally occupied the rear, the place of greatest danger. Down from the rise, knights and men-at-arms of the rear guard stood by their mounts, while footmen lazed on the ground, some of them dozing in whatever shade they could find, others joking or rolling dice or grabbing a last bit of food. The early morning sea breeze added a welcome coolness to the day. Gulls screeched and swooped overhead as though they were excited about the army's march as well.

Over his hauberk Roger wore his white surcoat with the red Death's Head—he didn't want to, but Tatwine had insisted on it. Henry's surcoat was, as always, plain and much mended. Both men wore conical helmets covered in cloth to keep them from getting too hot in the sun. The two Hospitallers wore black surcoats with the a white cross. "Forgive me, my lords," Roger said, "but aren't those black robes hot?"

Garnier laughed. He was a spare man in his mid-40s. He had been born in Outremer, and his face was deeply tanned and leathery. "We are monks, young sir, and we wear black as a symbol of earthly penance." The Hospitaller footmen were more sensibly dressed in light brown fustian with black crosses on the shoulders.

"How does it feel being back here with us, Henry?" Garnier went on jovially. "Not your usual station, eh?" He and Henry had known each other a long time. Garnier had been present when Roger and Henry had their confrontation with Richard and had been banished to the rearguard.

Henry placed a hand over his heart and bowed. "It is an honor to be in such distinguished company."

"If it's any consolation, I would have told the king the same thing you did about killing those prisoners."

"Thank you, my lord," Henry said, and he smiled. "That's the difference between you and the Templars."

From the van, a trumpet blew. "There's the signal for scouts out," William Borrel said. The swift, lightly armored Turcopole scouts would fan out ahead of the army. "We're getting ready to move."

Like a giant animal, the main body of the army shook itself to attention. Drums beat assembly, trumpets and horns blared. Banners blossomed over the host as they were unfurled. Armor and lance points glittered in the sun.

When all was ready, a gold-helmeted figure whom Roger knew to be the bishop of Beauvais rode out in front of the army's center. He blessed the crusaders and raised a silver cross to a great shout.

The bishop rode back to his lines, and a herald blew three blasts, setting the army in motion. One by one, the divisions started off—the Templars and some of the French in the van, the rest of the French, the Provenceaux, the English, and many more in the center, with King Richard. There were so many that it took a good while before the last center division, the Flemings under James of Avesnes, got under way.

"We're next," Garnier said. "All right, William, get them up."

The burly marshal, who had fought in his first battle at age fifteen, started off the rise. "Prepare to march!"

Knights and squires made a last check of their saddles and mounted. Footmen rose, donned-cloth covered helmets and formed up in marching order.

To Henry and Roger, Garnier said, "You two go first, we'll be right behind you. Keep the division in front of you in sight. Don't fall too far behind them or we could be cut off. Good luck, gentlemen."

"Thank you, my lord," they said. "Good luck to you as well."

As Roger and Henry started down the rise. Henry said, "My men are mostly horse, so I'll take the inside column. My footmen can march with yours on the outside."

"All right," Roger said.

Roger mounted his chestnut gelding. Knights usually rode stallions in battle but Roger was not sufficiently trained for that. He slung his triangular shield with the Death's Head symbol behind his back. Tatwine stood nearby with Slowfoot and the axe men. It was unusual to see a squire on foot, but Tatwine had never ridden a horse and he refused to learn.

Roger's two understrength companies of spearmen formed up four abreast, with the sections of axe men between them marching in twos because there weren't enough of them to make fours. The archers—most of whom Roger had gotten from Henry—filled in with the axe men. Roger's own men all had the Death's Head painted on their cloth helmet covers. To Roger's right, Henry's knights and men-at-arms formed in a column of fours, with the baggage train beyond them, near the sea.

"Ready?" Roger cried to his men.

"Ready!" replied Short Peter.

"Unfurl the banner!"

Tatwine shook loose the white banner with the red Death's Head.

Henry cried back to Garnier. "Much as I'd like to display my banner, I'll keep it furled for now, Lord Garnier. If Saladin knows I'm with you, he's like to come after us with everything he's got."

"He may well do that anyway," Garnier replied, "but thank you."

To Roger, Henry said, "Take them out."

It was an honor to issue the order to march. Roger watched the Flemings ahead of them, gauging the right moment, conscious of everyone's eyes on him. "All right, Shorty, start them off."

"Forward!" ordered Short Peter.

"Forward!" ordered Henry of Deraa.

"Forward!" cried William Borrel.

The Death's Heads started off, marching jauntily and singing "Girls of Falaise." Henry of Deraa's men rode alongside them, followed by the Hospitallers, singing psalms.

The Christian host snaked across the dusty plain toward the distant headland of Mt. Carmel, until they were lost in the dust and only the singing could still be heard.

Behind them, the first Saracens appeared.

PART II

Chapter 18

THERE WERE TWO of them.

They were a quarter-mile behind the rear guard, mounted, their light armor and conical helmets flashing in the sun. They didn't approach the marching column but kept pace with it, riding easily.

One of Roger's spearmen—Francisco, the young *morisco* who had painted the helmet covers—said, "Are those—?"

"Yes," Roger told him.

"Eyes front, there!" Short Peter yelled at the men. "If we wanted you to gawp around like monks at a knocking shop, we'd tell you to do it. This ain't no sightseeing trip."

Roger rode over to his father—still hard to think of Henry that way. "I didn't expect them so soon. We only broke camp a short while ago."

"Well, they're here," the one-eyed baron told him. "Foraging parties will need to go heavily armed if they want to come back in one piece."

Roger watched the riders. "What do you think they'll do?"

"Those two? Nothing. They're just here to remind us that Saladin's around. Oh, they might dash in and stick an arrow in someone or steal a horse if they get a chance, but that's about it. Don't worry, we'll see more of their like before the day's over."

"You think Saladin will attack us?"

"Not today. He'll harass us and try to wear us down, the way he did before Hattin. Then, when he figures we're weak enough, he'll move in for the kill."

The two Saracens continued to follow the column, and after a while the men got used to having them around and stopped paying attention to them. Already the men of the rear guard were covered with so much dust that they, and their animals, had turned a uniform shade of light brown. The men hadn't gotten into the routine of the march yet, especially the recruits, and they were more concerned with the heat and exertion than they were with the two Saracens. Sweat poured out of them.

"Easy on that water," the vintenars warned. "Won't be no more till we make camp."

Ahead of them the long column was strung out over several miles, with messengers riding up and down its length. The banners had been furled. A huge cloud of dust hung over the column. On the crusaders' left, the hills pressed close. To their right, high dunes separated them from the shore. Between breaks in the dunes the Pisan and Genoese fleets were visible in the distance, hard to make out in detail because of the glare off the water.

Towards tierce, a mist rolled in off the sea, which was unusual during the day. The men cheered the mist because it brought relief from the blazing sun. It made vision dicey, though. "Keep them moving, Shorty," Roger said. "Don't let those Flemings in front of us get out of sight."

The mist thickened to fog. The unseen sun gave the fog a pearly luminescence, made its droplets seem to swirl in undulating waves. The fog mixed with the thick dust from the column, severely limiting visibility. The men could no longer see the hills to their left. The sound of marching feet, the clatter of hooves, the rattle of wheels and creak of baggage carts were strangely muffled.

The black-robed Hospitallers Garnier and his marshal William Borrel rode up to join Roger and Henry. "I don't like this weather," Garnier said. "I don't like it at all. I fear our pagan friends may use it to cause us mischief."

"I agree," Henry said. "I wouldn't be surprised to see Sidesaddle gather his forces and launch a quick attack. He nearly carried our camp the last time he attacked in a fog."

"Be vigilant," William Borrel warned Roger. Roger's footmen were on the outside of the column and would bear the brunt of any attack.

"We will be, my lord," Roger said. He took a swig from his water bottle.

Garnier pointed east. To Henry, he said, "My home of Naplouse is just about halfway between this place and the River Jordan." He sighed. "Wonderful orange groves there, I wonder if I'll ever see them again. I remember when I was a—"

"Sh-h-h!" said Henry.

Everyone jerked to attention. "Did you hear something?" Borrel asked Henry.

Henry nodded with his chin. "Out there."

The men strained eyes and ears into the fog. Beside them, the Death's Heads filed by, the men quiet, alert.

"There it is again," Henry said.

Roger heard it now. "Horses?"

"They didn't waste any time," Garnier said. He turned to Borrel. "Pass the word—no man is to leave the ranks for any reason. Alert the baggage train to the enemy's presence."

William turned and disappeared into the pearly mist as Roger and Henry issued similar orders to their men.

"But I got the flux," one of the axe men complained to Roger. "I 'ave ter shit somethin' fierce."

"You'll have to do it in your braies," Roger told him.

Tatwine jogged back to Roger from the front of the column. "Can't see them Flemings ahead of us no more."

Garnier bit back an oath. "We can't go any faster in this fog. We'd lose cohesion and get jumbled up. Our formation would fall apart and we'd be easy pickings."

"Probably what Saladin's hoping for," Henry told him.

"Fog's bound to burn off soon," Tatwine said hopefully.

" 'Soon' might be too late," Henry said.

Garnier returned to the Hospitallers, and Henry to his men. The rear guard kept marching, eyes fixed to the left.

Roger saw something move. At first he thought it was a trick of the mind; then he saw it again and knew it was real. A shape, ghostly in the golden mixture of mist and dust, and made all the more sinister because of that. Roger tapped Tatwine and pointed. Tatwine nodded; he'd seen it too.

Something thunked into the dirt nearby.

It was an arrow.

Another.

Somebody gave a nervous laugh.

Men up and down the line were pointing now as the shapes grew numerous. They appeared to be men on foot, though in reality they could have been anything, so vague were their forms. Some looked to be no more than fifty yards away.

"Look at that one," said one of the spearmen, a young tough named Joseph who had joined up to avoid the gallows. "Look how close he is." With a laugh, he turned to his friends. "Let's get him."

Before Roger could stop them, Joseph and two other men dropped their cumbersome spears, drew their knives and dashed out into the fog.

"Get back here!" Roger cried. He made to spur his horse after them, but Henry appeared out of nowhere and held him back. "Let them go," Henry said.

Joseph and his friends became vague shapes in the fog. The column kept moving, men looking to the left where the three spearmen had disappeared. After a moment there were muffled noises. A blurring of shapes.

A scream.

A buzz of talk swept down the line. "Quiet!" Henry snapped.

They kept marching, everyone praying for the sun to reappear. More ghostly shapes loomed to the left. There was the muffled sound of hooves, the jingle of accoutrements. An arrow suddenly bounced off Roger's shield.

"They're taking our range," Henry said.

Footmen fingered their weapons. Knights loosened swords in scabbards. Roger touched the axe at his waist to make sure it was still there.

The men in the outside ranks unconsciously edged inwards, crowding the next line. The Hospitaller footmen in the very rear walked backwards to avoid being taken by a sudden rush, slowing the column even more.

Henry beckoned to Roger. "Let's find those Flemings. I don't want them getting too far ahead of us,"

Henry and Roger, accompanied by Henry's squire, Teary, rode forward. The ground was open here. More importantly, they couldn't hear anything ahead of them. Then Roger spied something on the ground to his left.

A body.

"Father!" Roger called in a loud whisper, pointing. He and Henry rode over to the body, dismounting, while Teary held their horses.

The body lay face down in a puddle of congealing blood. His armor marked him as European, a footman. Henry turned him over. He was a Fleming by his badge, but he was otherwise unrecognizable because his face had been gouged out.

"They're between us and the Flemings," Henry said. "We're cut off."

Chapter 19

NO SOONER HAD Henry uttered those words than the Saracens attacked.

In the fog Roger felt, rather than saw, the rear guard come to a hurried halt. He heard Short Peter's voice, remarkably calm under adversity. "Face left—two ranks! Spears level! Axe men in the gaps! Archers ready!" All that practice that the men hated so much was being put to the test. To the rear, the Hospitaller commanders called out similar orders. From Henry's knights came the call, "Squires to the rear! Wheel left!"

This was followed almost simultaneously by the rattle of shield against shield, by the clash of metal, by yells and cries as men hacked at each other. Arrows rained down, wounded horses bucked and plunged.

Roger took his shield from behind his back and turned his horse to rejoin the Death's Heads, when there was more noise behind him.

"They're in the baggage train!" Henry cried. "Come on!"

Roger pointed. "But my men. I should be—"

"This is more important," Henry told him. "Come on!" To his squire, Teary, he said, "Bring our men. Quick as you can."

Roger followed Henry to the baggage train. A large party of Saracen cavalry had gotten through the gap between the Flemings and the rear guard, and they were overrunning the defenseless baggage train, killing the wagon drivers and muleteers, slaughtering valuable stock and pack animals, plundering supplies, killing or stealing spare war horses. They were led by a giant whose gilded armor marked him as an emir of note. The giant, who must have been seven feet tall, wielded an enormous spear, stabbing with it overhand, felling men left and right before being swallowed up by the fog.

With a cry, Henry and Roger charged into the action. The sound of thudding hooves told Roger that Henry's knights were close behind.

Roger lost sight of Henry. He chopped his axe into a Saracen's back, pulled the axe free, and with a crossbody blow struck a man to his left just behind the ear. By now Henry's men had lost the element of surprise. The Saracens turned to fight them, and Roger dodged a slash at his head, swinging his axe in return but hitting nothing.

This was not like an infantry fight, where men lined up in more or less orderly ranks. After the initial charge, this was a melee in the fog and dust, men wheeling and slashing, both sides jumbled together and barely able to see each other. A figure loomed out of the murk. Roger raised his axe, then realized it was one of Henry's knights and stayed his hand in mid-strike. The knight saw him and his eyes widened as he realized what had almost happened, and then their horses carried them past one another.

A spear struck Roger's shield, jarring him violently and almost knocking him from his saddle, and he spurred his horse into an open space, out of danger for the moment. He looked back and through the fog saw it was the giant who had hit him, but the giant didn't pursue because he was fighting one of Henry's knights now. He took a blow from the knight's sword on his round shield, then drove his huge spear into the knight's face and out the back of his head.

Closer to Roger, one of Henry's men was assailed by two Saracens, flailing his sword from side to side to ward them off. Roger came to the man's aid, shattering one Saracen's collarbone with his axe. The Saracen cried and slumped in his saddle as Roger's momentum carried him past.

Behind him there were horns and cymbals and pagan yells as a new wave of Saracens fell upon the beleaguered rear guard.

Saladin had isolated them, and now he was going to destroy them.

Chapter 20

𝕿HE CENTER DIVISION of the Christian army moved along in good order despite the fog. Gullies and hillocks forced them to go slower while the obstacles were negotiated—the ox carts had to be manhandled over the rougher parts—and King Richard, who rode with the knights in the middle column, fretted over the loss of time. Suddenly there was a muffled racket from the rear.

Richard looked that way but could see nothing in the fog. Other men looked as well, but their vintenars and centenars ordered them to turn back and keep marching.

The racket grew louder.

"The rear guard's in action," said Alart of Vouzin.

Andrew of Chauvigny squinted through the swirling mist. "Should we go to their assistance?"

"No need for that," said Guy of Lusignan. As putative king of Jerusalem, Guy commanded the center division. "They haven't sent for help."

"Maybe they're too hard pressed," Alart observed.

Richard beckoned a young herald. "Ride down there and find out what's happening."

As the herald rode away, the earl of Leicester and the duke of Burgundy joined the group. "No sign of the enemy opposite us," Graveyard Leicester said, "though with this blasted fog it's hard to tell."

"It's a diversion," Guy warned them. "Saladin wants us to weaken our center and send men to the rear, then he'll launch his main force against the center and try to cut the army in two. That's why it's so quiet—he wants us to think he isn't out there."

The herald returned, lathering his horse and reining to a halt, causing the horse to slide. The horse stamped and pawed the air, and the herald curbed him. "Couldn't get through, sire," he told Richard. "Once you get past the Flemings, the way is blocked by Saracens, lots of them. No sign of the rear guard, but there's heavy fighting down there by the sound of it."

Richard stroked his bearded chin, then to another herald he said, "My compliments to Grand Master de Sable, and tell him to halt the column."

"Yes, sire." The herald galloped off toward the army's van.

Guy of Lusignan said, "Sire, I'm telling you, this is a—"

Richard ignored him, calling to a formation of knights nearby, led by William of Tancreville. "Tancreville, I'll have your Normans, if you please."

"Yes, sire," William called.

"I'm coming too," Leicester said.

"And I," cried the grizzled duke of Burgundy.

To Guy, Richard said, "Have the footmen open a way for us."

"Sire—"

"Do it, damn you!"

"Yes, sire." Guy rode toward the footmen, shouting orders.

The Norman knights and men-at-arms formed up, close to a hundred of them. Richard would have preferred his own

Poitevins, but the Normans were traditional bodyguards to the king of England, and it was a position they guarded jealously.

One of Richard's squires handed him a lance. "Alart, Andrew—with me!" Richard shouted. To the Normans he cried, "Forward!"

Then, in column of fours, Richard and his knights galloped through the newly formed gap in the infantry and down the long line of men, toward the rear guard.

21

THE SUN GRADUALLY burned off the fog, revealing an impending disaster. The rear guard was surrounded. The Death's Heads and the Hospitaller footmen held their lines, but barely, because mounted Saracen archers were behind them, peppering them with arrows, while Saracen footmen assailed them from the front. Henry's knights were too outnumbered to do anything more than fight for their lives, while the knights of the Hospital had to be held in reserve against a collapse of the infantry lines.

The trick in a meleé was to outnumber an opponent. Thus, two or three men would join to attack one, five would attack three. Roger had been part of a group of three but had become separated from them in the chaos. A helmetless Saracen horseman came at him. Roger swung his axe at the Saracen horseman, but the man blocked it with his shield. The two riders circled and Roger tried to close with the man. He swung his axe again but for some reason Roger's horse shied away at the last moment and Roger missed the Saracen, lost a stirrup, and almost fell. Before he could recover, something pounded him in the back and he ended up on the ground.

He dropped his axe in the fall. He scrambled to his feet, drawing his sword, his shield hanging uselessly by its neck strap, just in time to see the mounted giant bearing down on him, the huge spear held overhead and pointed straight at his face. Roger dodged out of the giant's way, swinging his sword wildly, hoping to hamstring the giant's horse but missing.

The giant wheeled and came at Roger again. Before he could get to Roger, another horse crashed into his. The horse was ridden by Henry of Deraa. The two mounts screamed and fell to the ground, taking their riders with them. Henry rose first and attacked the giant. The giant had lost his spear. He took Henry's sword slash on his armored shoulder, then he picked Henry up, held him over his head and threw him to the ground. Henry landed on his back, hard. The giant drew his curved sword; he had lost his helmet and his long dark hair flew wildly around his face. As he went after the stunned Henry, two of Henry's men attacked him from horseback. The giant knocked the first man from his saddle with a sweeping blow, and Roger didn't see any more, because someone banged his helmet with a mace, knocking it askew and staggering him.

Roger turned in the direction of the new attack, knowing even as he did that he would be too late to save himself, and that he had made a beginner's mistake by watching someone else fight instead of paying attention to his own situation, and he was right because his mounted assailant had the mace raised again and was bringing it down, but before the spiked mace head struck Roger, the point of a lance punched through the Saracen's chest. And the lance belonged to a Christian knight, and suddenly all around Roger the Saracens were running, and knights and men-at-arms were chasing them, killing them, and through the dust Roger recognized the red-clad form of King Richard.

Chapter 22

ℜOGER TURNED TO go to Henry's aid. But the fight with the giant was over. Henry and one of his men were next to the fallen Saracen. Henry was bent over, hands on his knees. The other man—it was the man Henry had been playing chess with when Roger had visited his camp—stood sucking in great gulps of air. Both men were covered with blood; their swords dripped with gore. Roger realized that he was covered with blood as well. Arrows peppered his hauberk. Around them the battle receded—the Saracens were in full retreat.

Roger looked at the fallen giant. The man was not handsome in any sense of the word. His huge dark eyes stared sightlessly; his long greasy hair was spread in a fan around his head. "Any idea who he was?"

Henry straightened, still breathing hard. "His name was Ayas al-Tawil. I met him several times. He was an honorable man. Damned strong, too—I thought my back was broken when he threw me down."

The knight beside Henry ribbed him good naturedly. "He threw you so far, it looked like a contest at the village fair."

Henry picked up the giant's enormous spear. He held it up, admiring it. "What are you going to do with it?" his companion asked.

Henry hefted the spear. "Damned thing's so big, I think I'll build a ship with it, sail it down the Red Sea and burn Mecca."

The two men laughed like that was the funniest thing they'd ever heard.

When they were done laughing, Henry turned to Roger and gestured at the sword in his hand. "You give that thing a name yet?"

Roger had not been expecting the question. "Not yet."

Henry growled with displeasure.

Roger sheathed the sword. "I suppose I should thank you for saving my life."

Henry's eyes met Roger's. "No more than I'd have done for any Christian. Mayhap you can return the favor one day."

From the plain came the sounds of battle as Richard and his knights pursued the Saracens. The Hospitaller knights had joined them. Henry's men were too weary from fighting to be of any assistance; they had borne the brunt of the attack and had taken most of the casualties.

Roger searched for his horse and saw him not far away, shuffling along placidly, nosing for grass. Roger took off his mail-backed gauntlets, unlaced his helmet and removed it, along with his mail coif and arming cap, letting fresh air blow through his sweaty hair. Roger's water bottle was empty, so he took a water bottle from a dead knight's saddle, poured some in his helmet, carried it to his horse and let the animal drink. When the horse was done, Roger finished the rest of the water bottle. After much searching, he found the chased axe that he had taken at Acre. He wiped blood from it and put it in his belt. Then he gathered his gauntlets, his arming cap and helmet, and he led his horse back to the Death's Heads.

The Death's Heads looked like they'd come through the fight pretty well. They had maintained their ranks. There were a number of enemy dead in front of them and the enemy wounded were being dispatched. There was no taking of prisoners.

Tatwine hurried over to greet him, wide eyed. "Where you been? We thought you must be dead."

"I got caught up in the fight for the baggage train and couldn't get back here," Roger told him. "How'd we do?"

Tatwine plucked arrows from Roger's hauberk. "Nine dead, seventeen wounded so bad they'll need treatment. Would've been worse if the king hadn't come when he did." Tatwine was bleeding from a gash on the right forearm; that wasn't considered a wound that would need treatment.

Twenty-six casualties; that was a tenth of Roger's force. They couldn't afford many more battles like this. After seeing to his men, Henry joined Roger, followed by Garnier of Naplouse and Willaim Borrel. Like Roger and Henry, the two Hospitallers were splashed with blood. "We were lucky," Garnier told Roger and Henry. "We were attacked by Qaymaz's division, Saladin's best troops—I recognized their banners. We were only hit by Ayas's wing, though—that must have been all Qaymaz could gather on short notice. Had he thrown his entire division into the fight, we would have been overrun."

On the plain, a horn blew recall. Richard's knights returned in loose order, laughing and bragging about their deeds, the wounded receiving aid from squires and comrades.

Then Richard himself rode up, with the earl of Leicester on his left and Hugh of Burgundy on his right, Andrew of Chauvigny and Alart of Vouzin close behind. Richard was flushed with the joy of battle, but his demeanor darkened as he approached the leaders of the rear guard.

Garnier greeted the king warmly. "Thank God you came when you did, sire. A bit more, and we'd have been dead."

"What happened?" Richard asked him in a sharp tone.

"The heathen got between us and the Flemings of the rear division."

"How did they do that? Why couldn't you keep up with the main body?"

"We tried, but we had to go slowly in order to keep our formation. We couldn't see much in that fog."

"Everyone else managed to keep up," Richard said.

Garnier had no answer for that.

Richard went on, and he was not happy. "What were you thinking? You could have gotten yourself and all your men killed. There's no excuse for this, Garnier. I can't be stopping the army every few hours to save you."

Garnier stiffened in his saddle. "No, sire."

"The march to Jerusalem will be arduous enough as it is. I'd like to get there before Judgment Day, but I can't do that if my rear guard dawdles like a bunch of children on their way to Mass."

Garnier blushed, and Roger spoke up. "It was my fault, sire. I was in the lead, I was the one who lost sight of the Flemings."

Richard studied him. "I expected better of you, Huntley."

"I expected better of myself, sire."

"Well, you're young yet, and young men make mistakes. There's no excuse for the men of the Hospital, though—or for you, Deraa." He trained his gaze on Henry. "You're quick enough to be insolent. Maybe you should put some of that energy into your duties in the field."

Henry bit back a retort and said nothing.

To Garnier, Richard said, "We'll give you time to get reorganized, then we start the army forward. And try to keep up this time."

Garnier said, "What about our baggage train? Half our animals are killed. The wagons will be filled with—"

"Do I get nothing but excuses from you, sir!" Richard thundered. His face had turned bright red. "You hold a post of honor. If you cannot handle it, I'll find someone who can."

Garnier stood up for himself. "It's not an excuse, sire. I can't conjure animals out of the—"

"Manage as best you can. And don't take all day doing it. I won't come back here to save you again."

Richard wheeled his horse, Fauvel, and he and his party rode off. The men they left behind looked at one another. "He wouldn't have waxed so wroth had it been his precious Templars," William Borrel consoled Garnier.

Henry said, "You heard him—let's get reorganized before we're left on our own."

Men were already taking water from the dead—they didn't have to be told to do that. There was no time to bury the Christian dead; they were stacked in wagons to be buried when the army made camp that night. Those of the wounded who could not walk were placed in wagons, as well. They would be transferred to the fleet later and returned to Acre. This took up a lot of their wagon space, so more baggage and supplies were forced onto the remaining pack mules, and the men were forced to carry extra, as well. The Saracen dead were stripped of valuables and left where they lay. Their co-religionists could dispose of them—or not, as the case might be. Henry kept Ayas's huge spear as a souvenir. Others of his men took the giant emir's armor, sword and helmet.

Short Peter approached Roger. "What about Joseph and the two that went with him? We ought to recover their bodies. They were fools, but they deserve a Christian burial."

Roger looked back down the trail, trying to estimate how far back the three men would be. Half a mile? More? He guessed that the Saracen cavalry, while no longer visible, were just out of sight behind the hills and would pounce on a small party.

"There's no time," Roger said. "And it's too dangerous."

"The men won't like it," Peter warned. "They—"

"I don't care what they like! I don't like it, either, but we've no choice. Like you said, Joseph was a damned fool and so were the two that went with him. They can take the consequences."

As if to accent Roger's words, a trumpet sounded from the army's van. "Ain't giving us much time, is he?" Tatwine said.

The army got under way, and the rear guard scrambled after, marching along once more in the heat, almost as if nothing had happened. Roger walked his weary horse, letting it get some rest.

"Roger," Tatwine said. He pointed to the rear of the column.

The two mounted men had returned.

Chapter 23

EIGHT DAYS LATER

TWO TURCOPOLES GALLOPED down the long line of marching men. They halted in the center, where King Richard rode. Words were exchanged, then Richard, Alart, Andrew of Chauvigny, their squires, and two heralds galloped back up the line with the Turcos.

The party reached the forward group of scouts and dismounted alongside them. The king and his two companions were unkempt. Their surcoats had been brushed and their armor polished that morning, but they were now covered with a thick layer of dust. The men's hair and beards were untrimmed and tangled and gritty with dust. They had no helmets, spears or shields—the squires carried them. They wore broad-brimmed straw hats with conical crowns, as did most of the nobles, to protect their eyes from the blazing sun.

The scouts' commander stood looking south. He didn't say anything to Richard. He didn't have to.

To their front, a seemingly endless line of banners stood outlined against the sky.

"It appears we'll have a battle tomorrow," Richard said.

"It's about time," said young Andrew of Chauvigny.

The army had suffered eight days of hit and run attacks, of men and horses killed. Eight days of men dying from the sun and dysentery. Of sand fleas and biting flies. Of men battling snakes and venomous scorpions. Two footmen of Bordeaux had even been eaten by crocodiles while bathing in a river near Caesarea. Foraging and water parties had been cut off, the captured men tortured hideously. Sentries disappeared, their mutilated bodies found later on the route of march. The pace had been excruciatingly slow, and it hadn't been helped by the rear guard, which seemed to suffer most of the attacks and used that as an excuse to lag behind the rest of the army.

This was not the kind of war Richard was used to fighting. The army was large and unwieldy, and there were too many things to occupy himself with besides actual combat. He had to worry about supplies, about sick men and about men feigning sickness so they would not have to perform their duties. About deserters trying to get on the ships and return to Acre. He had to deal with the never-ending animosity between the followers of Guy of Lusignan and Conrad of Montferrat, between the Templars and the Hospitallers, between the Pisans and the Genoese, not to mention the sullen opposition of Hugh of Burgundy and the French to everything he did.

Ahead of them, so the scouts said, was a village called Arsuf, where fresh water was plentiful. To their left were wooded hills. To their right, cliffs overlooked the sea.

Richard studied the distant line of banners. He would not attack. That was a long distance for knights to ride in the heat. And the Saracens could always withdraw, lead tired men and horses on still farther, then attack them. Worse yet, the Saracens could get behind the knights and cut them off from the footmen.

"We'll go into camp here," he told the heralds.

When the army had made camp and the men had eaten, Richard called a council of the chief barons and clergymen. As they gathered around, he picked an open spot to stand, and when the council was ready, he borrowed a baton from a herald—he would have used his sword but it was bad luck to draw a blade unless you intended to use it. With the baton, he drew a wavy line in the dirt, and to its left, a circle. "This," he said, indicating the wavy line, "is the sea. And *this*," he pointed at the circle "is the village of Arsuf." He drew a straight line below the circle, pointing toward it but not touching it. "This is our army, and this," he drew another line parallel to the first but ahead of it, "is Saladin.

"There is water at Arsuf. The village is held by the Saracens, but the Turcos say it's lightly defended. It is essential that we have water. Resupply from the sea is impossible right now because of the cliffs. My plan is to capture the village, base our center upon it, then let Saladin do his damndest."

Hugh of Burgundy made a face. "You mean we're not going to attack? We'll just sit there and take whatever that pagan throws at us?"

"Oh, we'll strike them," Richard said confidently, "but not until the time is right."

Richard drew a line from the top of Saladin's army across the forefront of his own, blocking it. "I expect Saladin to hit our van with his hardest blows, to try to keep us from the village, which is why I'm reinforcing the van with the Poitevins and Normans." He glanced at Garnier of Naplouse.

"I expect the rear guard to be hit as well, to further slow us down."

He tapped the baton against his leg. "Saladin has chosen his field well. He will try to keep us from water, weaken us from thirst, and then destroy us, as he did to our army at Hattin." There were surreptitious glances at Guy of Lusignan, who had been responsible for that disaster. "But that will not happen. It is imperative that we get to the village and capture it, and that we do it tomorrow. Everyone must keep up the pace, no matter how difficult."

Richard looked over the assembled nobles and churchmen. "Questions?"

There were none.

"Very well. We march before dawn. Hot work tomorrow, my lords. May God be with you all."

As the council broke up, Richard turned to the now-dark hills. *So, friend Saladin, at last we will see which of us is better.*

Chapter 24

NIGHT.

Some men prayed, some tried to sleep. Some sharpened weapons or polished armor. Some of the prominent nobles made the rounds of their equals.

Balian of Ibelin, one-eyed Henry of Deraa and the count of Champagne approached James of Avesnes, who sat on a camp chair outside his yellow tent, tinkering with his helmet. It was a new helmet, and he was adjusting the bolts on the nose guard to make it a bit longer. The big Fleming saw his three friends, rose and embraced them.

"We've come to wish you joy of the morrow," Balian told him.

James was in an anticipatory mood. In his toothless voice, he said, "Something tells me that this time we'll see off Old Sidesaddle for good."

The count of Champagne said, "Your company is just ahead of the rear guard, James, it may prove busy for you."

"The busier the better," James said.

Henry of Deraa grinned, "Remember—don't bite anyone."

"Ha, ha," James said.

Champagne went on. "The king has given me charge of the baggage train."

"Hard luck," James said.

The youthful count shrugged. "It's a job that has to be done. If the Saracens break through our lines and capture our supplies, we're lost. I'll be on the far left wing, right behind you."

"You don't think the main attack will come against the van?" Balian asked him.

"I'm not sure, but I want to be prepared if it doesn't."

"Too bad Geoffrey's not here," Henry said. "He waited a long time for this day, and now he's going to miss it."

"He didn't look at all well when last we saw him," Champagne said. "I hope he pulls through."

"You wouldn't look good, either, if you had his wife," James cracked.

The other three men laughed. Balian said, "A she-devil if ever there was one."

Henry of Deraa said, "We'd best see to our men, my lords. We have an early night. And an even earlier morning."

Chapter 25

ROGER, TATWINE, SHORT Peter, Slowfoot and some
of the old hands sat around as much of a fire as they'd been
able to build given the scarcity of wood. There was a forest—
or what passed for a forest in this part of the world—nearby,
but the Saracens controlled it, so there was no question of
getting wood there.

The fires from Saladin's army made the eastern sky glow.
The fires of their own army stretched up the coast in an
undulating line, like an enormous serpent from some pagan
myth. The Death's Heads had eaten a meal of mutton, black
bread and oranges, sent up from Acre by Fauston, who'd
fulfilled his promise to spend half his profits from the relics
on supplies.

"Good old Brocky," Tatwine said. "Knew he'd come
through for us."

Now they were passing around a jug of arrack that
Tatwine had scrounged from God only knew where. "Go
easy on that," Roger told them. "You'll need clear wits
tomorrow."

Tatwine took a swallow and wagged a finger at the
group. "I been thinking."

"There's three words no one wants to hear," Slowfoot
muttered.

Tatwine was undeterred. "I been thinking about Heaven.
You know how the priests are always telling us about how

Heaven is sitting around on clouds and playing harps and singing hymns for eternity? Well, that ain't my idea of fun. I'd rather be chasing whores, drinking and gambling. So what I been thinking is, what if the priests got it wrong? What if *Heaven* is chasing whores and drinking, and *Hell* is sitting on clouds and singing hymns?"

The men looked at one another. Short Peter made a face and shrugged. "Makes sense to me."

"Me, too," said a red-bearded spearman named Bern.

Slowfoot was impressed. "Surprised nobody's thought of that before. Tell the truth, I always been kind of worried about Heaven. Sounds boring."

A vintenar named John the Fifth—no one knew how he'd come by the name—took the jug and drank from it. "Way Tatty tells it, it almost makes you want to die."

There was head nodding and murmurs of agreement, and Slowfoot slapped Tatwine's back. "Tatty, me lad, yer a genius."

"A religious scholar of the first order," Bern pronounced.

"A prophet," said a Suffolk centenar named Oli.

The jug had made its rounds, and John the Fifth passed it back to Tatwine. "They should make you Archbishop of Canterbury."

"Hell, make 'im Pope," Slowfoot said.

Tatwine swallowed from the jug, and Short Peter took it from him. "Still," Peter said, "it means we got to be on the straight and narrow while we're here on earth."

"No worries about that," said Oli. "Not if it means spending eternity with some comely whore—or better yet, two whores. Maybe even three—why not, it is Heaven."

Bern rubbed his grimy hands together, warming up to the idea. "I bet the ale up there won't be watered down, neither."

Oli drank from the jug. "This'll be good news for all the lads what bought it during the siege."

" 'Cept that Welsh twat Uwen," Slowfoot said. "Hope he's sittin' on a cloud right now, singin' his ass off."

Proud of himself, Tatwine expounded. "A lot of these sourpuss priests are in for a rude awkening. Can't wait to see the looks on their faces when they go through the Pearly Gates and find themselves in a brothel."

Bern frowned thoughtfully. "Wouldn't that make St. Peter a pimp?"

"Better'n bein' a fisherman," Tatwine said.

The conversation went on, but Roger paid no attention. He couldn't stop thinking about the morrow. There was a tightening in his gut as he watched the glow from the Saracen fires. Those men believed they had God on their side, just as the crusaders did. But how could that be? There were intelligent men over there, how could they not see that their god was false? Then he realized that some of them were probably thinking the same thing about the Christians right now.

This was the kind of speculation that led to madness. The only thing for certain was that many men on both sides would not live to see tomorrow night's campfires.

The guard shift changed, and the group by the fire broke up. Roger lay on his blanket and tried to sleep, but couldn't. He wished the dawn would never come, and at the same time he wished it were dawn already and they could get it over with. Because tomorrow the fate of the crusade—the fate of the Holy Land—would be decided.

Chapter 26

THE ARMY ROSE well before dawn, but Roger was already awake. His nerves were on edge and he was anxious to be doing something. He heard Mass, forced himself to eat a piece of hard bread and wash it down with a little water. He didn't understand how some men could stuff themselves with food before a battle.

He put on his thick leather haubergon, then bent while Tatwine pulled his short-sleeved hauberk over the haubergon and adjusted the laces until it felt comfortable. Then came the white surcoat with the red Death's Head. With Tatwine's help, Roger pulled his mail coif over his arming hat and put his conical helmet on over that. Tatwine drew the mail aventail across the bottom of Roger's face, lacing it to bolts on the bottom of his helmet. The aventail was uncomfortable and hot, but it kept your teeth from getting knocked out. Roger buckled on his sword and stuck his axe in his belt. He put on his old mail-backed gloves and slung his shield over his neck and shoulder, adjusting it to hang behind his back until he needed it.

The battle was expected to begin at dawn, so it was still dark when the Death's Heads took their places in line. Down from them, the Hospitaller footmen were doing the same. Roger inspected his men, checking their equipment and wishing them luck. Then he mounted and rode over to where Henry of Deraa sat his horse in front of his assembled knights. Roger held out his gloved hand. "Good luck, Father."

Henry took the hand. "Luck to you as well, son."

Far ahead of them, a horn sounded.

The sentries hurried in. "Column right!" called the captains.

The men faced right, forming column of fours.

"Forward!" cried Garnier of Naplouse. "Forward!" cried Roger and Henry of Deraa. "Forward!" cried the captains and centenars.

The army lumbered into motion. As Roger understood it, the plan was to march to a village called Arsuf, where there was supposed to be water, and take up a defensive position there.

The pace was steady. Dawn came, then passed, and there was no attack. The sun rose, with not a cloud in the sky to block it. It grew hot. There were no sounds but the tramp of marching feet, the clop of horses' hooves, the tired creak of wagons in the baggage train.

Still no sign of the Saracens. Gradually the tension eased and men felt free to complain about the heat, about marching, about the thousand and one things soldiers complain about. "Maybe Old Sidesaddle won't fight today after all," they told each other hopefully.

Roger felt equal parts relief and disappointment. Relief because, if Saladin didn't attack, it meant that Roger would live to see the sun set, disappointment because they were just putting it off till another day. Better to get it over with.

The sun rose higher. The heat worsened. The huge army trundled on.

Not long past prime, they heard a low rumble to the west.

Soon after, men began pointing at a dust cloud in that direction.

The rumble grew louder, the dust cloud grew larger.

Suddenly Saracen cavalry came boiling over the low hills, yelling and shooting arrows at the marching Christians. The arrows rained down, clattering off upturned shields. One stuck in Roger's hauberk. Another glanced off his aventail. Still another stuck in the skirt of his saddle.

Whinnies and cries as horses were hit. Two of the Hospitallers' mounts went down, leaving their mailed riders on foot in the heat. The Saracens rode away.

Roger dismounted and had his horse taken to a safer location near the baggage train. He wondered if the entire army was being attacked or just the rear guard. The dust was already so thick it was hard to tell.

Another attack. The Saracens got close enough to loose their arrows then wheeled and galloped away. They were too far off for the Christian horsemen to chase them.

Henry rode up to Roger. "They're trying to slow us down," he said. He turned in his saddle and called to the men at the head of the formation. "Keep moving! Keep those Flemings in sight!" A flutter of wind blew away the dust for a moment and Roger saw that the Flemings ahead of them were being attacked as well, as was the entire Christian army, or as much of it as he could see.

Another attack, more arrows, and this time as the attackers rode away, a mob of African spearmen charged out of the dust behind them, yelling strange war cries.

"Halt!" the captains cried hurriedly. "Face left! Spears down! Archers loose your bows!"

The column halted. Once again, the Death's Heads performed their evolutions smoothly, without panic, and Roger was proud of them. A glance ahead told Roger that the Flemings were under foot attack, as well. He saw their leader, James of Avesnes, riding behind the lines, waving his sword.

Some of the Africans fell to arrows and crossbow bolts. The rest slammed into the crusaders' wall of shields. Cries and yells turned to grunts and oaths as men hacked and stabbed and killed each other. Roger adjusted his shield strap around his neck and slipped his hand through the grip. He stood behind the footmen with his axe drawn, waiting to deal with anyone who broke through the line. But no one did. The Africans were lightly armored and the Death's Heads and Hospitaller footmen beat them back with little loss to themselves.

To their right, the Flemings had formed up and were marching again.

"Form column!" Roger cried.

Henry of Deraa yelled, "Lively now, boys! Keep up with those Flemings!"

⁓

A Templar herald galloped up to King Richard and his retinue. "Grand Master de Sable's compliments, sire, and the vanguard has the town in sight."

"Very well," Richard told him.

The herald rode off gratefully. Grateful because King Richard and his staff sat their horses in the open, well outside the protection of the marching army, completely exposed to Saracen arrows. Richard stood in his stirrups and looked up and down the column, trying to gauge what was happening. He could see neither the head nor the rear of the army, and all the dust stirred up by marching men and the constant attacks of the Saracen horsemen made it almost impossible for him to get a read on the situation.

This was insanity. How was he supposed to determine what to do when he couldn't even see his entire force? Why couldn't this be a proper fight where the knights just lined up opposite each other and charged? Why did it to be so complicated?

Despite the attacks, the army was keeping up the pace. They'd had to halt and fight off the Africans, but that was more of a nuisance than anything else. They needed to get to that village and anchor first their right flank, then the center. Then they could draw the Saracens in close and counterattack.

Here came horsemen attacking the Christian center again. Arrows whizzed by Richard, they bounced off his mail, but he ignored them.

He peered down the line once more. The attacks seemed heaviest on the left wing and rear guard, but it was hard to say for sure, and it was probably a diversion anyway. Saladin was waiting for him to reinforce the rear, then he would strike the van with his main force.

Alart rode closer and took Richard's arm. "Sire?"

Richard followed his friend's gaze. An entire company of Saracen horsemen was galloping straight at them. Richard waved a friendly salute to the oncoming Saracens, then he and his staff wheeled their horses and trotted back behind the wall of cheering footmen.

∾

The Saracens attacked again.

Roger put the axe in his belt, slung his shield behind his back and turned to Tatwine. "My crossbow, please."

Tatwine handed Roger the dragon-tillered crossbow that had once belonged to Helvise. He passed him the quiver of bolts. Roger had practiced with the bow while they were in camp. It was easy to use, but it took a long time to reload. With his right foot in the bow's stirrup, Roger bent and placed the bow cord on the hook in his belt, then he straightened, using his body weight to draw the cord up till he could hook it behind the nut. He seated a bolt in the channel. He found a gap in the line of marching men, took a place just in front of the line—so he wouldn't get run into by his own people—and looked for a target. The half-obscured Death's Head on his dusty surcoat made him a tempting target for the Saracens, but there was nothing he could do about that.

He aimed at a Saracen who had just shot his arrow and was in the process of wheeling his horse. He fired—and the bolt went wide.

He ducked back behind the line of marching men. He was with the brown-jacketed Hospitaller footmen now, so he had to hustle back up the line to the Death's Heads—no mean feat while wearing armor. He stopped and went through the laborious process of reloading the bow—how had Helvise managed this for days on end during her march through Anatolia? He took a place just outside the line of spearmen again and marched with them, waiting for a good target. Another arrow stuck in his mail; he felt a jolt when it hit. He saw a Saracen who had stopped his horse in order to take better aim at his target.

The target was Roger.

Roger leveled his bow and pulled the trigger. The bolt hit the Saracen in the face and he topped backwards off his horse, his own arrow fluttering into the dirt. Men cheered and clapped Roger's back as they marched by.

Roger made his way back to the Death's Heads and reloaded. He wouldn't be able to keep up this pace for long, not in this heat. He had Tatwine unlace his aventail and he took a long drink from his water bottle. Meanwhile, the Hospitallers' archers and the few archers with the Death's Heads kept up a steady fire at the horsemen. They brought down some, but not enough. The horsemen kept coming closer and closer, and more and more of the column came within range of their bows, even the baggage train. Roger had to admire the way the Saracens rode, seemingly one with their mounts, reins in their teeth as they shot their short bows. Christian casualties weren't bad yet, mail and armored jacks kept most of the arrows from doing damage to the men, but more and more of the horses were being hit.

More and more of the knights and men at arms were walking, and when they were afoot they grew tired. More importantly, when the knights were afoot they were no longer an offensive threat, and the knights were the only means the crusaders had of striking back at the enemy. The screen of footmen and archers guarding the rear of the column was being forced to walk backwards again, and that slowed the column down.

"We need to attack these fellows," Garnier told a hurried council of his commanders. "We can't just stay here and let them shoot at us." He beckoned to a herald. "Ride to the king. Give him my respects and ask him for permission to attack."

❧

"Grand Master Garnier sends his respects, sire. We are losing horses at a rapid rate. The Grand Master begs to be allowed to attack, else we may not be able to keep pace with the army."

"Tell the Grand Master he must keep up," Richard ordered. "I don't give a fig how he does it, but he must. Tell him we will attack, but only when I give the order. Make that clear—only when I give the order."

"Yes, sire," the herald said. He wheeled his horse and galloped off.

❧

The attacks were almost constant now, wave after wave of them, with the Saracen horsemen withdrawing to refresh themselves, while the Christians got no rest but were forced to endure the marching, the heat, the thirst. Each attack came a bit closer to the marching formation. Roger's aventail was laced again; his hauberk was stuck with so many arrows he no longer bothered to pull them out. Everyone else was the same. They looked like a column of hedgehogs.

The African footmen attacked again, and that forced the column to stop. More horses went down. Men were falling now, too. The dead were left where they lay, the wounded carried to wagons in the baggage train.

Henry rode up to where Roger plied his crossbow. He pointed through the dust to a blue Saracen banner. "That's Qaymaz's flag. I'd give anything to get my hands on that bastard."

The banner was well out of range of Roger's crossbow, so there was no chance of getting a shot. "Are we facing his whole division this time?" Roger asked.

Henry studied the mass of men opposite them, much larger than the force they'd faced the first day out. "I believe we are. I think they mean to destroy the rear guard, then roll up the army's left flank."

"King Richard thinks the main fight will be with the van."

"I wish he'd tell that to Saladin. Let the old boy know he's doing it wrong."

❧

"The king says to keep moving, my lord," the herald told Garnier. "No attack till he gives the word."

Next to Garnier, William Borrel bit back an oath. "At the rate our horses are going down, our entire force will be on foot soon," he told Garnier.

The Grand Master's black surcoat was the color of ochre from the dust. "The king does not understand how desperate we are. I'm going to see him myself."

Garnier rode up the long column, staying inside near the baggage train, which at this point of the line was largely untouched by the fighting. The army's center was being attacked, but with nothing like the ferocity of the assaults on the rear guard and the left wing.

Garnier searched for the red banner with three lions, saw it through the dust, and found Richard with his staff— Burgundy, Lusignan, Alart and Andrew of Chauvigny, along with a crowd of heralds and squires. Alart's filthy cheek was gashed and bleeding. Richard's hauberk bristled with arrows, his brilliant blue eyes peered out at Garnier from beneath the cake of sweat and dust that covered his face.

Garnier wasted no time on formalities. "Sire, we must be allowed to attack. All of my knights will be on foot elsewise."

Instead of the hot temper he had shown the last time they'd met, Richard was patient now. "We will attack, Grand Master, but we must wait for the right moment. The main body of Saracens isn't close enough yet. We must take the village and let the Saracen main force come to us. When they're close enough, we will charge them and we will crush them. The signal will be two blasts from my horn, then two blasts from the right wing and two more from the left."

Garnier said, "You don't understand, sire. Saladin has sent Qaymaz's entire division against the rear guard. We're being cut off from the main body, and I'm afraid we'll be overrun."

Richard took another look down the line, but that told him nothing. He couldn't see the left wing, much less the rear guard. "It won't be long, Grand Master, I assure you. Until then you must keep up the pace."

Garnier said, "But—"

Richard snapped, "That is an order, my lord."

Garnier said nothing. He bowed his head curtly and rode away.

"Old woman," Guy of Lusignan muttered.

"What did the king say?" William Borrel asked.

Garnier reined in and took some water from a squire. "He said to keep moving."

Henry of Deraa had joined them. "Doesn't he understand—"

"He has his plan and he's sticking to it. It matters not to him what's really happening."

Horses were still going down. More and more footmen and knights were dead or too wounded to fight, the cumulative effect of being hit by so many arrows.

One of Henry's knights rode up to the group. "We've lost sight of the left wing, my lord. The Saracens have cut us off. Roger is deploying half of his Death's Heads across the front of our advance to protect the baggage train. There is a line of our knights—those who still have horses—behind them."

William said, "That stretches our line of footmen dangerously thin."

"That's what Qaymaz wants," Henry said. "When it's thin enough, he'll break it with his infantry, then send his cavalry through, and that will be the end of us. Then he'll attack the left flank, and that will be the end of the army."

Garnier said, "Richard must strike soon, or we are lost."

❧

Roger fired another crossbow bolt into the seething mass of horsemen and dust. They were so close now that he couldn't miss. "I hope your idea about Heaven was right," he told Tatwine.

"Looks like we're about to find out," Tatwine replied.

❧

For what must have been the hundredth time, Richard looked down the line, judging the moment for his counterattack.

What kind of battle was this? The vanguard, which Richard had thought would bear the brunt of the fighting, had seen surprisingly little action, and said they had entered Arsuf. Indeed, they were setting up their tents to make camp. The rear guard claimed they were about to be massacred. This wasn't how it was supposed to be. The Saracens opposite the center were still not close enough to charge. How was a man to know what to do or who to believe when he couldn't see for himself what was happening?

Saladin's best chance for victory had been to keep the Christians from water, and for some reason he had thrown it away. Very well, Richard would make him pay. He would let the Saracens opposite him get a bit closer, let them get confident, and then the chivalry of Christendom would fall on them and erase them from history.

The rear guard could hold on, that was their job.

Just a bit more . . .

"We can't take much more, my lord," William Borrel pleaded.

"We have our orders," said Garnier, resigned.

The rear guard had halted. The men covering the very rear of the column were assailed so closely by Saracen footmen that they had to stand and fight hand to hand, and many of the dismounted knights had joined them. The formation was losing its cohesiveness. Men were collapsing from thirst and from the effects of the sun. Garnier and

William saw the Africans massing for another attack. The line was stretched so thin that the Africans would break through this time, and Qaymaz's horsemen would be right behind them.

"It has been a pleasure serving with you, my lord," William said.

"And with you, William. Please God we will meet tonight in Heaven."

Roger's first quiver of bolts was gone and he had another brought from the baggage train. Across from the halted rear guard, many of the Saracens had now dismounted to take better aim. The falling arrows were like a steady rain that threatened to wash away all before it. So omnipresent were they that men paid them little attention. Apart from the few archers who were still shooting their bows, the footmen and knights could only raise their shields and endure, waiting for the Saracens' final charge.

Through the dust Roger saw a mounted man directing a company of Saracen footmen, pointing at the Death's Heads' banner as if he had a special interest in it. The man's right hand was heavily wrapped. He wore Saracen armor but he was bigger than most of his fellows and his beard was blond.

"Dirk!" Roger swore incredulously.

"Where?" said Tatwine.

Roger pointed at the mounted figure.

Dirk, the traitor.

Dirk, who had abducted Ailith.

"My horse," he told Tatwine.

Tatwine brought the horse as arrows showered around them. "What are you going to do?" he asked Roger.

Roger tossed him the crossbow and bolts. "What I should have done a long time ago." He threw himself onto the horse and shifted his shield into position. "Out of my way!" he yelled at the footmen in front of him.

The surprised men jostled aside and Roger charged through the opening they made.

"Roger!" Tatwine cried.

Nearby, Henry of Deraa saw what was happening. He swore and rode through the opening after Roger to try and save him. Loyal to a fault, Henry's men followed him.

William Borrel saw Roger and Henry ride through the line and he thought the horns must have blown. "Attack!" he cried. "Attack!" The Hospitallers who still had horses gave a cry, made their way through the footmen and fell upon the dismounted Saracens opposite them.

On the left wing, James of Avesnes saw what was happening. He thought the horns must have blown, too, and he charged. So did Henry of Champagne, leading his knights from the baggage train. The next unit down the line from the Flemings, the Manceaux, attacked as well.

In the center, King Richard saw the attack of the left wing. At first he was enraged because they had disobeyed his orders. Then he understood that this was his chance and he had to make the most of it.

"Sound the horn!" he bellowed. "Form line and attack!"

Chapter 27

THE KNIGHTS OF the rear guard and left wing caught many Saracens on foot and killed a number of them with the first shock of their charge. Those Saracens who were on horses turned and attempted to flee, but, overconfident, they had gotten too close to the crusader lines and they were caught from behind by the charging knights and slaughtered. The footmen who had been attacking the very rear of the Hospitaller formation were cut off from their fellows, and a number of them tried to save themselves from the vengeful Christians by jumping from the cliffs into the sea. The rest were killed without mercy. The infantry advanced in a steady line behind the horsemen, dispatching any Saracens left alive.

In the center, Richard led the charge, Andrew and Alart to either side of him, Burgundy and Lusignan close at hand. The Saracens weren't expecting Richard's attack, and the initial shock of the charge—heavily armored knights riding side by side, spears leveled—shattered the Saracen center. Men were killed or unhorsed, the Saracen line smashed wide open. When the fighting grew too close for spears, the Christians switched to swords or, in Richard's case, his Danish war axe. There was a brief meleé, but the Saracens were no match for the Christians in hand to hand fighting. The Saracen survivors fled, and the crusaders pursued them, cutting them down from behind.

From his vantage point in the hills, Saladin watched the action unfold. He watched with a small staff—all his senior commanders were involved with the fighting. He had planned to smash the Christian left wing, then, when Richard shifted his forces to meet the threat from the left, he would flank the Christian van and attack it. He would encircle Richard's army the way he had encircled the Christian army at Hattin, and he would destroy it.

Now he saw what had appeared to be victory turned into defeat in a matter of minutes, his invincible army running for its life.

"We should leave here, lord," said Beha ad-Din, his long-time chronicler. "All is lost."

Saladin could not believe what had just happened, but he didn't allow himself to show it. "No," he said. To his staff he said, "Beat the drums and keep beating them. Our men must know we are still here. That will give them heart."

From his vantage point in the hills, Saladin watched the

The pursuit extended across the plain, the Saracen army in full flight, the Christians at their rear riding for all they were worth. The Christian line grew ragged, the faster horses forging ahead, the slower ones falling behind. A huge cloud of dust covered the battlefield, obscuring vision. Units were jumbled up. Men no longer fought as a group but as individuals.

Richard and the first elements of the pursuit neared the pine forest. In the forest they could be trapped, Richard thought, picked off one by one. That's what he would have done were he in Saladin's place. The knights would be vulnerable to archers and footmen in the woods. They wouldn't be able to form a line, and their cumbersome war horses would be a liability.

He reined in Fauvel, and his staff reined in around him. "Sound the recall," he told a breathless herald.

"Recall?" cried Burgundy. "That's insane. This is our chance to destroy—"

"I suspect a trap," Richard told him. "Our knights will be at a disadvantage in the trees."

Ignoring an arrow in his shoulder, the unarmored herald raised his horn and blew.

Gradually the knights halted their charge, and the fleeing Saracens disappeared into the dust cloud and the woods. At Richard's order, the knights turned and started back toward the count of Dreux's men, who had followed behind the main charge in a steady line, acting as a reserve, and whose banners now formed an assembly point for the disorganized crusaders.

The charge had covered miles. Richard's knights were scattered like seed in a high wind. They rode back slowly, enjoying their triumph, men and horses winded. When they had reorganized, they would take place behind their advancing line of footmen, where they could get water and give their tired horses a rest.

❧

The feringhees were entering the forest in pursuit of Saladin's men, when suddenly a horn blew and they ceased their attack.

Saladin had been rallying his fleeing troops, riding back and forth, exhorting the men to re-form. His brother al-Adil and son al-Afdal helped, so did Qaymaz, who used a whip to halt his men's retreat. Through their efforts, what was left of the sultan's army was brought under some semblance of order.

Saladin halted his black horse and watched the crusaders' leisurely withdrawal, and he saw a way to salvage a day that had appeared to be lost. "Form your men and attack the feringhees," he ordered his generals. "Quickly, while they are not expecting it."

❧

The retreating Christians were relaxed and unprepared for further fighting when the Saracens came at their backs from the woods, loosing arrows, striking with swords and maces.

Now it was the surprised Christians' turn to flee, their turn to be cut down from behind. James of Avesnes tried to rally the left wing, but in doing so, he was cut off by a party of the enemy.

In the center, Richard was surrounded, along with Alart and Andrew. Every infidel wanted to be the one to slay

Malik Rik. That was fine with Richard. Instead of retreating, he wheeled and charged into his foes, laying about him with his Danish axe, Alart and Andrew guarding his flanks, the three of them holding up the Saracen attack by themselves. The rest of the knights saw them and took heart. Led by Burgundy, Lusignan and the earl of Leicester, they formed a hasty line with the count of Dreux's men and charged once more. And now from the Christian right wing appeared the knights of the vanguard, who had so far seen little action.

This second charge was even more devastating than the first. Sensing victory, the Saracens had come on as a yelling mob. Their momentum, and the momentum of those behind them, drove them straight onto the spears of the charging knights, who bowled through them like a battering ram might go through the walls of a thatched hut. Then the Normans and Poitevins of the vanguard struck them in the flank, smashing their formation to bits and forcing the survivors once more into headlong flight.

Richard was out in front of his men, fired with the joy of battle, striking with a fury unmatched on the field. Even so, he had presence of mind to keep an eye on his battle line, which, as it had done before, quickly lost cohesion in the dust.

This time the force of the Christian charge carried them well into the woods. There was fighting among the pine trees and boulders. The land was broken and it was difficult to see any distance. The battle resolved itself into a series of individual combats and small group skirmishes.

Somewhere drums beat steadily, and that drumming worried Richard. As before, he was fearful of an ambush. He knew enough about Saladin and his tactics to suspect that this was the kind of maneuver the sultan would employ, feigning retreat and drawing the Christians into terrain highly unfavorable to them, where he could fall upon them with his reserves. Perhaps that had been Saladin's aim from the first. Richard had no idea how many more men the sultan had—it could be few, but it could be many. Richard could not establish a battle line in these woods. He had only a small field of vision to either side. This was no ground for knights, and his footmen were far behind. He had won a great victory, he did not need to lose it here.

"Heralds! Sound the recall!"

Saladin watched his defeated troops fleeing past his banner. This time the constant drumming and the exhortations of their commanders did not stop them. It was only by the grace of Allah that the army maintained any organization at all. Many of these men would not stop running for days.

Qaymaz, no diplomat, stated the obvious. "This is a disaster."

Saladin made no reply. He did not have to. His face was flushed with the shame of defeat.

The chronicler Beha ad-Din glanced over his shoulder as though expecting to see the Christians ride up at any moment, which, indeed, was exactly what he was expecting. "I beg you, lord, leave this place before Rik catches you."

Reluctantly Saladin nodded. He was about to give the order when the infidel horn sounded again.

"They are pulling back," Qaymaz said in astonishment. The blue sash on Qaymaz's helmet was in shreds. His hawk-nosed face was splashed with blood. His black horse limped from a long gash in its flank.

"By the grace of Allah, we are saved," said Saladin's son al-Afdal, the Bull, who had fought well this day.

Saladin's brother, al-Adil rode up. "What are your orders, lord? Shall we retreat beyond the River Jordan?"

Saladin's jaw clenched. His dark eyes burned. "No, we stay here. Bring back as many of the men as you can and make camp in these woods."

The commanders looked at one another. Al-Adil said, "Are you sure?"

Grimly, Saladin said, "You heard my order, brother. Obey it."

Chapter 28

𝕬FTER THE SECOND recall, Henry of Deraa retreated behind the infantry line, where he reorganized his exhausted men. His squire, Teary, had somehow managed to stay by his side during the second wild charge and the fighting in the woods, and Henry gave the lad a thump on the back.

"Now that's what I call fun—eh, boy?"

"If you say so, my lord," a wide-eyed Teary said. Henry had a reputation for going through squires. They were either killed in battle or made knights. Either way, he did not keep them long.

Henry's jocularity was feigned—he did it because the men expected it of him. He had followed Roger to keep the boy safe as he charged into the middle of the Saracen army. He had been so intent on watching Roger that he hadn't paid enough attention to his own surroundings, and because of that he had been unhorsed by a spear thrust from the side of his blind eye. Henry's knights—whom he had not known were following him—had dispatched the man who had unhorsed him, while Teary recovered Henry's horse.

Shaking the cobwebs from his head, Henry had remounted, but by then the battle had turned into a massive brawl. There was no sign of Roger. If he had not been killed, he would be far ahead of Henry by now. There was no question of finding him, so Henry and his men had joined the general fighting, filling in with the knights of the Hospital.

Now the sun was setting over the sea. Henry bade his second in command, a scarred veteran named Guiles, lead his men to camp while Henry got a fresh horse.

"Where are you going?" Guiles asked him.

"To look for Roger."

Teary made to accompany him, but Henry waved him off. "See to my tent," he ordered. "Have a meal prepared for my return."

Henry rode back across the wide battlefield, which had for the moment become a neutral site, as men from both sides retrieved the dead and wounded, observing the unspoken truce that sometimes followed these engagements. On occasion, parties from one side would even help parties from the other place the dead and wounded on horses, when a short time ago they had been trying to cut each other's throats. Christian footmen had broken their formations and were looting bodies from both sides. Henry thought he recognized Roger's squire, Tatwine, among them.

Henry still had arrows in his mail from earlier that morning, which seemed so long ago. He retraced Roger's path into the battle, as near as he could remember it, walking his horse back and forth over a wide swath of ground. He searched the Christian bodies, resigned by now to his son's fate.

He prayed that Roger was only wounded—that his life could be saved if he was found in time—but in his heart he knew it wasn't true. Roger had charged into the heart of the infidel army to kill an old enemy. It had been a foolhardy move, and it could have had only one ending. Henry was sad, but he was proud of the boy. It was something Henry himself might have done. Now all he wanted was to find his son's body and give it a proper burial.

Why didn't the young fool stay at the abbey like he was supposed to? Why did he have to come out here?

Because he was my son. Because it was in his blood.

He came upon two figures standing over a body. Through the dust and blood that covered the two men, he recognized Balian and Henry of Champagne.

Henry walked his horse over to them. Balian and the count looked up, but gave him no word of greeting, and suddenly Henry's blood ran cold because he thought the body must be Roger's. Then he saw that the dead man was taller and heavier than Roger, and his hauberk ended in mailed gauntlets, whereas Roger's hauberk had short sleeves. And the bloody surcoat was yellow, not white, as Roger's had been.

Henry dismounted. The dead man's face was unrecognizable because it had been hacked to pieces, but Henry recognized the green eagle on the slashed surcoat.

"Oh, God," Henry said, and he made the sign of the Cross.

It was James of Avesnes.

Henry hung his head. Both Balian and the count of Champagne had tears in their eyes.

No one spoke. There was nothing to say. There was nothing but memories . . .

At last the count of Champagne turned away. "I'll get someone to take care of him," he said.

Balian said, "I'll wait with the body," and he knelt beside it to pray.

Henry rested a hand on Balian's shoulder. Then he mounted and resumed his search of the battlefield.

Where was Roger?

Chapter 29

As HE RODE, Roger kept his eyes fixed on Dirk, unaware that his father and the entire Christian army had followed in his wake. Saracens tried to intercept him and he lashed at them with his axe. He wasn't trying to kill them, he just wanted them out of his way.

Ahead of Roger, Dirk became aware that a Christian knight was coming toward him. Shock flared on Dirk's face as he realized who the knight was. He stopped directing his men and began edging his horse backward.

Roger closed on Dirk, swinging his axe at anyone in his path. Arrows struck him and his horse, but Dirk was the only thing he could see—Dirk and what he had done to Ailith. Roger knew he was going to be killed, but it would be worth it if he could kill Dirk first. His flagging horse took another arrow, missed a step, then went on again.

Suddenly the Saracens around Roger were fleeing, and Dirk was fleeing as well. Roger didn't know what had caused the enemy to run, and he didn't care. He spurred his horse, trying to keep Dirk in view while at the same time dodging blows aimed at him by passing Saracen horsemen. Roger lost sight of Dirk in the confusion and roiling dust, then found him again. Dirk was riding away, with an occasional glance over his shoulder to see if Roger was still there.

The chase led across the wide plain. The Saracens didn't care about Roger now, so intent were they on saving themselves, and Roger rode amongst them with impunity, keeping Dirk in sight all the way. Roger's horse slowed from his wounds and Roger urged him on. He had lost Dirk once before, during the siege, and he wasn't going to let that happen again.

Then they were in the forest, among pine trees and boulders. There was shade in the forest. It was cooler. Roger heard drums pounding ahead, a horn blowing urgently from behind.

Ahead of him, Dirk had suddenly halted and turned his horse. He looked like he was waiting for Roger now, a grin on his ham-like face. Roger went toward him, but his way was blocked by a group of Saracen footmen. He fought his way through them, chopping down furiously with his axe.

The Saracens footmen withdrew. There was a shower of arrows. Roger was struck. His already wounded horse made a plaintive noise and went down, throwing Roger. Roger lost his axe in the fall. He stood, drew his sword and started toward Dirk once more.

Dirk was taunting Roger now, enjoying himself, beckoning Roger to come on. Two horsemen rode by, shooting arrows. One arrow stuck in Roger's mail, the other grazed his cheek. More footmen rushed at him. He struck at them with his sword, cleaving shields and armor and bone, cleaving helmets and skulls. And every time he put a man down, another took his place and Dirk was just as far away as he had ever been, and he was laughing now and that made Roger all the madder, and he went after Dirk all the harder.

Yelling faces with yellow teeth and fetid breath, oiled hair and beards—these were Roger's fleeting images as he fought his way toward Dirk. His shield was hacked to bits, his helmet dented and knocked askew with blows from sword and mace, his chain mail split. Blood gushed from his nose.

He fought on. Dirk sat on his horse and grinned at him smugly, and Roger vowed to drive the blade of his sword through that ugly face.

Roger sucked in air. He grew unsteady on his feet, his throat burned with thirst. His right arm was too tired to lift the sword anymore, so he threw off his shield and switched the sword to his left hand, and kept fighting. Sweat blurred his eyes and it was hard to keep them focused. The Saracens had stopped fighting him now; they backed away, keeping just out of his reach, laughing as he swung his sword wildly at them. Laughing—that was the worst part, and he wanted to kill them all. Then the world was spinning, and suddenly Roger found himself on his hands and knees in the cool earth and pine needles.

He tried to push himself to his feet, got partway up and fell to his knees again, blood from his nose spattering the dirt. He was surprised that no one rushed at him to finish him off, then realized they were enjoying this spectacle. He tried to get up once more, took a few steps forward, swung his sword at the laughing Saracens one last time, then stumbled and collapsed full length on the ground. He couldn't move. He was finished. And the rage burned inside him more fiercely than ever because he had not done what he had set out to do.

He lay on his face, awaiting the inevitable, blood from his nose pooling beneath him. The drums were still pounding. Roger was surrounded by grinning faces.

Somebody kicked him in the ribs, then yelped because Roger's mail hurt his foot. Roger had a disjointed view of a man on a black horse, a whip in his hand, a cut-up blue scarf around his helmet. He saw a face he had last seen on the walls of Acre, when the man had smashed Deaf Martin's skull with a sledgehammer.

Qaymaz looked at Roger with eyes that showed no emotion. "Kill him," he told his men. "Take your time with it."

"I'll do it," Dirk said. He dismounted and took a spear from one of the footmen. "So nice to see you again, Roger. Sorry we don't have time for a chat. Maybe I'll start with your hand, as you did with mine. That would be symbolic, don't you think?"

From the ground, Roger stared at Dirk contemptuously.

Two Saracen footmen pinned Roger's right arm to the ground, and Dirk raised the spear for the downward thrust through Roger's hand.

"Wait," said a voice. The voice wasn't deep, but it was steely with authority.

Dirk halted and turned toward the voice.

Roger turned as well. He saw a tall, slender man on a horse lathered from heavy riding. The man's armor was plain but finely crafted. He had a regal bearing and was surrounded by bodyguards.

Saladin.

Saladin inclined his chin toward Roger, and the two Saracens let go of Roger's arm and hauled him to his feet.

Saladin gestured at Roger's tattered surcoat. "You wear the red skull."

Roger straightened. Through thirst-cracked lips he croaked, "I do."

Saladin's deep eyes narrowed. "Are you commander of the Red Skulls?"

"I am, and we are called Death's Heads." Suddenly he was more proud of that Death's Head emblem than he had ever been proud of anything in his life.

"This man deserves to live," Saladin announced to those around him.

Qaymaz attempted to protest, but Dirk beat him to it. "Lord sultan, he is an enemy. He—"

Saladin silenced him with a look. To Qaymaz he said, "My spies report that the leader of the Red Skulls argued with Malik Rik against killing our prisoners at Akko. That was a noble deed, and for that he shall keep his life. You may take him as a slave, but I do *not* want him killed. Is that understood?"

Qaymaz was impassive. "As you wish, lord."

Disgruntled, Dirk remounted his horse. Qaymaz gestured to Roger with his whip. "Surrender your dagger."

Roger nodded acquiescence.

The two men who were holding Roger let him go. Roger tried to steady his wobbly legs. He reached for the dagger at his left side. Summoning all his strength, he pulled the dagger from its sheath and with a fluid motion he sent it sailing through the air the way Fauston had taught him.

The blade sunk in Dirk's throat.

Dirk grasped at the dagger, tried to pull it out, couldn't. His arms windmilled. He fell from the saddle. His legs thrashed, then he was still.

Roger steeled himself, waiting to be cut down for his deed.

To his surprise, Saladin showed no reaction. "It is of no matter," he said. "That man was a traitor." He indicated Roger to Qaymaz. "Take him away."

Chapter 30

ℜICHARD RODE THROUGH the camp, accompanied by Alart, Andrew of Chauvigny, and a party of heralds. Progress was slow because men crowded close to see Richard, to touch him. Nobles great and small, along with common foot soldiers, vied with each other to congratulate the Red King on his victory.

On impulse, Richard dismounted and plunged into a group of Angevin knights. The knights had been in the process of removing their armor and getting themselves cleaned up. Now they clustered around Richard, who grinned broadly as they slapped his back and shook his hand. "Adelbert, isn't it?" he said to one man. "You were with me in the Perigord?"

Adelbert's bearded face was split by a smile. "I was, sire."

"Jean," he said to another, "you didn't lose that hand after all."

The man-at-arms held up his left hand, flexed it and winked. "Grew me a new one, sire."

Richard laughed.

Richard mingled with the footmen, as well. "Christ on the cross—Gilles, you old thief! Are you still alive?"

"Still alive, my lord. Them buggers can't kill me."

He recognized another face, tried to think who it was, then snapped his fingers. "Patrice!"

The gnarled spearman beamed, pleased that the great king had remembered him. "That's right, sire."

161

"I know you from . . . ?"

"The Ballans campaign."

"That's right. I spoke with you one night when you were on sentry duty. I remember because it was raining like Noah's Ark."

"That it were, sire. You lent me your cloak, as I recollect."

"And I recollect you never gave it back."

"Well, sire . . ." Patrice lowered his head sheepishly to gales of laughter, the heartiest from Richard himself.

Richard had previously campaigned with many of the men in the Poitevin, Angevin and Norman camps, but he'd met men from all over Christendom since his arrival in the Holy Land, and he had an especial fondness for one group of English archers.

"Ah," he said, approaching them, "it's Master Rob and his merry band of poachers." He said this with a big smile, and the archers—even those who understood little French—grinned.

"Did you enjoy yourselves today?" he asked Rob.

Rob spoke French well. He was either a quick learner or he'd spent time around the nobility. "Not as much as you, I expect, sire. We killed enough of 'em, though. Here, John, show the king what you got."

John was a big fellow—they had to be big, to draw those Welsh longbows, but John was bigger than most. He handed the king a dagger, the curved blade of which was made of fine Damascus steel. Its hilt was crusted with precious jewels.

"Took that off a dead one," Rob told the king. "An emir, like as not."

John looked on anxiously as Richard admired the dagger; though Rob, who knew the king better, didn't seem worried. As king, Richard was entitled to take the dagger for himself if he chose. He handed it back to John. "Keep it safe," he advised.

John let out a breath of relief. "I mean to, sire. I'll use it to buy me a farm when I get back to Yorkshire."

"A farm?" Rob said incredulously. "Why, man, you can buy yourself a manor with that."

Richard laughed. "A manor? You can buy all of Yorkshire!"

There was laughter and Richard went on, slapping John's back. "I expect to find you presiding at the next assizes."

It was dark by the time Richard reached the rear guard. He acknowledged Garnier, William Borrel and Henry of Deraa, then he spotted the Death's Heads' banner and went to it. The English soldiers mobbed him, eager to shake his hand—because what other king, or noble of any sort, shook the hands of footmen?

Richard looked around. "Where is Roger?"

One of the men, a sharp-eared fellow, replied glumly. "Gone, sire."

"Never come back from the attack," added a taller man.

Richard drew in his breath. He had posted young Huntley with the rear guard as punishment. If he hadn't done that, if he had left him in the center with the earl of Trent's men, where he was supposed to be, he might be alive now. Had it really been worth the balm to Richard's anger to see the boy killed?

"He had the makings of a gallant knight," Richard said. Then he corrected himself, "No, he was already a gallant knight." He added, "How are you men doing?"

"Be doing better if we had some food," said the sharp-eared fellow, emboldened.

Richard frowned. "What do you mean? There's plenty of dead horses around. Eat them."

"That's just it, sire. The Goat Fuckers'—beg pardon, the Saracens'—horses taste queer. Must be something they feed 'em. Gives us the runs. There's enough of our own dead and bad wounded horses about, but the nobles won't let us take 'em less we pay."

Richard looked around the knights in the audience. "Is this true?"

Downturned eyes and lack of response gave him all the answer he needed. He turned to his entourage. "Heralds—go round the camp and issue this proclamation: For every dead horse given to the footmen this day, I will provide the animal's owner with a new mount."

His words were greeted with cheering from the footmen, while Alart and Andrew exchanged glances, thinking no doubt about the cost.

164

❧

When Richard rode on, Slowfoot said to Tatwine, "Good on yer, Tatty. Speakin' up like you done."

Tatwine looked shocked as the enormity of his act sank in on him. "Never spoke to no king before."

Short Peter said, "There's a tale you can tell your grandkids—assumin' any of 'em's actually yours." He added, "We're going to eat well tonight."

Slowfoot was already sharpening his knife in preparation. "And for many a night thereafter, I'm thinking."

Tatwine said, "Too bad Roger ain't here to join us."

Short Peter nodded. "Aye, poor bastard."

"What do you think will happen to the company now?"

Slowfoot started off to look for a dead horse. "I'll worry about that after I eat."

Chapter 31

THAT NIGHT A council of the army's principal barons was held in Richard's pavilion. Inside, there was boisterous laughter, shouts and boasting.

Outside, in the darkness behind the pavilion, Richard brooded.

The battle had been a great victory, but he had not ordered the charge that won it. Should he have? Or should he have waited longer? Had he waited, the victory might have been greater still. But what if he had waited too long? The rear guard might have been overrun. Saladin might have turned his flank and rolled up his army from the left. His triumph had been a near-run thing that could easily have gone the other way, and that troubled Richard. Was Saladin actually capable of beating him? The idea had seemed preposterous not long before, but it couldn't be discounted now.

Richard was the only man who could lose the crusade in a day. The emperor Barbarossa was dead, and King Philip was on his way back to France. There was no one to take the blame for failure but Richard. That was a terrible burden to bear and one he had become more and more aware of. He had a responsibility not only to himself and the army, but to all of Christendom. They were looking to him to succeed, but even more importantly, they were looking for him not to fail.

A soft voice disturbed his thoughts. "Richard?"

It was Alart. His mentor, his confidant, his oldest friend. "They're waiting," Alart said.

Richard nodded. He paused before the pavilion entrance, threw his shoulders back, and barged in ebulliently.

He strode to the center of the tent, cheering nobles making way for him. Even old Burgundy seemed to be in a good mood. Richard hopped on a camp stool and raised a hand for silence. When the crowd had quieted, he began. "We give thanks to Almighty God for our victory this day, my lords, but that victory could have been greater."

He paused. He didn't know if he believed what he was going to say next, but he had to say it if these headstrong men were to respect his authority going forward. "Had we waited for my signal to attack, we could have destroyed Saladin and his entire army. We could have ended our holy pilgrimage here on this field." He paused again. "Unfortunately, a few of us felt the need to take matters into their own hands."

His eyes sought out Garnier of Naplouse. "Grand Master? Your Hospitallers attacked in defiance of my command. What say you in defense of your action?"

Garnier stood straight. He had removed his armor. His black surcoat had been hastily brushed but it was torn and blood stained. Before he could say anything, Henry of Deraa stepped forward. "I led the attack, sire. The Hospitallers followed me in the mistaken idea that you had given the order."

Richard studied him distastefully. "I cannot say this news surprises me, sir. Why did you disobey my order?"

Henry held his ground. "For one thing, the rear guard would have been dead in a few more minutes of waiting for that order. The left flank would have been destroyed next, and the army would have been destroyed with it. For another, I saw an old enemy, the emir Qaymaz. I'm sure you remember Qaymaz? You entertained him during the siege and forbade my killing him. I didn't want to get cheated of that pleasure again."

Red-faced, Richard jumped from the stool and bulled through the crowd toward Henry. "You arrogant peasant. I'll have you—"

Garnier interrupted. "Don't take the blame, Henry. Your son led the attack, not you."

Richard looked to Garnier and back to Henry. "Your son?"

Henry shot Garnier a glance. Garnier said, "Roger of Huntley, sire, commander of the Death's Heads."

"Huntley?" Richard turned to Alart, who shrugged, uncomprehending. To Henry, Richard said, "I was not aware that Huntley was your son."

"I found out only recently, sire."

Richard's temper cooled as quickly as it had risen. In a low voice he said, "I understand the boy was killed."

"Apparently, sire. We have yet to recover the body."

Richard stared at Henry a long moment, saw the anguish on his face. "It must be terrible to discover a son after so many years and then lose him."

Henry's expression answered for him.

Richard drew a deep breath. "Very well. We will speak no more of the matter. What's done is done, and those who did it have paid the price. You have my condolences, Lord Henry."

"Thank you, sire," Henry said.

Richard addressed the rest of the council. "On to other matters. We will rest here two days, then resume our march on the Holy City."

❧

Some miles away, an entirely different scene was being enacted. There was fruit and sherbet in the sultan's tent, but no one partook of it. The Saracen commanders were lost in gloom. Even Saladin's arrogant son al-Afdal, the Bull, was subdued.

To one side of the tent, Saladin paced back and forth, deep in thought. The army of the faithful had been utterly routed. They were in no shape for battle or for anything else. The way to Jerusalem—the way to Damascus—was wide open.

At last al-Adil, Saladin's brother, spoke. He was the only one who possessed the nerve. "So what do we do, brother?"

Saladin stopped pacing and faced them, and to the surprise of all, he said, "We attack."

Chapter 32

ON SEPTEMBER 9, the day after the feast of the Virgin Mary's birth, the army set out once more. They were in high spirits. As far as they were concerned, the war was over. Many of the knights didn't even bother to put on their armor. Formations were ragged, men were singing.

Suddenly, from the rear of the column, came the sound of galloping horses, followed by surprised shouts, blowing horns, warlike yelling.

Heads turned. In the center of the line, where Richard and his retinue rode, Andrew of Chauvigny said, "What the—?"

"The Saracens are attacking the rear guard," Alart of Vouzin said in disbelief.

Richard and his staff rode a distance from the column, trying to get a better view, but all they saw was dust. Guy of Lusignan, with the golden circlet on his helm, said, "How can this be? We've beaten them."

Richard struck his saddle pommel with his fist. "Saladin has forces in reserve—I knew it."

Alart said, "The question is, how many?"

Alarms sounded up and down the column. Knights got rid of their jaunty straw hats and hurriedly donned their mail. Footmen buckled on helmets and tightened their formations. Richard and his staff were joined by Balian of Ibelin, who commanded the native Christians, and Hugh of Burgundy.

"This is a ruse," Balian told Richard. "Saladin wants us to think he can still put up a fight."

"But what if it's not a ruse?" Alart countered. "What if the king is right, and Saladin has fresh men?"

Grizzled Hugh of Burgundy snorted. "If the bastard had more men, he'd have used them two days ago, when we destroyed his army. Balian's right—this is for show."

"Perhaps," Richard mused. "Perhaps not. Saladin is a wily fellow."

"That he is," Guy of Lusignan said, "You were right to call off the battle when we reached the forest, sire. We might well have been massacred in there."

"You should know," Balian said to Guy. "You're an expert at getting an army massacred."

Guy's face flushed with anger. Before he could reply, Richard interjected. "Gentlemen, gentlemen. We have enough to do fighting our present battles. Let us not refight old ones."

The hit and run attacks went on for two days, now on one part of the Christian column, now on another. The attacks weren't particularly damaging in terms of casualties, but they slowed the army down and they eroded the morale of men who had thought the fighting was ended and that they would soon be going home.

At about nones on the second day, a Saracen herald appeared in the distance with a white flag. Richard sent his own herald, along with an interpreter, to talk with the man.

The visit was brief, and Richard's herald cantered back. "They wish to talk, sire," the young man said excitedly.

Richard considered. "Tell them we agree."

As the herald and his interpreter rode away, Hugh of Burgundy said, "Is this wise, sire?"

"It won't hurt to talk," Richard said. "Maybe they've had enough."

Soon a richly anointed rider appeared from the direction of the Saracen army, mounted on a fine white horse. He was accompanied by one other man, probably an interpreter, and they halted a quarter-mile from the Christian force.

"I'll speak to him," Alart said, gathering his reins.

"No," Richard said. "I'll go."

Andrew of Chauvigny said, "You don't fear treachery?"

Richard grinned. "From two men? Hardly."

Richard beckoned the interpreter—a Greek priest—and rode out. He slowed his pace as he approached the Saracen, who was unarmored, wearing a green silk tunic and white turban. He was tall and well built, good looking in a manly fashion, while his interpreter had the well-fed appearance of a merchant. Richard came level with the men and halted. The Saracen flashed an easy smile that showed straight white teeth. He salaamed from the saddle, and through his interpreter he said, "I am—well, my full name is quite long, but you may call me al-Adil. I am governor of Egypt and brother to Sultan Yusef."

Richard nodded acknowledgement. "I am Richard Plantaganet, king of England, duke of Acquitaine and Normandy, count of Poitou and—" he flashed his own smile—"as you say, it is quite long."

Al-Adil nodded in return. "The sultan wishes to congratulate you on your magnificent victory of four days ago."

"Give the sultan my thanks," Richard said.

"He says that only you, of all the Christian lords, could have achieved such a feat."

Richard bowed at the compliment.

Al-Adil went on. "The sultan has no desire to prolong the fighting. He desires a negotiation to end hostilities."

Richard tried not to show his eagerness. He was leery of marching through the Judean hills in this heat. From what he had been told, there wasn't much water on the approach to Jerusalem and the ground was unfavorable for his knights. After the other day's battle, Richard had hoped to enter the Holy City unopposed, but if Saladin had fresh reserves—as seemed to be the case—who knew what could happen?

As if reading Richard's thoughts, al-Adil went on. "The sultan instructs me to tell you that what you seek may be obtained without fighting."

Richard took that cryptic remark to mean that Saladin wanted to surrender Jerusalem, but was looking for a way to do it that did not make him appear weak. Which made sense. Acting as though he did not care one way or another, Richard shrugged. "Very well, we can talk."

"Shall we say, two days hence?"

"I am prepared now," Richard said.

"Alas, the sultan must take council with his emirs to make sure we are agreed on our position."

On your terms of surrender, you mean. "And that will take two days?"

Al-Adil held out his hands heplessly. "It is our way." He cleared his throat. "Plus, some of our emirs who fled the battle have a distance to travel for their return."

Richard laughed heartily. "Very well, then—two days."

"Good. I will have a pavilion erected." Al-Adil waved a hand. "Here, if it suits you."

"How many men are to be involved on each side?" Richard said.

"As many as pleases your highness, though I must say my preference would be to speak with you alone, as you are the commander of your army, as well as its greatest warrior. I find that involving too many people in this sort of thing leads to arguing, and nothing gets accomplished."

"It sounds like you've attended some of our council meetings," Richard joked. The last thing he needed was Philip's creature Burgundy or hotheads like Leicester and Beauvais, or even a popinjay like Lusignan involved. "I shall be more than happy to come alone. But will the sultan not come himself? His fame is great, and I should very much like to meet him."

"Sultan Yusef desires to meet you, as well, but that is for a later date. For now, he prefers that I do the talking."

Richard wasn't happy with that, but he nodded agreement.

"Excellent!" said al-Adil. "At noon, shall we say? It will be the heat of the day, but I assure you we will make it cool for you."

"Very well," Richard said. "I shall see you in two days."

Al-Adil salaamed, Richard bowed, and the two men rode back to their armies.

Chapter 33

"WHY ARE WE stopping?" the bishop of Beauvais complained to Richard. "We just got started again."

The council of barons was being held outside this evening, to take advantage of the cool sea breeze. Balian of Ibelin spread his hands pleadingly, "Saladin's playing for time, sire, can't you see that? We can negotiate after we've taken Jerusalem."

"Conrad wouldn't negotiate," Henry of Deraa added.

There was a loud growl of assent to that remark.

Richard reddened and, with difficulty, held his temper. "A few days cannot hurt," he said. "We may save time in the long run if Jerusalem can be taken without a siege."

"We may not need a siege," the duke of Burgundy said. "There may not be anyone left to defend the place."

"We don't know that's the case," Richard snapped. "Besides, my lord, I thought you would have welcomed a delay. Didn't Philip put you here to prolong my stay in the Holy Land as long as possible?"

Now it was Hugh's turn to redden. With his gruff voice and burly physique, he resembled an old bear. "I swore a vow to liberate the Holy City, sire. The city is ripe for the taking, and every minute we sit here talking makes its capture more difficult. We're wasting time. Were Conrad in charge, we'd be there by now."

And so it went. Others could speak of bold action and say that Conrad would do this or that because the responsibility wasn't theirs. Four days earlier, these same men had called Richard the greatest commander who ever lived; now they complained about his caution. Richard would be glad when the waiting period was over, and he could get away from these people and meet al-Adil again.

Two days later, as promised, a pavilion—more of a huge silk awning, really—was set up at the spot where Richard and al-Adil had met previously. "Red," al-Adil told Richard, waving a hand at the pavilion, "in your honor."

"You are too kind," Richard said, though he was secretly flattered.

In the welcome shade, thick carpets had been laid down, along with plush cushions to sit or recline upon. Servants handed al-Adil, Richard, and their interpreters plates of fruit and cups with cool drinks.

"It is good to see you again," the handsome al-Adil told Richard.

"It is good to see you, as well," Richard replied sincerely. For some reason, Richard felt closer to this Saracen whom he had only known for a few days than he did to many of the nobles in his own army. He could picture himself and al-Adil hawking together, or hunting.

The two men made themselves comfortable, sitting cross legged on the cushions. They traded small talk about the weather, about horses and falcons, then Richard got down to business. He was affable but direct. "So, on what terms does your brother propose to surrender Jerusalem?"

Al-Adil pursed his lips. "I will be frank. Our army is intact, but we would prefer to avoid another battle. We suffered serious losses a few days ago, thanks to your skilled leadership." He bowed to Richard in compliment. "A defeat like that makes the provinces . . ." he searched for the right word, "restive. Something we wish to avoid."

"Yes," Richard said. He knew all about pacifying restive provinces. That's why he was in a hurry to get his crusade over with and go home before King Philip could stir up trouble.

Al-Adil went on. "The sultan hopes you and I may reach an arrangement suitable to both sides, with no more fighting."

"Is the sultan willing to give back everything he has taken from us?"

"That is asking a bit much," al-Adil said. Then, tantalizingly, he added, "At least, at first. We cannot be seen to be surrendering. It makes the provinces . . ."

"Restive," Richard finished for him.

"Exactly. You must remember, al-Quds is a holy city to us, as well."

Richard nodded. "I have heard that."

Al-Adil said, "There are limits beyond which we may not go—again, at first. We have our share of religious . . . I will not call them fanatics, but they are extremely true believers. I expect you have the same problem."

Richard thought of men like Leicester and the bishop of Beauvais, men who would kill a Muslim just because he was Muslim, and consider themselves blessed for doing it. "We do."

Fresh drinks were brought, and Al-Adil said, "So, how do we reach a peaceful resolution?"

They proposed one solution after another, but none solved the core problem of Jerusalem to both party's consent. Things seemed at an impasse when, of a sudden, Richard had an idea. He didn't know where the idea came from, it popped into his head. But as Richard thought about it, it seemed like an idea that could end this crusade with no more bloodshed and get them all home by next Easter. He sat forward eagerly. "Tell me, my friend—for I consider you a friend—are you married?"

Al-Adil frowned slightly, as though that were a strange question to ask. "I am not."

Richard raised a forefinger. "I have an unmarried sister named Joanna. She is quite beautiful. You could marry her and the two of you could be co-rulers of Jerusalem."

Al-Adil was taken aback. "Are you serious?"

"Quite serious," Richard said.

"This sister of yours—Joanna?—would she be agreeable to such a match?"

"Joanna will do what I tell her," Richard said, though he wasn't exactly sure that was true. Joanna was headstrong, like Richard himself, like all the Plantaganets.

Al-Adil stroked his short beard. "Would your sister be willing to accept our faith?"

"Would you be willing to accept hers?"

Al-Adil was apologetic. "A good Muslim may not stray."

"Neither may a good Christian," Richard admitted.

The proposal seemed a non-starter, then Richard had another idea. "What if . . . what if you both keep your religions and rule that way? That might even work better. Think of it—a city sacred to both faiths, with rulers from both faiths. There would be no need to ever fight over it again."

Al-Adil smiled. "Muslims are forbidden to marry outside the faith. So, I believe, are Christians. And what about our children? What faith would they follow?"

"You raise good points, but I'm sure something could be worked out. It always can be if there's will to do it."

Al-Adil nodded and sipped his drink. "It is an intriguing offer, I admit, and as you say it would solve many problems on both sides without any more blood being spilled. I will take it to the sultan, and we can meet again to discuss it in—two weeks?"

"Two weeks?" Richard was dismayed. He wanted to get this over with as soon as possible. "Why so long?"

Al-Adil spread his arms. "A proposition such as this must be ruled upon by our religious authorities. I assume you have the same constraints?"

"Yes," Richard realized. Of course the priests would want to argue about it.

"It is a clever idea," al-Adil went on. "Brilliant, even. I believe the sultan will like it."

The two men rose. "We will meet in two weeks," al-Adil said. "He placed a hand over his heart. "And tell your beautiful sister I send her greetings."

They parted, and Richard returned to his army full of hope. It was an outlandish scheme, but it just might work. Joanna would be angrier than a hive of disturbed bees when she heard about it, but Richard didn't care. She would come round in time, and even if she didn't and he had to force her, it would be worth it for him to get out of the Holy Land quickly.

INTERLUDE

Chapter 34

ℰPIPHANIUS LOOKED SMUG. "Name the nine orders of angels, in rank from highest to lowest."

"That's too easy," Anselm scoffed. "First Choir— Seraphim, Cherubim, Thrones. Second Choir—Dominions, Virtues, Powers. Third Choir—Principalities, Archangels, Angels."

They were in a tavern near the cathedral of St. Thomas— Epiphanius, Anselm and abu Flath, who currently went by the name Michael. They were priests in training, attached to the house of a great lord, and tomorrow Father Manue was going to examine them on the nature of angels.

Epiphanius was compact and red haired. He had been born Rikard but had taken his present name because it sounded more religious. With his family connections, he would be a bishop one day—if the Muslims didn't kill them all first. Abu Flath knew that Epiphanius would visit the tavern's prostitutes later, something the ultra-religious Anselm would never consider. Epiphanius raised a forefinger and posed another question. "Can two angels occupy the same space?"

"Of course they can," Anselm said. "Angels are pure intelligence, pure spirit. In theory, all the angels in Heaven could occupy the same space at one time. They could fit on this table top, they could fit in the palm of your hand. Why, they could fit on the tip of your finger, an it came to that."

Anselm was tall, dark and wide eyed, and it seemed as though it were impossible to satisfy his thirst for knowledge.

"Can angels can assume corporeal form?" Epiphanius asked him.

"No one can say for certain," Anselm replied.

"The Archangel Gabriel appeared to Mary," Epiphanius said. "Surely he wasn't a spirit then."

"He could have been," Anselm retorted. "Nothing explicitly states that Gabriel assumed a form that had substance and could be touched when he appeared to Mary. It's never been proven one way or the other whether angels can assume bodily form."

"So you're saying that angels cannot assume corporeal form?"

"I'm saying it has never been proven."

"Ah, but it has," Epiphanius said triumphantly. "I myself have seen a feather from the wing of the Archangel Raphael."

Anselm frowned. "You have? Where?"

"In a little church outside Rome, when last I was there."

While Anselm mulled that over, abu Flath pretended to sip at his wine. Here, in the midst of war, these two were arguing about angels. There was a time when abu Flath might have enjoyed this kind of argument, especially as angels were a part of his own faith. Abu Flath had once aspired to be a Hafiz, one who had memorized the Koran, and as a boy he had loved to hear the holy men debate. Since he had been taken in by Sinan, however, all that had changed. Now the only angel he cared about was Azrael, the Angel of Death.

While Epiphanius had a long pull of wine to refresh himself after so much talking, Anselm, who drank sparingly, took his turn at playing Father Manue, tilting his head to one side and giving his voice an aristocratic drawl the way Manue did. "The angel who spoke to Moses through the burning bush is referred to both as 'the Angel of the Lord' and as 'the Lord.' How can this be possible?"

Epiphanius thought for a moment, twisting a finger absently though his hair. Like many redheads, he was going bald early, and he was constantly touching his hair, as though to assure himself it was still there. At last he came up with an answer. "He is called 'the Lord' because he is the messenger of God, and God speaks through him. So when Moses addresses the angel, he is actually addressing God at the same time."

Anselm turned. "Michael, you haven't said much. Father Manue will be hard on us tomorrow, you know."

Abu Flath smiled. He had taken to his priestly training well, much as he despised the false religion it served. "Let me offer an alternate answer to your question. The prophet Isaiah termed Christ 'the Angel of Good Counsel.' So is it not possible that the angel of the burning bush was the Angel of Good Counsel—that Moses was speaking to Christ Himself? That way he could be both an angel and—" he caught himself, he had almost said "Allah"—"and the Lord."

Anselm smiled at Epiphanius. "I like that."

"I like it, too." Epiphanius said. His future was assured, he could afford to be generous with his praise. "You will go far, I think, Michael. Perhaps you will become famous one day."

Abu Flath shrugged modestly. "You are too kind." He intended to become famous, but for a different reason.

Anselm and Epiphanius wrangled on about angels, but abu Flath paid slight attention. He had been told to bide his time and wait for the signal to fulfill his mission, but the waiting was difficult. He knew what his job would be, and he wanted to do it now. This moment. He wanted to enter Paradise and sample its delights. But he waited, because waiting was also his job, and he did not want to disappoint the master who had trusted him with so much responsibility.

PART III

Chapter 35

"IN THERE," THE guard snarled.

He shoved Roger through the door of the crude hut. Roger stumbled, and by the time he looked back, the door was closed. The hut was constructed from poorly fitted blocks of baked earth. Inside were a dozen filthy straw pallets with thin, lice-ridden blankets that were stiff from age and lack of cleaning and were no doubt passed from one man to another as their owners died. The stench was overwhelming, combining the scent of unwashed men and unwashed bedding with the contents of a bucket that served the hut's occupants as a latrine.

Roger wore only his shirt, braies and hose. His cloak and Death's Head surcoat had been taken from him. He was still taking stock of his new surroundings when there were noises outside and the rest of the slaves returned from work.

The men shambled in. They were ragged and diseased, wasted by hard work and malnutrition. They regarded Roger with dull curiosity.

"Hullo, what's this?" said a wiry, sharp-eyed fellow with thick forearms.

"Fresh meat," said a short brawler who eyed Roger with what looked like anticipation.

An old man stepped forward. He had a long grey beard and was missing most of his teeth. His skin was covered with sores aggravated by heat and dirty clothing, and there was a white film over his right eye. He took Roger's hand in both of his with a grip that was surprisingly strong. "Greetings, my son. I am Father Lambert. Who are—"

A big, dark-haired fellow shouldered his way between them. "What's your name, boy?" he asked Roger.

Roger bristled at being called "boy," but he didn't let it show. "Roger," he replied. Then he added, "What's yours?"

The dark-haired man drew himself up with an air of authority. "I am Borchard. I am a man-at-arms and thus in charge of this hut. What is your rank?"

Roger gave a little smile. "Knight."

The sharp-eyed fellow said, "Uh oh, he outranks you, Borchy."

"Shut up, Pentecost," Borchard said. He stared at Roger for a moment, as though digesting this information and what it meant for him, then he said, "Knight by birth?"

"Battlefield," Roger said. "I was knighted by King Richard of England."

A rippled murmur went round the hut. Borchard put his fists on his hips. "You don't really expect me to believe that, do you?"

"I don't care what you believe, you buffoon," Roger said. He was already tired of Borchard. He looked around the hut. "Unless anyone here is a knight of higher standing than me, I am now in charge."

"What if we don't want you in charge?" said the short brawler.

This was not the reception Roger had anticipated. He didn't want to be in command, but there was no way around it. A knight could not take orders from a man of lower rank. "What you want doesn't concern me," he told the shorter man. To the hut at large he said, "My name is Roger of Huntley. I am English, and I command a company of footmen called the Death's Heads. I was captured at the big battle outside the town of Arsuf."

"We heard something about a battle," said a young man whose dress marked him as a Turcopole. The Turco's sweaty face was drawn and pale with illness.

"Mahmoud says our army was destroyed," said Father Lambert.

Another man added, "He claims King Richard fled and left the Holy Land."

Roger snorted. "The last I looked that day, the Saracens were running for their lives." That was greeted with a murmur of approval. "As for King Richard fleeing, I have met the king. He has his faults, as we all do, but I know that he would die before he fled the field of battle."

"Told you," the sharp-eyed man said to the others.

Roger turned to him. "Your name is Pentecost?"

"That's right," said the man.

"You're a crossbowman?"

Pentecost's eyes widened. "How did you know?"

Roger gestured. "Your forearms."

Pentecost grinned. "Well, I'm buggered. I'm one of Balian of Ibelin's men; been in this palace since the fall of Jerusalem."

Roger turned to the ancient priest Lambert. "What about you, Father? How long have you been here?"

Lambert shook his head sadly. "In truth, I no longer know. I came to the Holy Land as a young priest with Louis VI of France and Queen Eleanor. I was captured by

Qaymaz's father when we tried to take Damascus. I have been at one of his family's castles ever since."

"It's a miracle you've stayed alive so long," Roger marveled.

"Some might call it a miracle, others might call it a curse. At any rate, I am happy to serve God."

"What kind of work do you fellows do here?" Roger asked the men in general.

"Hard work," said the sick Turco. "And then we work some more. And if we don't work hard enough, Mahmoud beats us."

"Who is this Mahmoud you keep talking about?"

"The chief guard," Pentecost said. "A real piece of work, Mahmoud is."

The young Turco said, "The other guard for our hut, Yasir, he isn't so bad."

"What's your name?" Roger asked the Turco.

"Aimery. I was taken during the early days of the Acre siege. We've heard the city has finally fallen, is that true?"

"It is. I was there." He peered closely at the sick youth. "Have you seen a doctor?"

"No doctors for slaves," Aimery said ruefully.

The hut door opened and two guards entered—a frog-faced older man whom Roger took to be Mahmoud and a younger one who must be Yasir. Mahmoud carried a dirty bucket. Yasir had a chipped plate piled high with flatbread. They left the food by the door and withdrew.

There was a rush toward the food. The rush ended in pushing and shoving, with Borchard and the brawler winding up in front of the pack, Father Lambert, Aimery and two natives bringing up the rear, and everyone else jumbled in between. By the way Borchard and the brawler were piling their plates, eating as they went along, there wouldn't be much left for the men at the rear.

"Stop!" Roger ordered.

Borchard and the brawler ignored him. They kept filling their plates and eating.

Roger kicked Borchard's plate out of his hands and onto the floor. "I said stop."

Borchard turned on Roger, fuming.

Roger said, "What's going on here?"

"What does it look like?" Borchard said. "We're eating."

"I can see that. How is the food shared out?"

"Grab as grab can, and Devil take the hindmost." Borchard jerked a thumb. "Especially those two Goat Fuckers."

"Not anymore," Roger said. "From now on, everyone receives an equal share."

There was excited approval, then Borchard said, "I don't think so."

"Thinking doesn't appear to be one of your strong points," Roger told him. He indicated Borchard and the short brawler. "Do you two always get the most?"

Borchard shrugged. "Most of the time."

"God wills it," said the brawler. He and Borchard seemed to find this remark quite funny.

"And who are you" Roger asked the brawler.

"Tillo, if it's any of your business, which it ain't."

"You're a soldier?"

"Sailor."

"Bit far from the water, aren't you?"

Tillo didn't answer, staring at Roger defiantly. Finally Pentecost said, "They captured him when Saladin took Acre. Dumb ass got drunk and missed his ship."

Tillo shot Pentecost a look. "I'll deal with you later."

"Be quiet," Roger told him. Borchard's food was on the floor, but Tillo still held a full plate. "Put that food back where you got it and we'll start over," Roger told him.

Tillo dropped his plate and came at him, as Roger had expected him to. Tillo feinted a punch and tried to kick Roger in the balls. Roger had been in enough sailors' brawls that he expected that, too. Tillo was slowed by lack of good diet and overwork, while Roger's reflexes were finely honed by a year of battle. He easily sidestepped Tillo's kick and with his right foot swept Tillo's left leg from under him.

Tillo fell on his back. Roger kicked him as hard as he could in the balls. Tillo cried out, and before he could double up, Roger stomped his gut so hard he was afraid he might have ruptured something inside. Tillo bent double on the floor, retching.

Borchard tried to attack Roger from behind—again, as Roger had expected. Roger whirled to confront him, and Borchard was brought up short.

The two men faced each other. Roger's eyes were locked on Borchard's, daring him.

Borchard breathed heavily, but breathing heavily seemed all he was willing to do right now.

Roger slapped Borchard hard across the cheek, the sound loud in the quiet hut.

Borchard started forward, then hesitated.

Roger backhanded him across the other cheek.

Borchard's dark eyes were on fire, but he bore the insult.

At last he relaxed and made a deprecating gesture. "Have it your way."

Roger's heart was pounding so hard, it was difficult for him to speak. He tried to look unfazed as he beckoned Pentecost. "Help me divide the food, will you?"

"My pleasure," Pentecost said. He gave Borchard a look as he passed him.

"Line up," Roger told the men. "And stop pushing. Everyone will get the same amount."

The men stood in line and Roger and Pentecost doled out equal amounts of food to all, Roger handing out flatbread and Pentecost ladling the food in the bucket—chickpeas in some kind of sauce—with a dark-crusted wooden spoon. "Thank you, my boy," the old priest Lambert said when he got his share.

"No thanks needed," Roger said. He was only doing his duty. Fate had made him the highest-ranking man in the hut, and he had no other choice. He would not have been a knight otherwise.

Others thanked him, as well, including the two natives, one of whom was an Arab named Ahmed and the other a Kurd called Zoran.

"This is the first full meal I have had since Borchard got here," Ahmed said. "Zoran and I always get the scraps."

Roger was surprised to find non-Christians in the hut, though he supposed he shouldn't have been. "How did you end up a slave?" he asked Ahmed.

"I got caught stealing chickens." Ahmed said, and he shrugged. "I was a thief—it was bound to happen eventually. I was sold in the market in Damascus."

Zoran smiled fatalistically. "Me, I was enslaved for being a Kurd."

"Is that a crime?" Roger asked him.

"It was that day."

"Isn't Saladin a Kurd?"

"That doesn't mean the Turks and Arabs like him."

The sick boy Aimery had a tear in his eye as he was given his food. Borchard was next in line. Roger stopped Pentecost before he could put chickpeas on Borchard's plate.

"Your food's on the floor," he told Borchard.

There was another tense moment, then Borchard began picking his flatbread off the foor, scraping up the chickpeas with it, heedless of the dirt that came up with them. Roger noted that he took Tillo's share as well, with Tillo still curled up and moaning.

"You've made an enemy there," Pentecost told Roger.

"No, he's the one who's made the enemy."

The door opened again, and the two guards came back, this time carrying long staves. "Where is the new man?" the frog-faced guard demanded.

He spotted Roger before anyone could answer and came over to him. "I am Mahmoud. You will obey me in everything I command. If you do not, this will be the result."

He lashed out with the staff, catching Roger alongside the head.

Roger staggered back. Before he could recover, Mahmoud hit him again. And again. He hit him on the shoulders, on the back, on the head. Roger dropped to his knees. Mahound struck him once more, across the face, then left.

Roger fell headlong. Before everything went black, he was aware of Pentecost crouching over him protectively. "Welcome to Hut Three," Pentecost said.

Chapter 36

OCTOBER 1191

THE SARACEN HORSEMEN ambushed them in a narrow defile. There was no warning. The Saracens raced out of a side canyon and fell upon them with swords and maces.

King Richard and his four companions were outnumbered three to one. Horses and men pressed in upon one another in a thick cloud of dust. There were grunts, the ring of metal on metal, the *chunk* of steel hacking into bodies. A sword blade cut through Richard's mail, penetrating the thick leather haubergon beneath it. He lashed at the perpetrator with his axe, shattering the man's shield. He spurred Fauvel forward, looking for room to maneuver.

A Saracen appeared to his left. The man raised his round shield to protect his face and upper body, so Richard struck him just above the knee, severing his leg. A Saracen to Richard's right aimed a spear thrust at him but was stopped by the young knight Etienne, who crashed his horse into the Saracen's mount, disrupting the Saracen's blow, then dispatched the man with a backhanded sword cut to the face.

Richard wheeled. The Saracens were pulling back. A blow to a retreating Saracen's collarbone left the man reeling in the saddle. The Saracens galloped away as quickly as they had appeared. It was over.

The Christians took stock. There were no dead on their side. Andrew of Chauvigny had a gash in his upper arm, and the Burgundian knight Aiger's helmet had been struck so hard with a mace that it was cracked and driven so low upon his brow that he couldn't get it off. Five Saracens were dead, two more grievously wounded.

Richard's companions laughed the nervous laugh of relief, glad to be alive, slapping each another on the shoulder. "Turbans got the jump on us that time," said Alart of Vouzin.

Andrew of Chauvigny spoke with boyish bravado. "Yes, I was actually worried for a moment."

Richard's heart sang. This was what he loved, the joy of combat, the total release of it, the freedom, the camaraderie, without all the worries about strategy and soothing hurt feelings.

"My thanks, Etienne," he told the young knight of Hainult. "You saved me from a dire fate."

Etienne bowed his head. "It was my privilege, sire."

Richard went on, pointing and laughing. "Aiger, my friend, I fear we'll need a blacksmith to get that helmet off you."

"I fear you're right, sire," red-haired Aiger replied. The helmet was cockeyed, its edge digging into Aiger's brow, and the others laughed at his predicament. Aiger glowed with pride, though, as did Etienne. It was a great honor to be chosen to join Richard on these expeditions into the hills.

Instead of leading the army to Jerusalem, Richard had taken it to Jaffa, confounding its leaders. Richard made these "hunting" trips outside the city several times a week. The

Saracens knew that he and his companions would be abroad, and their best fighters came to test their skills against the English king, though so far the results for their side had been disappointing. The Saracens could have sent a hundred men at a time, they could have sent a thousand, but that would have been dishonorable, and Saladin would never have allowed it. These cat-and-mouse contests were like miniature tourneys, albeit more deadly.

Aiger and Etienne plundered the Saracen bodies for valuables, including the swords, which always brought a good price. After ascertaining that neither of the wounded Saracens was likely to bring a ransom, the party left them to their fate and rode back to Jaffa.

A crowd gathered to watch them ride in. Some of the men were drunk. The army had grown indolent during its stay in Jaffa, lulled by the sweet-smelling orange groves and the pleasant sea breezes. There were women in the crowd, as well. Some were soldiers' wives but most were whores, drawn from as far away as Cyprus. Not a few of the whores were Muslims, because when all was said and done, money was money.

The common soldiers and knights cheered Richard as he rode through the city gate, and he acknowledged them with a wave. Richard's excursions into the hills were the talk of the army. Men bragged of the English king's deeds as if they were their own. They talked of how he always slew two, three, or more of the enemy, how he always overcame great odds. He might return covered with blood, or with his mail rent, but he always returned victorious, and the men loved him for that.

Chapter 37

Meanwhile the Negotiations over Joanna's marriage to al-Adil dragged on. Now there was something the Christian priests objected to, now there was something the Muslim priests—or whatever the pagans called their holy men—didn't like. Then Pope Clement died, and was succeeded by a new Pope, Celestine. Plump Archbishop Ubaldo was replaced as Papal legate by the dour bishop of Verona, and he demanded to examine Richard's plans for a peace settlement all over again. Why couldn't they just agree and be done with it?

And, of course, the complaints in council continued.

"The road to Jerusalem is open," shouted Henry of Deraa, "why aren't we taking it?" Henry had become even more truculent since he had lost his son.

Balian of Ibelin agreed. "We need to get there before the winter rains come. There's still time, but not much."

"Every day we sit here is an extra day for Saladin to fortify the Holy City," the bishop of Beauvais said.

"We will march when we are ready," Richard told them. He hadn't been attending the council meetings of late; he'd only come tonight because he needed to. "I've told you, we must secure our supply lines before we start for the Holy City. If the Saracens get behind us, they could cut us off." The truth was, Richard suspected Saladin was baiting him, trying to lure him into the rugged hills that lay on the approach to Jerusalem. He suspected a trap.

"The supply route is as secure as it will ever be," said Hugh of Burgundy. "We must march."

"Let us give the negotiations more time," Richard counseled.

"We've given them enough time," Henry said. "If Conrad were here, the negotiation would be: Give us the city now, and we'll let your people inside live. Otherwise we'll kill them all."

"That's what the first crusaders did!" shouted the count of St. Pol.

Hugh needled Richard shrewdly. "Aye, they had leaders more interested in serving God than in riding into the hills and seeking their own glory."

There were angry cries of agreement, and it was all Richard could do to hold his temper.

"Forgive me for being blunt, sire," said Balian, "but this idea of marrying your sister to Saphadin is ridiculous. The Saracens will never agree to it."

Richard smiled. "Won't they?" He was tired of hearing about that boorish oaf Conrad, tired of hearing his motives questioned by his inferiors. He gave his reason for coming tonight. "It may interest you to know that al-Adil—whom you call Saphadin—has invited our chief barons to a banquet at Lydda three days hence. There we will review—and with good luck finalize—our proposal for peace."

Richard had not seen al-Adil for some time. He missed him. He often wondered what would happen should they ever meet on the battlefield, and he prayed that would not happen.

Henry of Deraa was incredulous. "A banquet? We should be cutting these bastards' heads off, not having a banquet with them." Then his expression changed. "Tell me, will my dear friend the emir Qaymaz be present at this banquet?"

"He will," Richard said, "and you will not. I don't want trouble, and trouble is something you're sure to cause with Qaymaz there. Besides, Saladin has a ten-thousand-dinar reward on your head, and his envoys would take it as a sign of disrespect were you to be present."

"Then they would take it correctly," Henry swore, and there was a dark look in his eye that troubled Richard.

As if things weren't bad enough for Richard, his wife, Berengaria, and his sister, Joanna, came down from Acre to stay with him. Berengaria followed Richard around like a moonstruck cow, wanting him to get her pregnant. Joanna came because she had heard about her brother's plan to marry her off to al-Adil, and her response was predictable.

"What do you think you're doing!" she shouted as soon as they were alone in his quarters. "I won't marry a pagan! Not now, not tomorrow, not ever! How dare you even think such a thing? I thought you cared for me."

"I do. Al-Adil is a splendid fellow. I think you two would—"

She threw a vase at him. He ducked and it shattered against the wall. "He's a Muslim, you dolt! You can think all you want, but you're not going to get me near him, much less in his bed."

Richard straightened. "You forget, I am the head of this family."

"And I am a queen." She sneered at him. "You would need a Papal dispensation to marry me to anyone below my rank, much less an infidel—or hadn't you thought of that? I know Pope Celestine, by the way, and he's not likely to approve your scheme. I would deem the scheme harebrained, but that does a disservice to hares."

Richard sighed. "Why must you be so difficult?"

"Me, difficult! You're lucky I'm not Bonjute of Trent. She would claw your eyes out for even thinking of such a thing."

That was true, Richard admitted. Joanna was right about the Papal dispensation, as well. "Will you at least attend the banquet and meet al-Adil?"

"No, I will not." Joanna turned and stalked from the chamber.

Richard swore. He had taken the cross almost light heartedly, believing it the way to immortality. But immortality was proving much more difficult to attain than he had thought. More frustrating, as well. Not to mention the fact that he was sick all the time. He needed to get this crusade over with, get away from this pestilential land, go home and deal with King Philip. It still seemed like negotiation was the quickest way to do that. And the safest. Saladin was preparing a trap for him in the Judean hills—he had to be. That's what Richard would have done, were he the sultan.

If there were only a way to turn the tables, to lure Saladin out of the hills and destroy him . . .

Richard was tired of thinking. He summoned a page. "Find the count of Vouzin. Tell him to get Andrew and select a few worthy fellows. We're going hunting."

Chapter 38

THE TOWN OF Lydda lay two and a half leagues inland from Jaffa, on the plain of Sharon. It sat athwart the ancient caravan road between Babylon and Egypt, and was famed for its orchards and as the birthplace of the warrior saint, George. The town was dominated by a castle built by the crusaders and by a Greek basilica constructed over St. George's tomb. The basilica had been turned into a mosque by the Saracens. The castle had been reworked, as well. Its hall was not spacious enough to hold all the guests for al-Adil's banquet, so the event was held outside, on the plain, in two huge pavilions—one red, one gold—their sides partly rolled up to let in air.

At a distance from these two pavilions, and well separated from each other, were the tents of the guests. The Christian nobles had come up in a group from Jaffa, while the Saracens had arrived piecemeal, as it suited them.

In the outdoor kitchens, sweating cooks, naked to the waist, toiled over spits of roasting lamb and mutton. Others stirred great vats of soups and broths and sauces. The smells of spices, crisping fat, and fresh-baked bead wafted across the grounds. There were fruits and nuts, sherbets of all flavors, and that new drink called coffee, which most eschewed because the temperature inside the packed tents was too warm for hot drinks. Musicians from both sides entertained the throng of guests—it was rumored that King

Richard would sing a new song at some point—along with jugglers and acrobats.

Inside the pavilions the guests were seated alternately – Christian, Muslim, Christian—to encourage familiarity, but the language difference precluded that, save for the native Christians, most of whom spoke Turkish or Arabic.

No arms were permitted on the banquet grounds, only knives for cutting food. Muslims ate with three fingers of the right hand and used scented napkins to clean their hands afterwards, while the Christians ate meat off the points of their knives, shoveled in everything else with both hands, and wiped the grease from them on their tunics.

"Where the Devil is the wine?" wondered the purple-robed bishop of Beauvais as he accepted a grilled kebab from a servant.

"The Goat Fuckers don't drink," the count of St. Pol reminded him.

Gravedigger Leicester pointed at the kebab. "You may be eating one of their girl friends," he said in a rare attempt at humor.

The emirs who were seated between the three men smiled and nodded politely, unaware of what their Christian guests were saying.

Queen Berengaria was the only woman present. She sat at the high table, looking lost. The emirs and Christian nobles paid her deference, but Richard ignored her.

Nearby, Alart and Andrew of Chauvigny looked a bit lost, as well. They were used to being Richard's favorites, but he seemed more interested in his new friend, al-Adil, tonight, so they started a conversation with Berengaria, who seemed relieved to have someone to talk to.

The atmosphere in the pavilions was cordial, if not friendly. After the food was taken away the guests tended to congregate with their own kind, save again for those of the native Christians who had acquaintances on the other side. With no wine available, many of the Christians sought an excuse to go back to their tents and get into the wine or arrack they had brought with them. The banquet looked as though it would go on for a while, though, because Richard and al-Adil were huddled in deep conversation and it would be a sign of disrespect to leave before they did.

From a silver ewer, al-Adil drizzled pomegranate sauce over a rack of lamb. "Your wife is quite beautiful," he told Richard. "But your sister is not here?"

Richard cut a slice of the lamb, ate it, and licked his fingers clean. "No. She is indisposed. That womanly thing, you know."

"I am sorry to hear that. I was hoping to meet her."

"She feels the same way, I assure you."

The lamb juices and the pomegranate sauce mingled with the brown rice on al-Adil's plate. He stirred the rice to soak them up and took some in his fingers. "So she is acceptable to the marriage?"

"Yes, but there is a difficulty. Because she is a queen by her previous marriage, our Pope must rule on any new union she is entered into."

Al-Adil raised his brows. "And . . . ?"

"And there is a new Pope, so the process has to start all over." Richard spread his hands helplessly. "I have petitioned the Pope on this matter and asked for a speedy reply. In the meantime, his representative wishes me to demand the return of the True Cross you captured at Hattin as part of any peace settlement."

Al-Adil thought that over. "You still hold Meshtub and a few of our generals you captured at Acre. Will you release them without ransom in return for your Cross?"

"I believe I can convince our council to do that," Richard said. "Now what about Jerusalem? As an open city, I'm thinking we should specify there be no military presence allowed within a certain distance of its walls."

"What of your so-called 'military orders,' the knights of the Temple and the Hospital? They possessed much property in al-Quds. Would they agree to entering the city unarmed?"

Richard hadn't thought of that. "I will see what I can do." No members of the military orders had been invited—or would have accepted an invitation—to the banquet. Richard sighed. "Forgive me, but I was under the impression that we could get the framework of a treaty finalized tonight."

Al-Adil cut more of the lamb and smiled. "Have patience, my friend, these things take time. I promise you, you will be rewarded in the end."

"Time is something I do not have much of. My chief nobles clamor for me to march on the Holy City."

"I am sorry to hear that. There has been too much blood shed already, too many fine men killed. Many of our emirs demand that we attack you, as well, but my brother prefers not to fight."

Richard wondered if al-Adil was telling the truth about the Saracen leaders wanting to attack. Hugh of Burgundy and that pirate of Deraa would say that al-Adil was trying to make Richard think the Saracen army was in better fighting shape than it actually was. Either way, Richard, whose main striking force consisted of heavy cavalry, had no desire for a battle in the hills. "I feel the same," he said.

A blue-clad figure appeared beside them at the head table. "I hope I am not late."

"Qaymaz!" Richard exclaimed with delight, rising and pumping the newcomer's hand. "It is good to see you. That falcon you gave me is excellent, by the way. I hunt with him frequently."

Qaymaz placed a hand over his heart and bowed. "It pleases me that your majesty finds my gift to his liking."

Richard passed the emir a bowl of sugared almonds. "Come, my friend, tell me what you've been up to."

Outside the pavilions, a figure moved silently. The figure wore a black cloak and a hood covered his face, though the night was not cold. At his side was a dagger.

The moon was new. Only starlight provided illumination. The figure paused in deeper shadow thrown by a grove of date palms. His eye searched the two pavilions until he found the man he sought. He traced the path he would have to take to get to his quarry, walking it through in his mind, step by step.

He waited till the guards passed on their rounds, then he gripped the dagger and moved forward.

From out of nowhere a strong hand took his arm. "No," said Balian of Ibelin.

Henry of Deraa whirled. Like himself, Balian was dressed in black. "I expected you to try something like this," Balian said.

Henry attempted to pull loose but Balian held him tight. "I'm going to kill that bastard," Henry swore.

"You're just going to walk in there and stab him?"

"That's right."

"The guards will cut you to pieces."

"I'll take my chances."

Balian shook his head. "This is not the time for such deeds. We are under a flag of truce."

Henry's good eye blazed with anger. "You remember what Qaymaz did to my steward. There was a flag of truce then, too."

Balian's voice was calming but stern. "You will have your revenge, but not tonight. It would embarrass the king."

"I don't give a fig for the king," Henry swore. "He embarrasses us with these negotiations. Anyone with half a brain can see that Saladin is stalling for time. He knows Richard won't be here forever. All he has to do is wait him out, and Richard is playing right into his hands."

Balian sighed. "I know. But I cannot let you kill Qaymaz in this manner. We are men of honor and must behave as such, no matter how much it displeases us."

Gradually Henry's rage dissipated as he saw the truth in what Balian said. "I suppose you're right."

"Perhaps you should get away from the army and return to Deraa for a time?" Balian suggested. "Or maybe Acre? That's where I'm going. We could visit Geoffrey."

Henry thought about it. "No, I'll stay here on the off chance that Richard comes to his senses and moves on the Holy City. When do you leave?"

"In a few days." Balian said. "After that, I'm off to Tyre."

Henry perked up. "Tyre?" That was unusual.

"Yes, I have business interests there that must be attended to. That's the story, anyway."

As a long-time friend, Henry knew that Balian had few business interests in Tyre. Shrewdly, he said, "Will you see Conrad while you are there?"

Balian held out his hands. "Conrad is lord of the city. It would be a breach of courtesy if I did not pay him a visit."

"What will you talk to him about?"

"The future," Balian said, and there was much left unspoken in those words. "Shall I give him your respects?"

"By all means," Henry said.

"Good. Now go from here, before the guards catch you."

Chapter 39

BONJUTE BREEZED INTO the room where Geoffrey lay sick. Her riding dress was dusty and sweat stained. "Still alive, I see," she remarked brightly. She opened the curtains to let in the sea breeze. "I don't wish to be prophetic, but it's dark as a tomb in here."

Geoffrey groaned. "Shouldn't you be on a ship to someplace? The Antipodes, maybe?"

"I would be, if I could. There are no ships going farther than Cyprus because of the danger from pirates, and I have even less desire to spend the winter in Cyprus than I do to spend it here."

Geoffrey changed the subject. "How was your ride?"

"Hot. It's nearly impossible to get through the streets. Half the army has come back from Jaffa, it seems, and the city is overrun with whores, with more coming every day." She made a face. "They're probably all coming to see you. Pity you can't take advantage, isn't it?"

"I'm tired of you going on about my infidelities," Geoffrey said. "I missed the part about you being Our Lady of Chastity."

Bonjute drew herself up. "Anything I've done—well, almost anything—I've done for you. To advance your career."

"Maybe I don't want my career advanced."

"I'm aware of that, you boob, but I *do* want it. Mary Mother of God, don't you get tired of living in the woods?"

"We don't live in the woods, and I don't get tired of it."

"That's because you have doxies stashed all over the shire, especially that trollop at Carmel Priory. Well, I miss the court, or at least a place where people speak an actual language, like French, not that ungodly grunting you hear in Trentshire. But until you achieve higher office than Lord of the Sheep Herders, I'll never get anywhere beyond our little kingdom of mud."

"I should think you'd be happy in Acre, then. It's almost like the court is here."

Bonjute harrumphed. "There are no proper women here, save for Joanna and Berengaria, and Hugoline of Montjoie. I'm not crazy about Joanna, but I quite like Berengaria and Hugoline. Poor dear, Berengaria's in for a rude awakening if she thinks Richard is going to get her pregnant. She tries so hard to be a good queen, too." She shrugged. "Anyway, Joanna and Berengaria are in Jaffa now. The rains will be here soon, so I guess we won't take Jerusalem again this year. I have no idea what the army is waiting for."

"I'm sure Richard has his reasons."

Bonjute harrumphed again. Her opinion of the king had changed a lot in the last year, Geoffrey noted. She cast a glance at him. "I suppose you really are sick. Otherwise you'd be in Jaffa with your men. I know you're not staying here because of me."

"My fever may have eased a bit," Geoffrey said wishfully.

"Enough for you to chase me around the house? Oh, wait—it's other women you chase around the house, not your wife. How silly of me."

"Maybe that's because having sex with you is like being with a vintenar drilling his troops—'one, two, three.' "

"Maybe that's because you do it like someone who wishes he were somewhere else. Maybe if I dressed like a prioress, you would get more excited." She put her hands under her breasts, pushing them up. " 'Let us pray.' "

"I've told you, I'm not—"

"Don't insult my intelligence, Geoffrey. There may as many as a dozen women in Trentshire that you haven't bedded, but she's not one of them."

They were interrupted by Pero, Geoffrey's wizened chamberlain, who entered with an arthritic flourish and bowed. "My lord, you have—"

Balian of Ibelin strode into the chamber past Pero, followed by the count of Champagne. "Geoffrey!" Balian said, arms wide. "Good to see you!"

Both men bowed to Bonjute, and Henry of Champagne said, "Lady Bonjute. It is good to see you, as always."

Bonjute inclined her head. "You lie most delightfully, my lord." She straightened. "I'll leave you to whatever it is you men do. Meanwhile I'll go off and thrash some servants. That damned Jehan will have done something wrong, I'm sure. I'd throw her out if she wasn't such a good cook. Will you gentlemen be staying for supper? We can put you up during your stay in the city, if you like."

"We're staying at my house," said the count of Champagne, "but supper would be wonderful."

The two men bowed again as Bonjute left, then they took positions on either side of Geoffrey's sick bed. "You look well," the count of Champagne told him.

"As my wife says, you lie most delightfully," Geoffrey told him. Then he added, "I heard about James."

Balian let out a heavy sigh. "Count Henry and I were the ones who found his body—what was left of it. Poor fellow."

Henry tried to make the best of it. "He died a Christian gentleman."

"He still died," Geoffrey said gloomily.

There was an awkward silence, then Balian said, "So, how are you enjoying the good life?"

Geoffrey snorted. "I'd be enjoying it a lot more were there actually something good about it. But tell me, what's going on with the army? Why haven't you marched on Jerusalem? We hear all sorts of rumors."

"We know no more about it than you do," Balian said. "We beat the stuffing out of the infidels, and now we sit in Jaffa, doing nothing, while Richard rides around the hills seeking single combat. It's insane."

Champagne said, "Richard hopes Saladin will surrender the city through negotiation. His idea is to get Saphadin— you know, Saladin's brother—to marry his sister Joanna."

Geoffrey reacted with surprise. "What! How is Joanna taking that?"

"About as you would expect," Balian said.

"About as any Christian woman would take it," the count of Champagne added.

Geoffrey said, "You know Saphadin, Balian. Would he go through with something like that?"

"I don't know him all that well, but I doubt it. My guess is that he's making a fool of us."

216

"Then why the negotiation? Is Richard afraid of a fight? That doesn't sound like him."

"No, it doesn't," Balian admitted.

"Perhaps he was unnerved by our battle at Arsuf," the count of Champagne said thoughtfully. "It was a great victory, but it was a near-run affair. I was on the far left, and I can tell you that the Saracens came near to overrunning the rear guard and left wing, and had they done that, the battle's outcome might have been far different. Our counterattack came at the last possible moment, and it wasn't ordered by Richard."

"It wasn't?" Geoffrey said.

"Actually, it was led by one of your men," Balian told him.

Geoffrey frowned. "My men?"

"Yes, the commander of that company they call the Death's Heads."

"Roger?" Geoffrey said.

"If that's his name."

"My God, that fellow never ceases to amaze."

"He won't amaze you any more, I'm afraid. He was killed."

Geoffrey stared down at his blanket. "He was a good fellow. I'm sorry to lose him. Damn this war." He looked up. "No word of Ailith, I suppose?"

His guests shook their heads.

Balian glanced meaningfully at Henry of Champagne, then lowered his voice. "Geoffrey, there's something we need to talk about. I'm going to Tyre next week to speak with Conrad. I'm going to tell him that—"

From the harbor came the long troll of a horn. It was followed by another, then more. There were sounds of commotion is the street outside Geoffrey's window.

Balian and the count of Champagne went to the window as Geoffrey said, "What's going on?"

The door was flung open and old Pero appeared, breathless. "King Richard has called everyone back to Jaffa. He's marching on Jerusalem."

"Finally," Balian exclaimed. "And not a moment too soon. The rains will be here any day."

"We must go," Henry of Champagne told Geoffrey. "Tell Lady Bonjute we're sorry to miss supper."

Geoffrey held out a hand. "Help me up, I'm going with you."

Balian hesitated. "You're not well enough."

"I'm as well as I'll ever be. Better death in battle than the slow death of marriage. Pero, summon my squire."

Chapter 40

ℜOGER AND PENTECOST were digging a shallow hole. Their comrades from Hut Three looked on under the supervision of the black-robed guards Mahmoud and Yasir. They were burying the young Turcopole, Aimery, who had succumbed to fever, starvation and the beatings inflicted by Mahmoud. Aimery was wrapped in the filthy sheet on which he had slept—his blanket had fallen by lot to Alberic the merchant until a new slave was assigned to the hut, at which time Alberic would have to pass the blanket to him.

The hole lay in a large field of unmarked mounds. The watching men were emotionless; they had seen this many times before, and most expected to one day occupy spaces in this same field. In the background loomed Qaymaz's massive red sandstone castle, which for some reason he had named the Blue Fort and which the slaves called the Blue Fart.

Though it was not a warm day, Roger and Pentecost were sweating. Pentecost wiped his brow, leaving a streak of dirt across his forehead. "Think that's deep enough?"

"Has to be," Roger said. He nodded in the direction of the guards. "Frog Face is getting impatient. Looks like he's ready to come over here."

Roger and Pentecost climbed from the grave and four of the others—Borchard, Yves, Hillaire, and Zoran—lifted the body and placed it in the hole.

Yves, a native Christian farmer, and Hillaire, who had been a Hospitaller footman, filled the hole and tamped it with shovels. The old priest Lambert moved to the grave's head. Lowering his eyes, he began to recite a half-remembered Psalm.

Suddenly a long staff cracked across his shoulders. "Enough!" shouted Mahmoud. "Back to work!"

Lambert stood his ground. "I haven't—"

"I do not care!" Mahmoud struck Lambert again. "Your infidel rites are not permitted here. Move, or I'll beat you with an inch of your pathetic life."

Lambert started to reply, but Roger pulled him away. "Come, Father. It's not worth getting yourself killed. Aimery is in Heaven and that's what counts. Let's go."

Mahmoud scowled, as though he had been looking forward to beating the heathen priest; then he and the younger guard, Yasir, ushered the slaves back to work.

As the men shuffled off, Roger, who had dropped back to be last in line, stopped, bent, and with his finger drew a cross in the new-turned dirt. Unfortunately, Mahound picked that moment to turn. He saw what Roger was doing and whacked him with his staff. With the toe of his boot he vigorously scrubbed the cross from the dirt. Then he turned back to Roger. "Scum! Pig!" Blow after blow rained down on Roger, on his shoulders, on his head, against his ribs. Spittle flew from Mahmoud's mouth.

Roger fell to his knees, covering his head with his arms. "Get up!" Mahmoud screamed, and he struck Roger again. "Get up and keep moving!"

The other guard, Yasir, ran up and grabbed Mahmoud's arm. "Stop! You'll kill him!"

The enraged Mahmoud turned on him and Yasir said, "Remember what Qaymaz said—the sultan wants this one to live."

Mahmoud remembered, but he didn't understand. "What interest has the sultan in this dog?"

"I don't know, the sultan does not speak to me. I don't think you want the sultan for an enemy, though."

Gradually Mahmoud calmed, but rage still showed in his face. He kicked Roger in the ribs. "Move."

Pentecost helped Roger to his feet. Roger's eyes spun. There wasn't much pain yet, but the pain would come. He could barely walk at first, and Pentecost took his arm and helped him. Eventually Roger shrugged Pentecost off and staggered on by himself. He wouldn't give Mahmoud—or that smirking Borchard—the satisfaction of seeing that he needed assistance.

The little column shuffled along. When Mahmoud wasn't looking, Yasir took his water skin and held it to Roger's lips. "Drink," he said in a low voice.

Roger did. Again. "Thank you," he croaked to Yasir, passing the water back.

Yasir looked away, as if he didn't know how to answer. He was trying to grow a beard, but it wasn't coming in well. Then he turned back and, for Mahmoud's benefit, he yelled, "Faster, feringhee dog. Faster. The work will not wait."

Roger trudged on.

Chapter 41

NOVEMBER 1191

FAUSTON WAS IN a bad mood as he walked along the nearly deserted harbor of Acre. Winter was near; a cold wind blew off the sea. The last boatload of Fauston's pilgrims should have departed for home long since, but they had been held back by the weather. Once they were gone, there would be no more ships till spring, and Fauston would be out of work.

He reached the Golden Keys, which was nearly deserted because everyone was off on the march to Jerusalem. He took a table and ordered wine.

He had hoped to be long gone from Acre by now, but he was no closer to leaving than he'd ever been. The army camp had been razed when the troops set out for Jerusalem, so Fauston had been forced to take quarters in the city. Room prices had plummeted with the army's departure, but they were still high. At the rate Fauston was saving money, he'd be here till the Second Coming.

Not only that, he still couldn't make up his mind where he wanted to go. Byzantium, Cyprus, maybe Italy. Maybe Acquitaine. Someplace warm.

A big hand clapped his shoulder. "Fauston—is that you?"

Fauston looked up to see a bird's nest of dark, curly hair and a beard to match.

"Gregory!"

He jumped to his feet and the two men embraced.

"I almost didn't recognize you with that hat," Gregory said, indicating Fauston's wide-brimmed hat from St. James of Compostela.

Fauston beckoned for more wine, then said, "Where have you been? You look awful."

The swarthy Greek had lost a lot of weight. His clothes were worn and mended to the point of being shabby. He glanced around as though to make sure they were not being overheard, then he said, "I have been a pirate."

"Piracy doesn't seem to be very profitable these days," Fauston observed.

Gregory gestured with his hand. "Bah! We had bad luck. There are more pirates at sea than there are ships to plunder. So we decided to raid a town on Cyprus. Unfortunately, a party of Lusignan's knights were in the town when we struck. They killed many of my fellows, and the rest of us were lucky to get away with our lives. Now I am looking for a ship to Byzantium, to see if I can find work there. I stopped in for a drink, for old times' sake, and here you are. So tell me, my friend, how have you been?"

The serving girl brought Gregory wine, and Fauston told him about his job as a tour guide. He told how the Brabanters had wanted a relic for their church. "I looked all over for you, but you weren't in town."

"Too bad. I might have found you something. So what did you do?"

Fauston smiled casually. "As it turns out, I procured them an arm of St. John the Baptist."

Gregory was taken aback. "Really? How did you manage that?"

Fauston's smile widened. "I—"

At that moment the door opened and Fauston's tour group came in, loud and thirsty and grumpy because instead of going home, they were forced to remain in Acre, and they had seen everything of interest in Acre a dozen times. Most had originally intended to bring their wives, but because of the war the women had been left at home—much to the benefit of the whores the pilgrims had encountered on their way. The group was mainly English, and running out of money, and Fauston had procured them lodgings in a cheaper part of town than they'd been in before.

"Fauston!" one of them cried, and the group made its way to his table.

Fauston rose and greeted them. "How are your new lodgings?"

"Better than we could have hoped for at the price," said a fellow named Thomas Hasby. "Thanks for your assistance in finding them." Hasby was a master stonemason. He had worked on the cathedrals at Old Sarum and Ely, on Newstead Priory and the abbey at Donnington Wood. He had huge forearms and powerful hands. He looked at Gregory. "Who's your friend?"

Fauston said, "This is Gregory. He is—" what *was* Gregory?—"he is a relics finder. Forgive his appearance but he's just back from a collecting expedition."

"Relics!" said Joseph Demonde. Demonde was a carpenter, with an employment history even more peripatetic than Thomas Hasby's. He was so bald, his head looked like an egg with a beard. "Did you find any relics we could buy?" he asked Gregory.

Hasby added, "They'd need to be cheap. We don't know how long we'll be stuck here with this weather, and we've got to watch our money."

"Well . . ." Gregory pretended to think, but it was obvious to Fauston that he had no idea what was going on.

Fauston looked around the room, hoping for inspiration. He saw a plump canon from the cathedral gnawing a fingernail.

"Nail parings!" he blurted. "Nail parings of the early saints. There have been many collected in these parts, you know. These that I speak of are said to have been in the collection of—" he searched his memory for a name—"St. Augustine of Hippo."

Gregory stared at him like he was mad.

Joseph Demonde nodded sagely. "Would these nail parings be like those of St. Edmund? His martyred body was incorrupt, and once a year his acolyte Oswen opened his sepulcher and trimmed his nails and hair—because he was incorrupt, his nails and hair kept growing, you see. The nails and locks of trimmed hair are in churches all over England."

"Some of these are like that, I believe," Fauston said. "Others were collected at the time of the saint's death or martyrdom."

Thomas Hasby turned to his companions. "I'm certain there's many of us as would be interested in relics like that." There were nods and murmurs of approval from the group. "Would there be enough of these nail parings to accommodate all of our party?"

"I'm sure there would," Fauston said glibly. "Gregory was just now telling me about the collection."

Gregory's eyes grew even wider, if that were possible.

"Is that true?" a sharp fellow named Oswy asked Gregory.

Gregory glanced at Fauston, then answered. "I—yes. Yes, there are many."

"At what price in English shillings?" said Oswy. Oswy was a miller, and, as such, was disliked by his fellow pilgrims as much as he was disliked by the villagers at home.

Fauston cut in. " 'Twould depend on the stature of the holy man—or woman—but most would be one shilling, maybe two."

"Aye, well, that sounds fair," said Hasby, scratching his beard and looking at several of the closer men, who nodded approval. "When can we see them?"

"Tomorrow," Fauston said. "Gregory and I will get them this evening. We'll meet you here at this same hour."

The men nodded acceptance. Fauston drained his wine and stood. Gregory did the same. "Now if you'll excuse us," Fauston told the group.

He beckoned the bewildered Gregory, and the two men left the tavern. Before Gregory could open his mouth, Fauston said, "Please tell me you know how to write."

Chapter 42

"**I CAN WRITE,**" Gregory said.

"Latin?"

"A bit. Why?"

"I'll tell you later. Right now we need to purchase supplies."

They visited shops in the commercial district, acquiring parchment and inks and quills. They bought wax and some old, faded ribbon—which the merchant gave them for free—and a cheap ring with a seal, along with a number of small wooden boxes which they got from the same jeweler who sold them the ring.

"Are you going to tell me what we're doing?" Gregory said as they hurried from shop to shop.

"It's for the relics," Fauston told him.

"That much I guessed. But where *are* the relics?"

"You'll see."

They stopped at a small Greek church whose pastor gave them names of saints from the early days of the Church. Gregory copied the names onto one of the pieces of parchment.

"Why do you need this information?" the pastor asked. He was a jovial fellow, overjoyed to have his church returned from the clutches of the infidels.

"I am chronicler to the earl of Trent," Fauston said grandly. He indicated Gregory. "This is my apprentice."

Gregory gave him a look. "This information will be used as background to my lord's chronicle."

By the time they left the church it was near dusk. Fauston couldn't go to the Golden Keys because he might run into his tour group, so he took Gregory to a place called the Boar's Head, frequented by Genoese merchants.

Gregory said, "What are—"

Fauston held up a hand and led him in.

The tavern smelled of old sweat and olives and simmering garlic. A fire burned in one corner against the November chill. Fauston had two small leather sacks with him. He approached a crowded table and bowed with a flourish. "Good evening, gentlemen."

The merchants, who had been chattering away in Italian, stopped and eyed him warily.

Fauston held out one of the sacks and gave the men his most winning smile. "Could my associate and I impose upon you to pare your fingernails and put them in this sack? 'Tis for a worthy cause, I assure you."

The merchants looked at each other and frowned. "Are you some kind of queer?" said a big man with a heavy black beard.

"Not at all," Fauston protested. "I—"

"Yes, you are," said the merchant, "you're a queer. You have to be, to ask for my fingernails."

Another one said, "I'm not letting you touch my nails, you queer."

"He's not a queer," said a third. "He's a pervert."

"Go on, pervert, get out of here," said the big man, his voice rising.

Fauston said, "But—"

"Out!"

Attracted by the disturbance, the Nubian who enforced order in the tavern grabbed Fauston by the shoulders, frog marched him out the door and threw him into the street, where he stumbled and landed on his butt in the dirt.

"Do not come back here," the Nubian told him.

Gregory departed the tavern behind Fauston, hands up to show the Nubian he wanted no trouble.

In the street, Fauston got up, dusting himself off.

"That went well," Gregory said.

It was Fauston's turn to give Gregory a look.

Gregory went on. "So this was your great plan—we're making these relics ourselves?"

"That was the idea."

"Was that was how you acquired the arm of John the Baptist?"

"It was," Fauston said, wiping the filth of the street from his hands. "Though it seems that bones are more easily obtained in this city than fingernails."

"Forging relics is a mortal sin, you know. It is punishable by death if you get caught."

"Sin and I are old friends. Besides, who's going to catch us? We're simply filling a demand. Or we will be, if we can get anyone to part with his damned fingernails."

Gregory sighed. "Come with me."

Gregory led Fauston to a seedy tavern in the harbor, where, by the manner in which he was greeted, he was well known. By offering to pay a penny for each nail paring—finger or toe—Gregory got the customers to agree. A penny would buy a drink, and these men liked to drink. Indeed, he soon had them lined up to contribute to the cause.

"What's this in aid of?" a bowlegged sailor asked Gregory.

"Why do you care?" Gregory said. "You're getting paid for it."

These were working men—laborers and sailors—and their nails were ragged and cracked and dirty. "Excellent, just what we need," Fauston exclaimed from his stool as he struggled to saw through a particularly thick thumbnail. "Much more authentic than anything we would have gotten from those stuck-up fellows at the Boar's Head."

The tavern whores joined in, as well. One not unattractive redhead slipped her foot from its sandal and placed it squarely in Fauston's lap. "How does this look?"

Fauston traced his fingers across her foot, lingering on her shapely ankle. "Lovely."

He trimmed the painted nail of her big toe and put it in the sack. "You are a saint, my dear."

She eyed him knowingly. "It's not the first time someone's said that to me."

"I'll wager it's not."

She rubbed her foot against his crotch. "A penny a nail—sure that's all you want?"

Fauston smiled. "If we make this sale, I'll come back later and buy the rest of you."

She massaged his crotch with her toes, longer this time, achieving the desired reaction. "Don't wait too long," she advised.

When Fauston and Gregory had collected enough nail parings, they returned to Fauston's cramped quarters and set to work. Fauston cut the parchment into small scrolls. He sharpened the quills and mixed inks. He roughed up the women's nails as best he could with a file—the men's nails were already rough enough. Then he glued the nails to cheap brass casings and placed them in the wooden boxes.

Meanwhile, using the information they'd gotten from the priest, Gregory sat at the table and in strokes of black and red, he composed a declaration for each nail attesting that this relic of so-and-so was from the collection of St. Augustine of Hippo, that it was a true relic and blessed by the Holy Church.

"I didn't realize that writing was a necessary skill for a pirate," Fauston said.

"It's not," Gregory replied. "For a trader it is, though. If you can't read or write bills of lading, you won't have a long career."

"How did you learn Latin?"

"Lots of business is done in Latin, especially if the Church is involved, and it frequently is."

"Is that what you are? A trader?"

"I'm whatever turns a profit. I was born in Nicea. My father was a silk dyer and I was apprenticed the same way, but the dyer's wife was a tyrant who made life Hell for me. I spent more time doing her housework than I ever did learning how to color silk. One day I could take it no more and ran away to Constantinople, where I hitched on with a party of German merchants."

Gregory misspelled a word and swore. He crumpled the now useless parchment and tossed it to the floor with a rapidly accumulating pile of parchment balls caused by similar errors.

"Careful," Fauston said. "That parchment was expensive."

"I can't help it. I'm not a scribe." Gregory knit his brow in concentration and started over.

"Anyway, the merchants treated me little better than the dyer's wife, so I quit them at the first opportunity. I knocked around southern Germany for some years during the gold rush there, then I pooled my money with a friend and we headed north as iron mongers. I won't bore you with the details, but after many adventures I found myself in the Holy Land. Here I buy, I sell, I trade. Whatever presents itself."

"Why were you going all the way to Constantinople to look for work? Why not go to Tyre? It's a lot closer."

"One of my wives lives in Tyre."

"*One* of your wives? How many do you have?"

"Two. There was a third, but she ran off with a grain broker from Antioch."

When the scrolls were done, Fauston melted wax onto them and pressed the seal of his new ring into the wax. He still had the archbishop of Tyre's seal, but he could get in too much trouble for using that. "What's our imprimatur to be?" Gregory asked.

Fauston rubbed his chin and thought. "How about Theodosius, bishop of Aetherea?"

"Is there a bishop of Aetherea?"

"Who knows? This is the Holy Land. Every water hole over here has a bishop. This way they can't get us for forging a real prelate's signature."

Next to the wax seal, Fauston provided a creaky scrawl that stood in contrast to Gregory's stilted handwriting. It was more of an ink slash, really, since Fauston couldn't write, but it looked like something a doddering old bishop might have tossed off. When the scrolls were signed, Fauston and Gregory crumpled them and slapped them on the floor for aging. They bounced the wooden boxes off the floor and walls a few times for the same effect, then they affixed the scrolls to the boxes with the faded ribbon.

It was past daybreak when the task was finished and they were able to catch a bit of sleep. Fauston's eyes still stung and Gregory's hand ached as they carried the relics to the Golden Keys.

The English pilgrims watched eagerly as Fauston and Gregory spread the boxes on a table. Gregory read from the scrolls. "Here we have a thumbnail from St. Pionius of Smyrna. Here are two nails from Alpius of Thagaste; here, a lovely long nail from Anastasia Patricia; and another from St. Euphrasia. Here's a rare one from St. Suphronius, an early patriarch of Jerusalem. Oh, and here's something from the great theologian Tertullian."

He went through the collection, forty-three in all. Fauston set the last box on the table. He eyed it fondly because it contained the toenail from the red-haired whore who'd tickled his crotch. "Here is my personal favorite. This holy relic comes from St. Monica, blessed mother of St. Augustine."

Oswy the miller picked up the box and examined it. "Here. This nail's got bits of red polish on it." He eyed Fauston sharply. "Polish on the nail of a saint? That don't sound right."

Heads turned toward Fauston.

Fauston smiled and raised a finger to Oswy. "Ah, sir, you forget. Monica was a noblewoman of the Roman Empire. She would have worn polish on her nails as part of her social status."

"He's right," said bald-headed Joseph Demonde, nodding vigorously. "I heard about her in a sermon once. If you don't want that one, I'll take it."

Oswy pawed the box toward him protectively. "No, I want it. Just had a question, is all."

Fauston and Gregory settled the bill, then they bade the English pilgrims good day and left the tavern. On the street outside, they divided their earnings equally. "Fifty-two English shillings," Fauston said. "A tidy profit, even with what we had to pay for supplies."

"And for the relics," Gregory noted. "So now what?"

Fauston jingled the coins in his hand. "Now, I intend to visit that redhead."

"And after that?"

Fauston spread his arms, as though the answer was obvious. "After that, we sell more relics."

Chapter 43

THE ONLY GOOD thing about being a slave was that Roger no longer had the dream. The dream where he saw that first man he'd killed, on the walls of Acre, saw the man's face explode in blood and bone and teeth as Roger's axe clove into it. More times than he could count, Roger had awakened, covered in sweat, with that image in his mind. Right now, he was too busy staying alive to dream.

He reflected on this as he and his exhausted companions made their way back to the slave compound. They had spent the day starting an irrigation ditch that would lead to an expansive new garden behind Qaymaz's castle. The door of Hut Three had been left open for the day to let in fresh air, and the men filed in. When they were all inside, Mahmoud locked the door behind them. It would not be opened again till the call for work the next morning.

"Home sweet home," cracked Pentecost as he went to his pallet.

"Shut up, Pentecost," said the man-at-arms Borchard. "I'm glad you find this so funny."

Pentecost shrugged. "Have to laugh at something. I'd laugh at your face, but you're too ugly."

Borchard went at him. "You—"

Roger stepped between them. "All right. That's enough." He shoved Borchard back.

It was over as quickly as it had begun. The men were too tired. The Hospitaller Hillaire had been Mahmoud's target that day, and he sank painfully onto his pallet. "I had no land back in the Medoc, where I was recruited," he said, "and I ate grass at times to survive, but as God is my witness, I wish I had stayed there. Anything would be better than this."

Father Lambert looked toward the hut door. "I may be a man of peace, but I swear to you, I would kill that Mahmoud had I the chance."

"I do not see you getting that chance any time soon," said Zoran the Kurd.

"The Lord works in mysterious ways," Lambert told him.

"Wish He'd work a little harder," said the sailor Tillo.

Roger attended Hillaire's cuts and bruises as best he could, sponging them with water from a bucket, the same water they used for drinking. Their food arrived, the usual chickpeas and flatbread. The flatbread was called by the guards sometimes *aysh* and sometimes *raj*, though no one could tell any difference between the two.

Lambert blessed the food, as he did every night, while the others—save for Tillo and the two Muslims—knelt and prayed along with him. When Lambert was done, the men formed a line and Roger and Pentecost oversaw the food's distribution. There was no more pushing and shoving. Borchard and Tillo—and probably a few others—resented this new way of sharing the food, but it was a fact that there was now less sickness in Hut Three than there was in the other huts.

Since Roger had taken charge, the men now made an attempt at cleaning the hut with home-made brooms in the mornings before work; and all save Lambert, who was too old, took turns emptying the latrine bucket in the morning, which job had previously been reserved for Zoran and Ahmed. Indeed, Roger had been the first to empty the bucket. Borchard had drawn the duty the next day, and at first he refused to do it. "Maybe a jumped-up 'battlefield' knight does such work, but a noble-born man-at-arms does not."

"Fine," Roger had told him. "You don't have to empty the bucket, but you won't eat until you do."

It took a while, but Borchard emptied the bucket.

Now the men wolfed down their food, as they always did. As the dusk deepened, the men talked. They talked about their past lives, about the guards, about women, about war. Some, like the stolid native farmer Yves, said little. Yves had been captured when the Saracens overran the country around Castle Beaufort. His wife had been raped to death and his four children taken from him. He had no idea of his children's fate and knew that he never would.

Roger barely listened to what they were saying. He was thinking about his father, the one-eyed baron Henry of Deraa. What was Henry doing now? Was he still alive? There was so much Roger wanted to ask him, so much he wanted to know about him and about his mother. Now he was as far away from those answers as he had been when he was at Huntley Abbey. Maybe farther.

"We have to get out of here," he said abruptly.

"That's what I been telling the emir for two years," Pentecost remarked. "He never listens to me, though."

Borchard shot Pentecost an annoyed look, then said, "Why do you keep bringing this up, Roger? Because you're a knight and you think you must lead us to glory? Don't you think we haven't talked about escape? It's impossible. We can't get out of here—we don't even know where we are."

"Ahmed knows," said the merchant Alberic, who was squatting noisily over the latrine bucket.

Tillo spat. "Ahmed's a Goat Fucker. We can't trust him."

Ahmed's face flashed with anger. "I am a slave, like you. You think I do not want to leave this place?"

"So where are we then?" Tillo challenged him.

"We are maybe five days south of Damascus."

"Which means we're in the middle of nowhere," sighed Hillaire from his pallet.

It was now completely dark inside the hut. "Look," Roger told them, "it can't be that difficult. The sun sets in the west. If we follow the sunset, we'll eventually reach the sea and find our army."

"If our army's still there," Alberic grunted from the bucket. Like Tillo, Alberic had been taken when Saladin captured Acre. He was used to a more comfortable life than the others and folds of flesh hung about his face and body. "If what you say about that battle is true, there's a good chance King Richard has already taken Jerusalem, a good chance he and most of the army are even now on their way home."

Roger said, "In that case, the kingdom of Jerusalem will control all the land along the coast, so we'll still be safe if we reach the sea."

Borchard snorted. "I think there's a better chance that King Richard will retake the rest of Outremer before he leaves, including this place."

"The Blue Fart wasn't part of Outremer," Pentecost said.

"It will be when Richard captures it."

Alberic returned from the bucket, being careful not to knock it over in the dark. His exertions had left him even more drawn than usual. "If our army captures this place, the emir will kill us out of spite, you know that. If we had any value to our people, we'd have already been ransomed."

"Aye," said the peasant Yves with his dead eyes, "that's the way of it, no matter what your faith. The rich and powerful, they get to go on with their lives while the rest of us are left to rot."

Zoran spoke. "Escape sounds wonderful, Roger, but how would we accomplish it?"

"Tunnel under the wall of the hut."

"It's been tried," Borchard said.

"Then try again. We can use these spoons they gave us to eat with."

"Say we do tunnel out of here," Tillo said. "We come up in the middle of compound. Then what?"

"Overcome the guards and run for it."

"Overcome them with what? We have no weapons."

Pentecost said, "It might be easier if we just make a break for it during work detail."

Borchard said, "They'll chase us and run us down. We're too weak to outrun them."

Yves scratched a hard-to-reach flea bite. "Suppose everything goes right, and we do get out of here. It's a long way to the coast. What will we use for supplies?"

"We'll steal them as we go along," Roger said.

"We'll be pursued," Hillaire said. "We have no horses; we'll be caught in no time."

Roger would not be deterred. "Then we'll steal weapons and kill our pursuers."

"Beyond this place it is desert," said Ahmed. "We will die."

"We're already dead," Roger told him. "Don't you see that? If we don't get out of this place, we'll die here, like Aimery, like all the men you buried before I got here. We have to try."

The ancient priest Lambert sucked remnants of the chickpeas from the inside of a long, grimy fingernail. "You're new, Roger. You still have spirit. We were all like you once, filled with grand ideas. You'll be like us soon enough."

"The Devil I will," Roger said, though in his heart he feared Lambert was right, and that made him all the more determined to escape. Or die trying.

"I say we wait," Borchard said. "If Saladin's on the run, like Roger the Great claims he is, it shouldn't be long before the army of Jerusalem shows up here. Why risk our lives for nothing?"

"Or maybe there will be an exchange of prisoners," Hillaire suggested hopefully.

"I'm for getting out," Pentecost said.

"Me, as well," said Yves.

"I'll go," said Zoran.

"And I," said Ahmed.

The others were quiet.

Borchard barked a laugh. "There's your army, Roger—a clown, a farmer and two Goat Fuckers. Good luck getting far with that bunch."

Roger looked Borchard in the eye. "We'll make it."

"When do we go?" Pentecost asked Roger.

"As soon as we can."

Chapter 45

DECEMBER 1191

ℱAUSTON HAD BECOME a familiar sight around the city, with his wide-brimmed hat and pilgrim's staff. One particularly leaden afternoon, as he was on his way to visit the redheaded whore, whose name was Eugenia, he was approached on the street by a matron of about fifty. She was a handsome woman, her face deeply tanned, something a noblewoman from England or France would never have countenanced. She was dressed in the manner of the native Christians, and two burly servants who doubled as bodyguards accompanied her.

"Are you the one called Fauston?" she asked breathlessly.

Fauston removed his hat and bowed deeply. "I am, madam."

"Thank God, I've been looking all over the city for you. You need a shop or something, where you can be found. I've been at my wits' end."

"What is the matter?"

The woman drew herself up. Her voice steadied. "My name is Hugoline of Montjoie. I've been given to understand that you know where to find relics."

Fauston had heard of Hugoline of Montjoie, she was one of the richest women in the city. "I admit, madam, God has shown me favor in that regard." Since the departure of the last pilgrims, he and Gregory had eked out a living selling relics to residents of the city and to travelers.

Hugoline said, "My daughter is getting married tomorrow, and I want to give her a relic as a wedding present, to ensure a happy union."

Fauston hesitated. He had not expected this.

"I am willing to pay quite well for the proper relic," Hugoline said. "But there is little time."

Fauston bowed again. "I cannot promise anything, madam, but I will check my sources and see if I can find something suitable."

That rainy evening, over pots of warmed Cyprian arrack, Fauston conferred with Gregory in the Golden Keys. Gregory said, "Guess the Thirty Pieces of Silver won't do for this job?"

Fauston shook his head. Though he had once maligned their existence, the coins of Judas Iscariot had become a staple of Fauston's trade. They were easy to make and travelers expected to find them in Acre. His other offerings were bits of stone from Mt. Golgotha, where Christ had been crucified, and chips from the Ten Commandments. "We need something new for this, something special, something appropriate for a noble wedding. And we need it by tomorrow."

Gregory thoughtfully raked his fingers through his unkempt beard, dislodging old bits of food. "How about something associated with the Virgin Mary? Brides always like something to do with Mary. Maybe threads from the headdress she wore at the Annunciation? Something like that?"

"Hmm," Fauston mused, "that might do." Then it hit him. "How about a piece of the veil worn by the bride at the wedding feast at Cana?"

Gregory clapped his hands. "Excellent! I love it!"

From Eugenia's dust bin, Fauston procured an ancient, tattered piece of cloth, worn thin with age, its original blue color faded to an uneven grey. He found a box made of carved ebony for the reliquary, and he lined it with red velvet, while Gregory worked on the scroll.

"Theodosius of Atherea won't do for a relic like this," Gregory pointed out. "This scroll should be signed by someone noteworthy."

Fauston agreed. "What were the names of those old-time saints the priest gave us? Weren't a couple of them bishops?"

Gregory searched his work desk, found the scrap of parchment and read. "There is Ambrose—he was a bishop of Alexandria—and Macarius, bishop of Jerusalem."

"I think the bishop of Jerusalem sounds better for this piece. Let's use that. I'll buy a new ring for his seal."

"At this hour of the night?"

"People don't mind being inconvenienced if there's money involved."

For this scroll Gregory mixed more water with his ink than he usually did, to make it look faded. When the scroll was done and Fauston had signed it—he had found a seal so old that it was no longer legible—Gregory rolled it and whacked it against the table repeatedly, to soften it. He tore it, crumpled it and stamped on it. He burnt one edge with a taper, to make it look like it had survived a fire. Then he re-rolled it and bound it with a ribbon so faded it might never have had any color at all.

The next morning Fauston took the relic and scroll to Hugoline's house, which was near the cathedral. Like the dwellings of most wealthy people in the East, her home had a nondescript outer wall that surrounded a mansion full of fountains and statuary. The house still bore damage from boulders and other objects that had struck it during the siege. A famous emir named Qaymaz had used it as his quarters for part of the siege. To the emir's credit, he had hidden the statues away instead of destroying them for religious reasons, as so many other Saracen commanders had done in the houses they occupied. Right now the house was frantic with preparations for the wedding feast.

Fauston presented the relic to Hugoline, who opened the box reverently. "The wedding feast at Cana," she said, viewing the piece of cloth in awe. "This is perfect, simply perfect. How did you manage to find it?"

Fauston let out his breath in relief that she liked it. "Truly the Lord was with me in my search, madam."

Hugoline carefully unbound the ribbon and read the scroll. "My daughter will love this." She lowered her voice hopefully. "I don't suppose it will turn water into wine?"

Fauston gave her his most charming smile. "I can't say for certain, madam, but I think not. That is an expense you must bear yourself."

"I was so worried that you wouldn't find anything." She took his hand; her own hand was cool and smooth. "I am in your debt, young man. If there is ever anything I can do for you—anything—do not hesitate to let me know."

"Thank you, madam, I will." He added, "Perhaps if you come across anyone who is looking for relics?"

"I will be sure to send them to you"—her eyes twinkled—"if they can find you."

Hugoline rewarded him with two gold bezants. Fauston had never touched a gold coin; they were not even minted in western Europe. Geoffrey of Trent and other nobles used them over here, but they rarely fell to a person of Fauston's stature.

Hugoline was as good as her word. Thanks to her, Fauston began getting more requests for relics. Not only that, these requests came from wealthy residents of the city and high-ranking crusaders. This was good, but it presented a new problem. Fauston and Gregory would need better relics. They would also need better reliquaries than those Fauston could devise.

Once again, fate intervened. Fauston and Gregory were in the Golden Keys of an evening when a young man came to their table. The young man was well built but walked with a limp. He seemed to be a mixture of African and Arab blood. He had tightly curled hair like an African, but what had once been a straight nose had been broken and now canted to the right.

The young man stopped. "Is one of you named Fauston?"

Fauston was wary. "I'm Fauston."

"A redheaded girl at a stew in the harbor told me to look for you here. My name is Francisco. I was with the army, in the company known as the Death's Heads, till they mustered me out. Tatwine, the Death's Heads commander, told me to look you up when I got to Acre." His brow furrowed, as if he didn't understand the next part. "He said to ask Brocky if he could help me find work."

Fauston frowned. "Wait—Tatwine commands the Death's Heads? What about Roger? Did he get promoted?"

"He's dead. Killed in the great battle."

Fauston looked away, feeling ill. He remembered Roger as he'd first seen him, wet and bedraggled in his monk's robes, hiding under a rock shelf in Dunham Wood with Ailith. Poor Ailith—God only knew what had happened to her.

And now Roger was dead. It didn't seem possible. Roger had been one of those fellows you thought would live forever.

He turned back to Francisco. "Why did they muster you out?"

"During the battle a man fell into my right leg. Something popped in my knee, and now I can't keep pace on the march any longer. Some days I can barely walk."

"Is that when you got your nose broken—in the battle?"

Francisco nodded ruefully. "Goat Fucker clopped me in the face with a shield."

Gregory cleared his throat. "You are a Moor, Francisco. Forgive me, but shouldn't you be fighting for the other side?"

"My family are *moriscos*," the young man corrected proudly. "My grandfather converted to Christianity when he was a young man. I am from Spain. We have our own war against the infidels there, but I wanted to visit Jerusalem and see the Holy Sepulcher, so I came here."

"What made you join a company of Englishmen?" Fauston asked him.

"Those helmets, the ones with the death's head. I had to have one."

"And now you need work."

Francisco shrugged. "I have no money. I have to live."

"Do you have any skills?" Gregory asked.

"I'm good with my hands. Woodwork, stonework. I can draw and paint a little. I'd like to have been a painter, but that is not possible for a person of my background."

Gregory and Fauston exchanged glances, then Fauston rose and put an arm around the young man's shoulder. "Francisco, old son, you've come to the right place."

"So you'll ask this Brocky to help me?"

Fauston waved his free hand dismissively. "Don't you worry about Brock. Truth is, he's no better'n a common highwayman. Me and Gregory, we'll find work for you."

Even at his young age, Francisco was better at making reliquaries than Fauston was. He could fashion boxes and trim them with brass or silver or even gold, when they could get it. He fit them with panels of glass for viewing, so that customers wouldn't have to open the reliquary and expose the precious relic to air. He had a gift for the job, and he was only going to get better. The downside was that there were now three work tables in Fauston's cramped quarters, along with stacks of wooden boxes, reams of parchment, sheets of glass and various types of metal, as well as a litter of crumpled scrolls, old inkpots, quills, and wood shavings.

Business was picking up, but the money was being split three ways, and the cost of supplies, especially with the improved reliquaries, was not insignificant—not to mention the small fortune Fauston was spending on Eugenia. Fauston needed to make more money if he was ever to get out of Acre.

Standing amidst the chaos that was his quarters, Fauston made a decision. "Do you know what we need?" he announced.

Francisco looked around. "A cleaning woman?"

"No, gentlemen. As Lady Hugoline said, we need a shop."

Chapter 45

BET NABLE, JANUARY 13, THE FEAST OF
ST. HILARY

THE ARMY HALTED, waiting for King Richard's scouts to return.

The wind pelted their faces with cold rain. They were wet and bedraggled, with shaggy hair, long unkempt beards and rusting armor. Most suffered from dysentery or bloody flux. Some of the footmen were barefoot because their shoes had rotted away. Their once-proud banners were faded and tattered.

They had been on the march for two months. Constant skirmishes and raids had been interspersed with bursts of futile negotiation. The bad weather and muddy roads had slowed them. Their bread had rotted from the wet, as had the salt pork. There was no forage for the horses and many of them had died, while bones showed through the flanks of the rest.

They had chased Saladin out of Ramleh, then Latrun, and now they had now arrived at Bet Nable, the last village of consequence before Jerusalem. The Holy City was but four leagues distant. Had the sky been clear, they could have seen its towers. Many fell to their knees and prayed, others opened their arms wide and gave thanks to Heaven. A few priests started singing. The excitement was a living thing; it surged through the men, renewed them. Even the animals seemed to perk up.

"At last," said the count of Champagne, dismounting and stretching his cramped bones. Not far away, soldiers scoured the village for anything edible, but the villagers had wisely fled, taking everything of value with them. The young count usually went clean shaven, but now his beard had grown in. His surcoat was torn and stained, and there were dark circles under his eyes. "There were times during the last two years I thought we'd never get here."

"I, as well," said one-eyed Henry of Deraa. "By this time tomorrow we'll be at the gates of Jerusalem."

"It's a pity James of Avesnes and your son couldn't be here," the count said.

"They're here in spirit, believe me. As are all the poor fellows who have died to free the Holy City."

Next to them, Geoffrey of Trent wrapped his cloak tightly about him and stood in the mud, shivering. Geoffrey had stopped wearing armor because he had to empty his bowels so frequently. He had reached Jaffa for the start of the march, feeling more fit than he'd been at any time since the siege of Acre ended. It was good to be in command of his men again, good to be on the field of battle. The constant cold and wet had gotten the better of him, though, and his illness had returned, worse than ever.

Henry of Deraa said, "You look bad, Geoffrey. You should go back to Jaffa with the sick train."

"No!" Geoffrey said through chattering teeth. "I mean to enter Jerusalem with the army. That's what I came here for, and that's what I'll do." He attempted a grin, but because of

251

his shivering, it came out as more of a grimace. "Besides, Bonjute would never forgive me if Gravedigger Leicester got into Jerusalem and I did not."

"It's not going to do you any good if you get there dead," Henry pointed out.

"I'm not leaving," Geoffrey repeated.

Henry and the count of Champagne shared a glance, but said nothing.

At the front of the army King Richard stood lost in thought, heedless of the rain. His beard was bushy, his red surcoat faded. He had lost weight. He was sick again, and tired. Very tired.

"Here they come," said Andrew of Chauvigny, standing beside him.

In the distance, William of Mello, wearing only a helm and a leather jack, and two Turcopole scouts made their way up the muddy road.

"Summon the council," Richard ordered.

Heralds were sent down the long column; horns were sounded. As the army's leading nobles and churchmen gathered, a large awning was erected to provide cover from the seemingly endless rain. King Guy and Hugh of Burgundy were there, along with the earls of Leicester and Trent, the bishops of Turin, Evreaux and Beauvais, the counts of Champagne, Soissons and Dreux, Henry of Deraa, and many more.

William of Mello and the two Turcopoles dismounted, splashed with mud from their ride, and moved under the awning. To William, Richard said, "Report."

William bowed. A year younger than Richard and a proven warrior, he was one of Richard's most trusted knights. "Sire, the road to Jerusalem is wide open. There are no Saracens between us and the city. We could not tell how well the city is defende."

This elicited an excited murmur from the group.

William continued. "However, a large Egyptian army is camped in the hills surrounding the city."

Another murmur, this one surprised.

"How large?" said the duke of Burgundy.

"Twenty thousand men at least."

The murmur grew louder.

"Did you see this army?" Henry of Deraa asked William.

The knight shook his head. "Saracen patrols screening the hills prevented us from getting close, but we saw the smoke from their fires—that's how we arrived at their number—and their presence was all the farmers and herdsmen were talking about."

"Thank you," Richard said. William bowed again and left with his Turcopoles.

Beneath the awning there was an uneasy pause.

"What does this mean?" asked the bishop of Turin, a holy man who knew little of war.

"It means those Egyptians are in a position to move in behind us and cut us off from our supplies should we attempt a siege," Alart of Vouzin said gloomily.

"So what?" said the duke of Burgundy. "We're as good as cut off now. We have to send half the army to escort the supply trains up from Jaffa or they don't get through."

Richard rubbed his chin. This news, though bad, was not unexpected—at least not by him. "What shall we do, my lords?" he asked. He had already formulated his plan, but he wanted to hear their opinions, for courtesy's sake if nothing else.

Hugh of Burgundy, leader of the French, spoke without hesitation. Unlike most of the nobles, Hugh seemed to have gained energy as the arduous march from Jaffa wore on. "I say we advance, Egyptians be damned."

"I agree," said Henry of Deraa.

"I share their opinion," said the bishop of Beauvais. "We may never get this close to Jerusalem again."

Geoffrey of Trent mumbled something.

"Your pardon, my lord?" Richard said.

"Advance," Geoffrey said in a weak voice.

The always practical Henry of Champagne prevaricated. "I would like to hear from those who know the country around Jerusalem best." He gestured to the grand masters of the Templars and Hospitallers, the monastic orders that furnished the kingdom of Jerusalem with its best soldiers.

Robert de Sable, the Templar, spoke first. The arrogant Templars always got in the first word. "My lords, it grieves me to say this, but I believe we should fall back. To attempt a siege in this weather, with that Egyptian army behind us—maybe surrounding us—can only end in disaster."

The silence of the assembly on hearing these words was overwhelming.

De Sable, who was older than most of the nobles present, went on. "The countryside hereabouts does not produce enough supplies to support us, and our supply lines to Jaffa are tenuous. The siege engines are days behind us. It will take time to maneuver the wagons carrying them to the city in this mud, and we will have to have ammunition sent up from Jaffa. If this Egyptian army cuts us off from Jaffa, we will not have rocks for the trebuchets. Worse than that, we will starve, as will our animals. The animals are half dead already, the men are not far behind. It will be like the siege of Acre all over again, save the outcome is like to be different."

There were angry voices from the crowd. Rain drummed on the awning. Garnier of Naplouse, leader of the Hospitallers, raised his voice above the noise. "I agree with Grand Master Robert. It would be folly to attempt a siege in bad weather when we're cut off from supplies. We don't know how many men Saladin has to defend the city or how long it will take to capture it. We might be stuck here for months. And there is another point to consider. When we take the city, what then? You lords from the west will doubtless see your duty satisfied at that point, and you will go home. There are not enough of our local troops to hold the city against Saladin and twenty thousand men."

"Then what the Devil did we come here for?" cried the earl of Leicester in frustration. "Now you're saying that if we take the city, you locals can't hold it. Is there anything you people *can* do? Are we supposed to stay here forever to hold your hands and protect you?"

Garnier flushed with anger. "It will take time to build up our forces, my lord. We lost most of our army at Hattin."

"I wish Balian of Ibelin was here," the count of Champagne said. "I would like to hear his opinion on this matter."

"Where is Ibelin?" Leicester asked.

"Still in Tyre, the last I heard."

"What the Devil is he doing in Tyre?" Leicester snarled. "Buying new clothes? Having his hair perfumed?"

"I don't know," Champagne said irritably. "Why don't you go there and ask him?"

Robert de Sable said, "Were this new army from Egypt not present, I would be of a different mind. As it is—"

"That's a far cry from the advice your predecessor would have given," Guy of Lusignan said contemptuously.

"All the Templars save my predecessor had their heads struck off at Hattin while following his advice and *your* orders," de Sable pointed out. "So did a large number of the kingdom's knights. Which is why we cannot hold Jerusalem by ourselves at the moment."

"Enough, gentlemen," said the count of Champagne. "This arguing gets us nowhere." He turned to King Richard. "Sire? What are your thoughts on the matter?"

All eyes turned to King Richard. Not for the first time, Richard wished he wasn't burdened with the responsibility of command. His instinct as a warrior—his preference—was to ignore the risks, to advance and fight, but his judgment as a commander told him something different. "My lords, I acceded to your demands for a march on the Holy City, but from the beginning I suspected that Saladin would try to trap us. This latest news proves that my suspicions were correct. Saladin leaves Jerusalem apparently undefended, but a fresh army lurks in the hills. Saladin invites us to attack the city. Why? So he can draw us in, then spring his trap. I do not intend to fall for his ruse. We are at a major disadvantage in these hills. Our horses cannot maneuver. If our grain supplies are cut off, the horses will soon starve and we'll all be afoot, and then Saladin will have us where he wants us."

"What would you have us do?" said Andrew of Chauvigny.

Richard smiled slyly. "I intend to lay a trap of my own. I intend to lure Saladin out of the hills and make him fight on the plain, where our knights will have the advantage. If we can break him for good there, he'll give up Jerusalem without a fight."

There was shock. Most had expected a different answer from this most warlike of kings. After a moment, the count of Soissons said, "How do you propose to lure him out, sire?"

"We'll knock out the props supporting his empire. By doing that, we'll force him to come down from the hills and give battle." He paused, looking over the suddenly disheartened assemblage. "We'll begin with Ascalon. Ascalon dominates the road from Egypt. Saladin has torn down its walls, but if we fortify it, we can block him from his most valuable source of reinforcements and supplies. He'll have to try and take it back. And that's when we will destroy him."

If Richard was expecting cheers, or indeed any kind of positive response, he was sorely disappointed, because there was none. Nonetheless, he knew this was a sound move in the chess match between himself and the sultan. Time would be a factor in its execution, of course, but Richard could afford to remain in the Holy Land a while yet. It would be a closely run thing, but he could still win the immortality he had come here to achieve and get home to prevent King Philip from doing major damage to the Angevin holdings in France.

There was more silence. At last the duke of Burgundy voiced everyone's unspoken question. "What about Jerusalem?"

"Jerusalem must wait. As our friends from the military orders have pointed out, an advance now is like to end in disaster."

"You're saying we should retreat?" Burgundy growled.

"Not retreat. Withdraw."

Henry of Deraa yanked off his helmet and slammed it into the mud. "By all that's holy, we came here to take Jerusalem or die, and that is what we should do. I don't care how many armies Saladin has out there."

There was a roar of approval from the nobles.

Richard replied coolly. "That is easy for you to say, Lord Henry. You are responsible only for your own life and the lives of your men. I am responsible for the entire army. I am responsible to history."

"Conrad wouldn't turn back," Burgundy said.

"Conrad would have taken the city months ago," someone shouted.

"I'm tired of hearing about Conrad," Richard snapped. "If Conrad were in charge of the army, his head would be on a pole by now and all your bones would be rotting in the desert. You men are so confident of victory, you ignore the obstacles before you. You think they will magically disappear, that God will intervene to save you. If God would do that, why did He permit the Holy City to fall to the infidels in the first place?"

The earl of Leicester knew the answer to that. "Because the Christians of this country are sinners. Because they dress like women and fornicate and consort with Muslims. It was God's way of punishing them."

Richard sighed. Leicester was a formidable warrior, but he could be wearying at times. "Be that as it may, I refuse to lead the army into Saladin's trap. We will start back for Jaffa, then go to Ascalon."

There was silence in the tent. Without a word, the duke of Burgundy stormed out, followed by his barons. Gradually the others left, as well, until only Richard, Alart and Andrew of Chauvigny were left under the awning.

Word of what was happening spread through the army. It was met first by stunned disbelief, then by anger. The ecstasy these men had known only a few hours before turned to devastation, to rage. The nobles were met with boos and catcalls as they left the council, even the ones who had wanted to go on, and for a moment they feared for their lives, so enraged were their men. The slightest spark would have set off a mutiny. Fortunately, that spark was not forthcoming.

The army was turned around in the easiest way possible, reversing the order of march, with the Hospitallers assuming the van and the Templars bringing up the rear. Even that could not be accomplished without difficulty because each unit's marching order had to be rearranged before it could get under way, and pack animals had to be shunted aside to fall in at the end of their companies. The rain and the men's sullen mood did not help. Many of the footmen took off the badges of their lords and threw them in the mud.

"My men will go last," Henry of Deraa informed Robert de Sable, who was now in charge of the rear guard, and so foul was Henry's mood, the Templar dared not argue with him.

"Permission to go with you?" asked the squire Tatwine, who now commanded Roger's Death's Heads.

"Granted," Henry said.

King Richard stood in the rain at the end of the column and looked back toward the hills where Jerusalem lay. It was heartbreaking to have come this far and then have to turn around, but he knew he had made the right decision. Christian arrogance and underestimation of the enemy had led to a massacre at Hattin; there would be no repeat of that while Richard commanded the army.

Henry stood nearby, looking backward as well. The two men were alone, Henry's men being some little distance off, and the rest of army well down the road. Henry and Richard stood side by side for some time, then Henry murmured, "Time to go, sire. Saracen scouts will be here soon."

Richard nodded, then mounted and started off. He wished the Saracens would show up. He needed to take out his frustrations on someone. Behind him, Henry and his men followed.

From ahead came a cry.

Richard spurred Fauvel forward. "What's happened?" he said as he approached the mud-spattered Templars of the rear guard.

"It's the earl of Trent, sire," said Robert de Sable, pointing up the line. "He's gone unconscious and fallen from his horse."

❧

Huddled in their cloaks against the rain and cold, Saladin and his retinue watched the departing Christian army from a hilltop near Bet Nable.

"They fell for it," said Saladin's oldest son, al-Afdal. "They actually fell for it."

"Allah be praised," said Saladin's chronicler Beha ad-Din.

As usual, Saladin showed little emotion. He turned to Qaymaz and in a conversational tone, as though they were discussing the price of grain, he said, "That was an excellent idea of yours, Qaymaz."

Qaymaz bowed his head modestly.

In November Saladin had sent most of his army home for the winter. Then Richard had stolen a march on him by advancing on al-Quds. Saladin had been taken by surprise— he had not expected Richard to advance so late in the season. He frantically attacked the oncoming Christians with the few men left to him, then pretended to negotiate. Anything to slow the feringhees down. Anything to buy time. He had thought all was lost when the Christians took Latrun and approached Bet Nable, then Qaymaz had come up with his plan, and now the infidels were leaving.

There was no Egyptian army. There were campfires in the hills, but there was no one to man them. The farmers and herdsmen who had spoken to the feringhee scouts were Qaymaz's spies. For all practical purposes, al-Quds was empty of defenders. Rik and his soldiers could have entered the city without opposition.

Qaymaz studied the sultan. Saladin was unwell, and Qaymaz hoped the old man—funny thinking of him that way, he was only a few years older than Qaymaz—lived long enough to see the infidels off. Qaymaz had a bad feeling about what would happen when the sultan was gone. Saladin's oldest son, the Bull, was not fit to be a good ruler. His second son, al-Aziz, would be better; but his brother, al-Adil, would be better still. And therein lay the seeds of conflict. Plus there were deteriorating relations with the caliph of Baghdad, which meant the possibility of war on two fronts in the near future.

Normally a great lord like Qaymaz might aspire to seize the sultanate for himself with the succession so unsettled, but though Qaymaz had wealth and power and a keen military mind, he did not want the top spot. As sultan, you were always a target, you always had men scheming against you. Qaymaz did not enjoy statecraft, he liked war; and when he was not at war he preferred to be with his *harim* or hunting. He was especially enamored of the infidel woman Ailith. His loins ached at the thought of her, which was why he tried not to think of her too often.

To Saladin he said, "Do you think Rik and the other 'crusaders' will go home now?"

"They will go home at some point, but I know not when," Saladin said.

The Bull chuckled. "Then we shall only have to face the mighty 'King' Guy."

"What about *al-Markis*, Conrad?" al-Aziz said. "Do not forget him."

"I have not forgotten *al-Markis*," Saladin said. "He is the one I fear. Rik will go home one day, perhaps one day soon, but *al-Markis* intends to stay."

PART IV

Chapter 46

MARCH 1192

ⓆAYMAZ'S SLAVES, INCLUDING the men from Hut Three, were still working on the irrigation ditch. The new gardens were supposed to be ready for the birthday of Qaymaz's wife, but because of the weather, the ditch that would provide them water through the dry months was behind schedule. And when the ditch was finished, the slaves still had to build the windmill that would drive water from the river to the gardens. The slaves were covered with muck, which, since they never bathed, formed a more or less permanent—and growing—crust on their bodies and clothes.

Roger was chopping brush with a shovel—the only tool allowed to the men. He slipped in the mud, cut his hand and swore. Behind him, Borchard chuckled as he heaved a shovelful of mud outside the waterlogged ditch. "Thought you were going to escape, Roger? Why, I thought you'd be in Jerusalem by now. Hell, I thought you'd take Jerusalem single handed. Or maybe you'd already be back home, where they'd make you a duke or something on account of all your heroic deeds."

Roger shook the blood from his hand. "I am going to escape," he told Borchard. "I'll get out of this place or die trying."

"Me, I'm betting on the second result," Borchard said.

"Betting on it, or hoping for it?" Pentecost said.

"Same thing," Borchard replied.

Father Lambert stood above the ditch, carrying water and bread for the workers. He chastised Borchard. "That's an un-Christian attitude, Borchard. We need to be on each other's side here. Perhaps this denigration of your fellows is why you've never risen to knight from man-at-arms."

Borchard replied hotly. "A pox on you, old man. I've never risen to knight because—"

"Because you're stupid," Roger said.

"Stop talking!" Mahmoud yelled at them. "Work!"

In truth, Borchard was right. Escaping hadn't proved as easy as Roger had imagined. He and his comrades had first tried making a break for it. They had waited for the right time, but the guards had started mounted patrols to watch for that very thing. It was almost like somebody had warned them what the slaves might do.

Next, Roger and his men had tried digging a tunnel, using the wooden spoons provided them for their meals, but they hadn't gotten very far. The weather had been particularly bad that winter, and the ground was so wet that the initial hole's sides kept falling in before they could even start the tunnel. At last the hole had partially filled with water, rendering its use a moot point.

The slaves kept working on the ditch. Finally the sun began to set—or would have, had they been able to see it through the clouds—and the slaves were herded back to their huts.

Their path took them by the rear of the palace, on a balcony of which veiled members of the *harim* idled beneath an awning which protected them from the rain.

The sailor Tillo pointed. "Look—women. Wonder what kind of meat old Qaymaz keeps up there? I'd like to bend those bitches over and show them what a real—"

Mahound lashed Tillo across the face with his staff. "How dare you! It is forbidden for in infidel to look upon the women of the *harim*. I would put out your eyes, but we need you for work." He struck Tillo again. "Perhaps when the ditch is finished."

He hit him once more and the little column slogged on.

&

On the balcony, some of the women of the *harim* watched Tillo being beaten. Others ignored it. They had seen similar incidents most of their lives and only a few of those who watched showed any reaction. Lamiya, the Ethiopian, averted her eyes, sickened, while saucy Rasha chuckled, and Aysun, the Preferred One, laughed out loud.

Ailith stood apart from the others and looked on without interest. She was tired and sore from a long night with the emir Qaymaz, who had returned from attending the sultan. Suddenly she stiffened and watched more closely. There was something about the way the lead slave moved . . .

She studied the man intently. Where had she . . . ?

No, it couldn't be. It was impossible.

Her breath caught in her throat, and she struggled not to cry out or let the others see her reaction.

It was. It was Roger.

What was he doing here?

He had been captured, obviously. But when? How?

There had been rumors of a great battle in which the crusaders had been annihilated. Perhaps he had been taken there. But there were always rumors like that. In the *harim* you were isolated from the world outside and it was impossible to know the truth.

She knew one thing, though.

She had to contact him.

Chapter 47

THE NEXT EVENING, the men filed into the hut as usual, exhausted, hungry, sick. As the door was locked behind them, most wasted no time stretching out on their flea-ridden straw pallets. Pentecost, whose pallet was next to Roger's, spoke to Roger in a low voice. "Maybe Borchy's right. Maybe the only way out of here is to fly."

"Then we'll learn to fly," Roger told him.

The food came. Tonight the normally tasteless *aysh* was seasoned with something. "Ginger, it smells like," Pentecost said. "Maybe fennel as well."

"That's odd," said the native Christian Yves.

There was also a bucket of flavorful hummus instead of plain chickpeas.

"Odder still," Hillaire remarked.

Lastly the younger guard Yasir brought in a pail of something else.

"My God, that smells like broth," marveled Alberic the merchant. "To what do we owe this miracle?"

"Qaymaz probably had some bathwater he needed to get rid of," Pentecost said.

Alberic sniffed the steaming broth. "Smells like a piece of meat might have been dipped into it at one time."

"Maybe a stray cat fell in while they were cooking it," Hillaire said.

"Why so much food?" Roger asked Yasir before he left.

Yasir shrugged. "Doctor say."

"Doctor? What doctor?"

But Yasir was already gone.

Lambert blessed the food, then Roger and Pentecost doled it out. The starving men fell to with a will, spooning the broth noisily, dipping the seasoned flatbread into the hummus.

"This broth is actually decent," said Ahmed with an air of disbelief.

"Maybe Qaymaz has seen the light and become a Christian," Father Lambert suggested.

Outside, there was a commotion, followed by a raised voice.

"I am the emir's physician. He has sent me to examine his slaves."

"Why?" That was Mahmoud.

"Do I look stupid enough to question the emir's orders? You are welcome to do so if you wish, but for now let me get this ghastly task over with so that I may return to the palace and my regular duties."

A pause, followed by a *thunk* as the bar was drawn from the hut door. A creak. Lantern light in the dusk, and the doctor entered, wrinkling his nose and stepping back at the hut's smell.

Roger started. The doctor was Hassan.

Roger almost jumped up to greet him, but some inner sense told him not to. Hassan looked over the hut's inhabitants with a cold eye belied by his plump figure. His eyes met Roger's and lingered for a heartbeat, but he said nothing.

"Line up," he ordered the slaves. "Hurry, I do not have all night, and you people stink worse than the deck of a slave ship."

Hassan grumpily examined each of the men in turn, while Mahmoud watched him from the doorway, suspicious. Hassan gave some of the men medicine from a vial; others, like Zoran, he turned away without remark. Beckoning Pentecost to hold the lantern closer, Hassan pulled one of Lambert's remaining teeth and tossed it on the floor. The old priest winced, then rinsed out the blood with water from the communal bucket and spat it onto the dust of the hut.

Hassan next attended the men's latest bruises, applying salve to them and muttering. "You ungrateful fools insult your betters, then I have to make you well. The master wants you working, not lying in bed all day like a whore's cat."

When he was finished, he distributed oranges from a large sack he had brought with him. "These will keep your strength up. The master has need of you—at least until the gardens are finished. After that your lives will be meaningless, because by then we will have destroyed your infidel army and there will be thousands more slaves to replace you."

The men tore into the sweet oranges greedily, devouring them skin and all. With Mahmoud still watching from the doorway, Hassan examined Roger, applying salve to his bruises as well. "Another imbecile who makes work for me." Then he added in a low voice, "I heard you were here. I visited each hut to find you." He rubbed in more cooling salve. "The Lady Ailith sends her greetings."

This time Roger started so forcefully that Hassan had to pressure his shoulder to hold him still. "Stop acting like a child, infidel. That doesn't hurt."

Roger whispered, "Ailith? She's here?"

"Sh-h-h." Hassan glanced over his shoulder at Mahmoud. "She is a member of Qaymaz's *harim*. She saw you the other day from the balcony."

Roger tried to digest this. He had no idea Ailith was here. Dirk must have given—or sold—her to Qaymaz.

Hassan went on, rubbing in more salve. "She says not to give up hope. She will be in touch soon."

Roger said, "Tell her—"

Hassan slapped his face, hard. "Do not speak to me, dog. Give thanks to Allah that the emir shows you such mercy, for I most assuredly would not."

Hassan tossed Roger an orange, then, using a towel, he wiped the feringhee dirt from his hands contemptuously. "Now I must take a bath and burn my clothes."

He threw down the towel, strode past Mahmoud and left the hut.

Chapter 48

THE BATH WAS unlike anything Ailith had ever seen, unlike anything she had ever imagined before she came to the East. It was a pool surrounded by a tiled marble deck with a colonnade of filigreed, fluted arches. Light was let in through a glass roof. There were smells of jasmine and scented soaps and oils. A slave played an oud, a short-necked stringed instrument of the type that Ailith had been learning at Qaymaz's behest.

Before she had come to Qaymaz's palace, Ailith had only one proper bath in her life, and that was in the Saracen camp after Qaymaz had captured her. Back in England a bath had been a quick dip in the stream, and there had been few enough of those—none in the colder months. At Acre she had bathed in the sea and thought herself fortunate.

Now she bathed regularly, as did the other women of the *harim*. She liked feeling clean, liked being free of fleas and lice, though she didn't like the scrutiny of the other women, and of Narcissus. The big eunuch always seemed to be around when the women were bathing. His eyes seemed to take in every detail of their bodies, no matter how hard some of them tried to shield themselves from him.

The women were all here this morning, as they were most mornings. There was little else to do in the *harim* but idle and gossip and plot against one another, save for those who had borne Qaymaz children and who must make time for them.

Qawaya, second oldest woman in the *harim*, was leaving as Ailith entered. She was in and out of the bath quickly, thoroughly, like everything she did. She passed Ailith without a look, as though Ailith didn't exist.

All talk stopped as Ailith removed her robe and stepped into the pool. She felt the other women's eyes on her and tried to ignore them. After a pause, the other women stopped looking at her and talk resumed.

Ailith lowered herself into the warm water. Heated water was pumped into the bath from somewhere—Alilith didn't know how they performed such a miracle and she didn't care. It felt wonderful. At home, the lord of her manor and his wife bathed—when they bathed at all—in cramped wooden tubs, with buckets of water hauled from the spring, then heated in the kitchen and brought to the hall, slopping water everywhere. Ailith sat on a step that ran around the inside of the bath. The water came just above her waist. She splashed it over her face and shoulders, sponged her arms.

Lamiya, the young African who had tried to kill Ailith, was nearest to her, tall and willowy, lighter skinned than the Nubian slaves in the palace. Right now her shock of frizzed hair was wet and hung down her back like coils of rope. Aysun was at the pool's far end, a slave bathing her. As the Preferred One, she was the only woman allowed this privilege. The slave girl, a Nubian, maintained a blank stare while massaging Aysun's shoulders and back.

Dalaria the Kurd and Rasha preened and showed off their bodies, as though they were in a contest with each other, though who they were showing off to, Ailith couldn't fathom. Jasara and Zafina, the quiet ones, took turns bathing each other. Zafina, the taller girl, stood behind Jasara with a sponge. She cleaned Jasara's neck and back slowly, working her way down to Jasara's waist and below. Then she moved the sponge around to the other girl's breasts, cupping each breast and massaging it in a circular motion. Jasara leaned back into her, and Zafina's sponge ran down the other woman's belly and disappeared below the surface of the water. Jasara closed her eyes and Zafina moved closer, tight against Jasara now.

Ailith looked away. She leaned back against the wall of the pool, closed her eyes and pretended to relax.

She was waiting for word from Hassan. What was taking him so long? Had he been able to contact Roger? Was that really Roger that she had seen two days ago, or had it been a trick of her imagination? Had Hassan been caught? Was he even now undergoing torture to reveal who had sent him to the slave quarters?

A light splash nearby.

Ailith tensed. She'd thought they wouldn't try to do anything to her here, but she was ready if they did. She opened her eyes. Lamiya had come closer. The African girl glanced toward Aysun, who didn't seem to be paying attention to them. Without looking at Ailith, Lamiya spoke in a low voice, almost a whisper. "I—I am sorry for what I did."

Ailith stared.

Lamiya went on. "They made me. You know how it is."

"Yes, I know." Ailith couldn't think of anything else to say.

"The other women are jealous of you. They believe the emir is in love with you. They think you will become the Preferred One. Plus, you are an infidel."

There was a pause, then Ailith said, "Are you an infidel also?"

"Once," Lamiya said, "but I converted. I thought I could gain favor with the other women by doing it. Then I thought I could gain favor with them by killing you. But they hate me because of my color. That will never change. It wouldn't have changed even if I had killed you. I can see that now."

Ailith slipped off the step and lowered herself in the pool, over her head in the warm water. She came back up, brushed her blonde hair back from her face. "How did you become a slave?" she asked Lamiya.

Lamiya leaned against the wall, facing the oud player, who sat on a fringed rug, plucking the strings of his instrument. "Raiders came to my village. They took all the young men and women. They tied us together, marched us many days overland to the sea and put us on boats. They sold us in a port—I do not know its name. The boy I was supposed to marry was sold there, as well, and I never saw him again. I was sold again in Damascus, where Narcissus bought me for Qaymaz."

"Narcissus gives me an uneasy feeling," Ailith said. "Thank God he's a eunuch."

Lamiya lowered her voice till it was barely audible. "I have heard it said he is not really a eunuch, that something went wrong with the operation. They say he provides certain . . . services . . . to Aysun."

That explained a lot, Ailith thought.

Lamiya went on. "It is strange. Here I have luxury far beyond anything I could have imagined at home, yet I am unhappy. I would give anything to return to my old life."

Ailith did not say anything. She had run away from her old life and been glad to do it. "What was your life like?" she asked Lamiya.

Lamiya smiled wistfully. "We lived by the big river, in a hut made from tree branches. I was the daughter of the village head man. I had my family, I was treated with respect, and I was happy. What about you?"

"I come from a village in England. It was a poor village and my family were its poorest inhabitants. I was treated with less respect than some of the farm animals, and I was not happy at all."

Lamiya took that in, as though seeing Ailith in a new light. "England. I have heard that name, but I do not know where it is. Did raiders take you, as well?"

"No, I—"

A shadow loomed over them.

Narcissus.

The big Nubian had come up so quietly they had not noticed him.

He looked down at Ailith. "You will come now, feringhee, and make yourself presentable. The Preferred One desires to speak with you."

Chapter 49

ꕥILITH WAS FILLED with dread as she followed Narcissus down a corridor to Aysun's chambers. Hassan had been caught, he must have been. He had told Aysun and Narcissus why he'd been in the slave quarters. He had told them who had asked him to go there.

Ailith felt for Roger—if indeed that had been Roger—more than she did for herself. And for Hassan. Her actions always seemed to be getting other people into trouble.

As the Preferred One, Aysun had the largest chamber in the *harim*. The ceiling was high and airy, with windows of glass—something that, as far as Ailith knew, even the greatest lords in Europe didn't have. Fresh from the bath, Aysun reclined on a divan while a slave girl waved a fan over her head—the weather had turned, and it was the first hot day of the spring. From somewhere came the distant sound of children laughing.

Narcissus moved to a place at Aysun's right side, his dark, beefy face inscrutable. Aysun must have been strikingly beautiful once, and she was still attractive in her mid-forties, though her hair was dyed to keep out the grey and there were lines down her cheeks and around her eyes. Ailith could understand why she worried about the younger women. Aysun had lived on her beauty and sexual appeal and now those traits were being eclipsed by those of others.

If Aysun was panicking about her future, she didn't show it. Her attitude was cold and regal. "Ah, Ailith, our little Christian whore. So nice we could have this chat."

Ailith said nothing, and Aysun went on. "I saw you talking to Lamiya earlier. Poor child. She knows better than to speak with a feringhee."

Ailith felt a tightening in her stomach. "You're going to punish her?"

Aysun canted her head upward at Narcissus, who smiled.

"Leave her alone," Ailith said. "She meant nothing by—"

Aysun erupted. "Do not dare tell me what to do!"

Ailith was undeterred by this outburst. "She's just a girl. She—"

"The emir made her a woman," Aysun said, regaining her composure. "She needs to act like one, and no civilized woman would speak to a feringhee."

"You're speaking to me."

"Not because I want to. Believe me, I take no pleasure in your presence."

"Or I in yours," Ailith shot back.

Aysun looked like she was going to lose her temper again, but Narcissus stepped between them, moving smoothly for such a large man. To Ailith he said, "It is my responsibility to see that the *harim* functions smoothly. Since your arrival, here has been nothing but turmoil."

Ailith shrugged. "They tried to kill *me*, I didn't try to kill them."

Narcissus went on. "The *harim* has become like a hive of bees that has been disturbed. Things cannot return to normal until something is done about you."

"If I bother you so much, why don't you just let me go? I'd be more than happy to leave this place and return to my barbarian friends."

Narcissus smiled thinly. "I am afraid the emir would not countenance that. But since you bring the subject up, there is one thing that makes you stand out from the other women—you are an infidel."

"*You're* the infidels," Ailith scoffed. "You and Grandmother—" she indicated Aysun—"and all the rest of them."

Calling Aysun "Grandmother" had hit a nerve, Ailith saw. Narcissus went on. "I will not be drawn into an argument about theology. You must convert to Islam."

Ailith felt her cheeks redden. "That is something I will never do."

"We can force you," Aysun purred from the divan.

"How?" Ailith smiled confidently. "You can't hurt me. Qaymaz would never allow it."

"No, we cannot hurt *you*," Aysun drew out the word. "But there is someone we *can* hurt."

Narcissus snapped his fingers, and slaves led in a woman.

It was Margaret. The cast had been removed from Margaret's ankle, but she still walked with a limp. She shrugged out of the slaves' grip and gazed defiantly at Aysun and Narcissus.

To Margaret, Aysun said, "We have generously given your mistress the choice of submitting to the true religion, but she prefers to be a—what do you Christians call it?"

"A martyr, you cow," Margaret said, "and good for her. I'd be one, too, and gladly."

Aysun smiled and said to Ailith, "You hear? Your friend will gladly become a martyr should you not convert."

"You wouldn't," Ailith said, even though she knew that Aysun would.

Aysun's smile widened. "The emir doesn't want you hurt. He said nothing about her."

They had her. She couldn't see Margaret killed. She wouldn't. "All right," she said "I'll do it."

Margaret shouted "Ailith—!"

Ailith held up a hand. "I'll do it, I said." To Aysun she said, "Don't hurt her."

Aysun leaned forward, cold eyes alight. "Why does something tell me that your sudden zeal for Islam is insincere? Do you imagine you can pretend to be one of the faithful, then pray to your false god in your heart?"

That was exactly what Ailith had planned to do.

"Yes, I'm right, aren't it?" Aysun said. "That leads us to the second, and far more interesting, part of this interview. You are not to see the emir Qaymaz for the foreseeable future."

If only that were true. "What do you mean?"

"Exactly that. When he sends for you, you will find an excuse not to go to him. The other women are upset because you take up so much of his time. We may have rivalries among ourselves, but they are our rivalries. We don't want you to be part of it."

"You can have him and welcome," Ailith said, "but I have to go when he sends for me. I have no other choice."

"Of course you do. You're a clever girl, you'll find a way."

"And if I don't?"

Aysun stood. She took Narcissus's wooden staff, stepped from the dais and lashed Margaret's bad ankle. Margaret yelled in pain. Aysun hit her again, right where the ankle had been broken. Again. Ailith lunged to stop her, but Narcissus grabbed her arms and held her back.

Aysun hit Margaret again and again till Margaret dropped to the floor, crying in pain. Aysun kept hitting her until she ran out of breath. Then she threw the staff clattering to the floor, chest heaving from her exertions. Margaret moaned, sobbing and holding her leg.

"That will happen to her every time you go to Qaymaz," Aysun told Ailith.

"But if I refuse him too many times, he'll kill me," Ailith said.

Aysun gave a little shrug of her shoulders and smiled.

Chapter 50

$\mathfrak{K}$ING RICHARD STOOD on the newly repaired battlements of Ascalon, watching a boat rowing in from a ship offshore. Ascalon had no port; the only way to approach it was by sea. The boat's oars rose and dipped, rose and dipped, like some monstrous beetle making its way slowly toward them. Sunlight glinted off the water, hurting Richard's eyes, and he shaded them with his hand.

"What do you think it means?" said Alart of Vouzin beside him.

Richard put the hand down. "Nothing good, I expect."

Around them was hammering and sawing, the shouts of stone layers, the braying of mules, lowing of oxen. The smells of sawn wood and animals and grit. Saladin had torn down the city's western wall. He had broken up the stone battlements as best he could, burned the hoardings, walkways, halls and storage rooms. The stones for the wall, and the rubble that went between the two layers of stone, lay all around, but it was a time-consuming matter to get the wall back together again. Everything else had to be built from scratch, with wood sent down from Acre and Tyre. The storehouses had to be stocked with supplies, as well. All that was expensive, and even Richard's once bottomless coffers were feeling the strain.

Alart looked over at Richard. The two men had been together for many years, with Alart first as mentor, then as friend—well, more than a friend. Though Richard watched the boat, his mind seemed somewhere else. "What are you thinking about?" Alart asked him.

"I'm thinking about Philip," Richard said. "Wondering what deviltry he's up to while I'm stuck here."

"His going home does complicate our situation," Alart said.

Richard nodded. "I suppose I should hate him, but do you know, I rather admire the fellow. He's no fighter, but he's damned good at what he does—scheming, plotting, gathering power to himself. You have to hand it to him. When he became king, most of us thought France was finished as a country, but he's brought it back."

"More's the pity," Alart intoned.

Richard grinned. Though his handsome face had been tanned dark by the Mediterranean sun, his nose and cheeks had resisted, remaining red and flakey, and itching like the Devil. "Now, me, I prefer to bash somebody with an axe. That's my idea of statecraft."

Alart said, "Maybe we'll get lucky, and Philip's ship will be lost at sea."

"No, the little weasel's too wily for that. The sea won't get him." Richard turned away from the oncoming boat and studied the activity below him. "I confess, old friend, I never imagined it would be this difficult. I thought we'd win a few battles, do some hunting, then go home. We used to talk about capturing Damascus—maybe even Baghdad—but it looks as though Jerusalem's all we'll get, and even that's going to be tricky to pull off. Saladin has proved a formidable foe. The climate and the constant sickness haven't helped, either. I haven't been well since I got to this infernal country. By all that's holy, I don't see how Christ put up with the place."

Alart smiled at that.

Richard went on. "I feel like I've aged ten years since I've been here. Between lost teeth and—be serious—is there grey in my hair?"

"A few strands," Alart said diplomatically. God only knew what his own hair would look like if he didn't dye it.

"There's certainly enough grey in my beard," Richard said morosely.

Alart changed the subject. "I think you're overlooking the main obstacle to our success—and it's not Saladin or the climate or sickness."

"What is it then?"

"The barons. Their failure to cooperate—with you, and with each other. Why did they come here if all they wanted to do was argue amongst themselves?"

"Mm," Richard mused, "you're right, of course. Half these fellows act like they don't care whether we take Jerusalem or not. The other half, like Burgundy, want to rush off and do the job without thinking it through."

"Burgundy's the one who surprises me," Alart said. "I thought Philip left him here to slow you down, but he's the one leading the charge to march on Jerusalem."

"He's for doing the opposite of what I want, no matter what it is. If I'd wanted to march on the Holy City straight away, he'd have been against it. His job is to sow dissension in the army, and he's doing it well. He and that blockhead Conrad. I summoned Conrad to come down here and help us, and he refused."

"Just like him," Alart said.

"Now Burgundy and half the army have buggered back to Acre, complaining that I haven't paid them. Why do *I* have to pay them? They're Philip's men, shouldn't that be his job?"

Richard shook his head. "For all their talk, neither of those fools knows aught of war. I intend to make Ascalon the strongest fortress on the coast. When that's done, Saladin will be cut off from Egypt. Nothing will move north or south without our say. We'll have effectively split Saladin's empire in half. The old goat will have no choice but to come down here and try to take Ascalon back from us. That's when I'll bash him with the axe."

"Statecraft," Alart said.

"Exactly." Richard smiled, "And after that, Jerusalem will fall like a new-plucked fruit."

They made their way out of the castle, Richard stopping to speak with the men working on the walls, slapping backs, calling some by name, joking with them. Alart envied Richard's ability to connect with the common soldiers. It wasn't done for show, he genuinely liked the fellows. That puzzled Alart, who had rarely spoken to a foot soldier—why would he?—but it was part of the reason the men loved Richard.

They reached the little shelf of beach adjoining the castle. Because Richard was still bantering with some footmen, Alart got there first and studied the approaching boat. He looked over his shoulder as Richard joined him. "It's Mello."

Richard said nothing.

The boat beached and William of Mello stepped out, splashing through the wavelets. With a practiced flourish, he bowed to Richard. "Sire."

Richard embraced him. "William. It's good to have you back with us. I always feel better when you're around."

William must have lost twenty pounds since he had reached the Holy Land. His once jowly figure had grown lean and hard. "Thank you, sire, but I'm afraid I bring bad news."

"Is there any other kind?" Richard sighed. "Go on."

"Rioting has broken out in Acre. The—"

"Are my wife and sister safe?" Richard interrupted.

"Yes, sire. They're well guarded."

Richard motioned him to continue.

"It's the Pisans and Genoese doing the rioting. The Pisans support us, meaning King Guy and yourself. The Genoas are for Conrad, and they're being egged on by the duke of Burgundy. The Genoas are fair to overrunning the city, and King Guy asks for your help."

Richard looked at Alart. "This whole enterprise is falling apart. Now I'll have to go up to Acre and waste still more valuable time."

William of Mello went on grimly. "That's not all, sire."

Richard gave him a look.

William went on. "Humphrey of Toron was in Saladin's camp, as you instructed, to discuss new peace terms. While he was there, he encountered the lord of Ibelin."

Richard and Alart glanced at each other in surprise. "Balian?" Alart said.

William nodded. "Humphrey says Ibelin was there as Conrad's emissary."

Richard's brow darkened like a thunderhead. His jaws worked. "How dare Conrad send an emissary to Saladin, how dare he send an emissary to anyone? He can't admit that he's not king, that he never will be king. Well, it's time to end his meddling once and for all." To Mello, he said, "You're returning to Acre?"

"I am, sire."

"Summon my ship and suitable escort vessels. Have them meet me at Jaffa." He turned. "Alart, prepare my Norman guards and two companies of footmen—those Death's Heads and whoever else you choose. We're going to Acre."

Chapter 51

THE BELL OVER the door rang, announcing a customer. Outside, from the direction of the plaza, came the sound of the rioting that was threatening to tear the city apart.

Fauston made his way to the front of the shop and there he stopped.

The customer was the earl of Trent's wife, Bonjute. Bonjute had seen Fauston when he was the earl's chronicler, but she had paid him no attention then and he doubted that she would recognize him now. In the spring warmth she wore a belted blue kirtle with long sleeves trimmed in gold thread. Her hair was concealed by a lace wimple held in place by a gold circlet. With her was a pretty, but snobby looking, serving girl. Fauston was about to offer a greeting, but Bonjute beat him to it.

" 'The Street of Bad Cookery?' "

"My lady?" Fauston said.

"The Street of Bad Cookery," Bonjute repeated. "You couldn't find a better-named location for your business?"

"I had no part in naming the street, my lady, and I assure you, this is a quite desirable—"

"Yes, I can see it's a good neighborhood. I'm not blind."

"I didn't mean to—"

She cocked her head. "My, God is that an English accent I hear?" She pressed him. "Are you English?"

There was no point denying it. Fauston attempted to sound flattering. "I commend you on your—"

291

"It took no great skill. God knows I've heard that dreadful tongue enough. I'm surrounded by it in the wilds of Trentshire. How you people manage to communicate with all that grunting is beyond me. What is an Englishman doing calling himself Tolomei and Rico and selling relics in Acre?"

Fauston gave a well-rehearsed speech. "I've been in the Holy Land for a number of years, my lady. I inherited the firm from a distant cousin and, because it was well known, I kept the name. The firm originally started as goldsmiths but switched to relics because—well, because the Holy Land is a good place to find relics. That was before my time, of course."

His speech seemed to make no impression. Bonjute scowled. "I was told this was a reputable shop, yet I find it run by an Englishman. That's hardly a recommendation. You people can't even run your own country."

Fauston bit back his temper and replied smoothly. "Perhaps that's because your people stole it from us."

She made a dismissive noise. "It's not like you were doing anything with it. At least we've put the land to use."

"At the expense of good men's lives."

She stared at him, as if seeing him for the first time. "You're an impudent fellow."

He smiled and bowed his head. "While you, my lady, are merely rude."

The serving girl's eyes widened; she had probably never heard her mistress spoken to like that. She gave Fauston a warning look as Bonjute flared with anger. "I should slap you for that."

"You won't," Fauston said.

She glared at him, eyes wide, and he thought she was going to prove him wrong. At last she said, "You're right. I would never soil my hand by laying it on a peasant."

Fauston had wearied of this game. "Are you here for a relic?"

"No, I'm here to watch the sun rise. Of course I'm here for a relic, you idiot. You were recommended by Hugoline of Montjoie."

"Ah, yes." The countess of Montjoie, who was deeply religious, had become a regular customer.

Bonjute went on. "Hugoline said your merchandise was excellent. Does she know that you're English?"

"I don't recall her asking."

She harrumphed.

Fauston said, "Are you looking for something specific?"

"I need something for my husband." She hesitated. "He lies on the point of death."

"The earl?" Fauston said, surprised.

She frowned. "You know him?"

"I know of him. I'm from Trentshire myself, years ago. I've seen him about many times as governor of the city,– and yourself, of course. I'm truly sorry to hear about his condition." Fauston had always liked the earl. He remembered the earl saving him from the hangman in what seemed like another life. He went on. "The doctors can't—?"

"The doctors are imbeciles. All they do is babble nonsense and smell Geoffrey's urine. Now they tell me we should bleed him again. Can you imagine? The poor fellow is white as a sheet and they want to take what little blood he has left. The priests are no better. This crusade has become a nightmare. If Geoffrey lives, I'll kill him myself for going on a winter campaign when he was sick."

There was more noise from the plaza, louder this time, and Bonjute seemed to think she'd rambled on far longer than she had intended. She regained her cold dignity. "Hugoline reminded me that relics are sometimes known to work miracles and, a miracle is all I have left now. So are you going to dawdle here, or are you going to show me some relics?"

Fauston held aside a velvet curtain and ushered her into the middle room, where the better relics were kept—the front room held the cheaper material for tourists. The serving girl followed, turning up her nose at Fauston but managing to give him a saucy look at the same time. Fauston was still stunned by news of the earl. From what he knew of Bonjute, she bore no love for her husband, and her husband certainly bore no love for her. And yet here she was. He remembered the earl and Ailith, remembered poor Roger when he'd found out about it. Life was rotten sometimes.

"Would you care for a cup of wine, my lady?"

Bonjute nodded imperiously, and Fauston filled a pewter cup from a ewer on the sideboard and handed it to her.

The middle room was painted pale blue. Subdued candlelight rendered the scene reverential. Incense burned; a large crucifix hung on one wall. There were two cushioned chairs where customers could rest while they were being shown the merchandise, with carved stands upon which to place the cups they were given for refreshment. The relics occupied shelves and niches and pedestals around the room, with the very holiest grouped on display stands in the center of the floor. Another curtain led to a room in the back, where Francisco fashioned the reliquaries.

Bonjute walked around the room, taking it all in. "Are these relics genuine?"

Fauston pretended to take offense. "This firm has an impeccable reputation for honesty, my lady, going back long before I inherited it. If these relics were not genuine, I would not offer them for sale."

"An honest Englishman—what is the world coming to? Jehan—take your hands off that!"

The serving girl had picked up a thorn from the Crown of Thorns, and she put it down hurriedly.

"How come you by your merchandise?" Bonjute asked Fauston.

"Sometimes people sell the relics to us, but most we obtain through our collector, Gregory, who travels the Holy Land is search of material. Right now, he is in Samaria."

"Hmm," she said noncommittally. Then she added, "I must say these reliquaries are exquisite."

"Yes. They're fashioned by an elderly fellow—been with the firm for ages."

"What is this?" She indicated an enormous rock, centerpieced on a marble stand. The rock possessed an unusual, luminous gold color, with jagged black streaks running through it.

"That is the Star of Bethlehem," Fauston said.

She stared at him.

"It fell from the sky on the day after Epiphany. It was found in the bottom of a well many centuries ago." He spread his arms. "This is one of our most important items. We're—"

"I want something that would fit in Geoffrey's lap, where he could keep his hands on it and it could bring him comfort. Not something that's going to crush him."

"Yes, my lady." This was the part of the business that Fauston hated. He was showing the earl's wife these bits of bone and rock as though they were real, as though he and Gregory hadn't concocted them in the back room, as though the "elderly fellow" who did the reliquaries wasn't a young soldier invalided out of the army with a bad leg. Fauston understood the faith that people placed in relics, and he felt like a fraud. He *was* a fraud. At least when he'd been Brock the Badger, he'd been an honest thief, not a charlatan. Bonjute had come here seeking a miracle, and all he sought was her money.

Putting on gloves so that he wouldn't mar the reliquary's surface, he showed Bonjute an alabaster box carved in the shape of a cathedral. He opened the cathedral's hinged roof. "This is part of the ass's jawbone that Samson—"

"No, no. Nothing Old Testament."

She indicated a jagged piece of wood, set in a casque of carved mahogany with gilt trim. Like many of the reliquaries, it had a glass lid, so the relic could be viewed without exposing it to air. "What is this?"

"That is a piece of the lance of Longinus, the lance with which the centurion Longinus pierced Christ's side while he was on—"

"While He was on the Cross—yes, yes, I'm familiar with the Bible. What's it doing here?"

"It came from the estate of a baron killed at Hattin. The baron left no heirs and we were able to procure this from his widow, who needed money. As you know, the lance was found by Peter Bartholomew in Antioch during the darkest days of the first crusade."

She regarded him coolly. "I also know that the lance was whole when Peter found it."

Fauston thought quickly. "That is true, but unfortunately, the wood was brittle with age and several pieces of it broke off—one of which was this, which the baron's ancestor obtained. If you look closely you can see several dried drops of Our Lord's blood."

"And Longinus became a Christian and died a martyr," Bonjute mused. "Geoffrey has always liked that story—I've no idea why. How much?"

Fauston hesitated. He would normally have charged one hundred bezants, but he was so guilt ridden he felt like he shouldn't charge anything.

"How much?" she repeated. "Money is not a problem."

Despite his guilt, that irritated him. "I suppose not, since it comes from the sweat of English labor."

"Sweat?" she scoffed. "Labor? I've yet to see an Englishman perform actual labor. They're always dodging off somewhere and drinking ale. It's our poor bailiffs who do all the work, making them get back to the fields."

"I'm familiar with the 'work' your bailiffs do, my lady," Fauston said. "I've seen it all too often. And while you feast on the bounty from our fields and forests, the common men starve."

"Bah! Villeins live far better than they deserve."

"You wouldn't say that if you'd been one of them."

She sneered. "I didn't come here to be insulted by a—"

"You came here for a relic, and now you have one. That will be one hundred silver bezants." Any guilt he had felt was gone now. He wished he had charged her two hundred.

She produced a purse from under her cloak and counted out the money.

Fauston took the coins. "Will there be anything else?"

"No." To the serving girl, she said, "Come, Jehan. And put down that wine!"

Jehan had been drinking from the goblet Fauston had furnished to Bonjute.

The noise outside had grown louder, more insistent. Fauston felt compelled to say, "Begging your pardon, my lady, but the trouble outside sounds close."

"I'm not concerned with that. It's just part of the silly games you men play. You could have taken Jerusalem months ago, and we could all be back home now. Instead you spend your time like a bunch of roosters, preening and strutting and squawking at each other, all the while accomplishing nothing."

"All the same, my lady, you ought to wait here until the trouble has passed."

Jehan said, "I think we should listen to him, madame."

"Oh, stop being such a crybaby."

Bonjute might be an arrogant shrew, but Fauston didn't want to see her torn to pieces by the mob. "Please, my lady, it's too dangerous—"

"When I want advice from an Englishman, I'll ask for it. Which will be never. Jehan, open the door."

Jehan obeyed. The bell tinkled and the two of them went out.

Chapter 52

BONJUTE AND JEHAN made their way back to the earl's palace. Bonjute would be glad when they got there. The situation in the streets was getting out of hand. Why Geoffrey tolerated this sort of thing, she didn't know. If she had been in charge of the city, she would have—

"I'm scared, my lady," Jehan bleated.

"Oh, for God's sake," Bonjute told her, "stop acting like a child. We'll be home soon enough, and you can go back to swyving the stable boy—or all the stable boys, if that's what amuses you."

The Street of Bad Cookery debouched onto a plaza with a fountain in the center. Bonjute and Jehan reached the end of the street and stopped.

Across the plaza two mobs faced each other, yelling, chanting, waving banners and clubs. Now one group advanced and the other retreated; now the other group advanced and the first retreated. Rocks and paving stones flew between the two groups. A few bleeding men on each side dragged themselves to the rear.

Suddenly the group on the right launched a more determined attack. Most of the other group backed away safely, but those on the right caught one young man. They dragged him into their lines and began beating him with clubs. A counter charge from the left rescued the young man and hauled him away, his face red with blood, his embroidered green shirt torn and bloodied.

Before the young man could be passed to safety, there was another rush from the right. The group on the left fell back hastily, leaving the beating victim to his own devices. He staggered after his friends, but the other group caught him and pulled him back to their banners, where they began beating him again, stomping him, hurling paving stones down on him until he lay still, his legs splayed out.

Bonjute took an involuntary step back from the sight. She looked over at Jehan, but the little vixen wasn't there. She had run away.

Bonjute started back the way they had come, seeking another route home, when she found herself face to face with a man.

The man was big; he seemed to fill the passage. He had a squint eye and a filthy rag wrapped around his head and he smelled like a sewer.

"Well, well," said the man, whose accent sounded Genoan. He grinned, revealing his few remaining teeth. "Look what I found."

"Out of my way," Bonjute ordered him.

The man made an amused face. "And why should I do that, your ladyship?"

"Because I'm telling you to."

"Used to giving orders, are we?"

"Yes, and you'd do well to obey them. Now let me by."

She made to go around him, but the man blocked her way. "Not so fast, missy."

"Bah." Impatient, Bonjute turned the way she had come and was confronted by two more men, both of them grinning as well. Behind them, she saw more men coming, sensing fun.

She faced the first man, her back straight, voice quivering with anger. "What is your intent?"

The man snatched her wrist. "Oh, I think you can guess our intent."

She yanked her wrist back. "My husband is governor of this city. He will hunt you down and see you hanged."

The man scratched his grimy beard. "Well, now, you oughtn't to have told us that, missy, you really oughtn't. Guess we can't afford to let you go now." He chuckled. "Not like we was ever going to."

The man hauled her to him roughly, leering. Then a strange look came over him, and the tip of a blade punched through his chest. The man's eyes lost focus. He stumbled sideways, fell into the stone wall and thence to the street.

Standing behind him was that fellow from the relics shop—Fauston. He had a dagger with a foot-and-a-half blade in his left hand, and a sword in his right. The dagger's blade dripped blood.

"Run!" he told Bonjute.

She didn't need to be told twice. As she moved past Fauston, he slashed at the men behind him with his sword and Bonjute heard a cry of pain.

Fauston caught up to her and moved ahead. Another man blocked their way, and Fauston hit him in the mouth with his sword hilt, knocking him aside.

Sheathing the dagger, Fauston grabbed Bonjute's arm and dragged her along. "Faster!" There were footsteps behind them, yells. Bonjute was too scared to look back.

Fauston dragged her to the right down a narrow alley. Shoved her forward. "Go!"

Fauston waited at the corner. As the first man rounded it, Fauston swung his sword in an arc that would have decapitated the man had it struck him right. Instead it hit him in the middle of the face, cutting his head in half.

"Stop looking at me," Fauston yelled. "Go!"

Up a stone staircase Bonjute ran, though another plaza. Cries behind her. Fauston caught up with her again and dragged her along so roughly it seemed like her feet weren't always hitting the ground.

They ran down a narrow market street, abandoned because of the riots, overturning empty goods carts behind them to slow the pursuit.

The market street led them to a shaded path between rows of fig and palm trees. It was someone's park. The park must have been neglected during the siege, because mounds of dead leaves and palm fronds had been piled against the trees and the far walls by the wind. Their pursuers were still after them, and there was the sound of more men from ahead.

They were trapped.

Fauston pointed. "Over there."

He half threw Bonjute off the walk, like a sack of dry goods, pushing her to the far wall of the park, where he shoved her into an opening in thick fig roots and began piling dirt, old leaves and palm fronds over her. He burrowed in next to her, covering himself up. It was damp and moldy as they dug down. Things crawled over them. He put down his sword and clamped his hand over her mouth, the side of the hand between her teeth so she couldn't scream. His other hand tightened on his dagger. The long-bladed dagger was better for fighting in confined spaces.

Men entered the courtyard. Bonjute heard cautious footsteps. Mutters as whoever it was poked around the massive trees.

"Must have ducked down that last side street," said one.

"Swore I seen 'em come in here," said another.

"Well, you seen wrong. Come on."

The voices receded. Bonjute started to rise but Fauston held her down. She tried to protest but his hand in her mouth prevented speech.

Noise. The men were back.

"They have to be in here," said a new voice, a voice with authority. "That fucker killed my cousin. Now work your way to the back and take this place apart."

Using sword and knife blades, the men began poking through the mounds of leaves and dirt and tree roots. Bonjute's heart was beating so fast she thought it would burst out of her chest.

"I'll hold them off, you make a break for it," Fauston whispered in her ear. He took his sword and eased the dagger into her hand.

The men came closer. They were almost on them now. Bonjute sensed Fauston ready to leap to his feet, and she prepared to do the same.

There was a blast of distant horns. Shouts. More horns. The clatter of horses moving in formation.

"King Richard is in the city!" came a cry. "He's brought his army with him! Run for your lives!"

In the space of a few moments, the park emptied. From nearby came the sounds of fighting.

After a moment, Fauston dug out of the roots and rose to his feet. He helped Bonjute up, but she shook him off, spitting dirt from her mouth, wiping it from her eyes. Her lace wimple and circlet were gone; her hair was a tangled mess and her favorite kirtle was ruined.

"You followed me," she told Fauston accusingly.

"Yes," Fauston said. "I was afraid something like this would happen.

"I suppose you expect me to thank you?"

"That's the usual response when someone saves your life."

"Odd, I don't recall asking for your assistance."

"Your gratitude is noted." He turned her sideways, brushing dirt off her back. "Here, let me help you—"

She slapped him. "Don't you *dare* touch me, you—"

He pulled her to him and kissed her.

Chapter 53

𝕱AUSTON TOOK HER in the back room of his quarters. Biting, scratching, pulling hair. When they were done, they faced each other, covered with sweat and breathing hard, like wrestlers after the first fall of what was likely to prove a grueling match.

"Perhaps the English *are* good for something," she panted.

Fauston taunted her. "Are you ready to go home now?"

She got to her hands and knees in the bed. "Hardly."

Later he escorted her home, carrying his unsheathed sword for protection. Neither of them spoke. Richard's troops were in the streets, including men from Geoffrey's company called the Death's Heads. Two of them stopped the couple.

"Nobody supposed to be on the streets, Brocky," said the leader. "Curfew."

Fauston said, "This lady got caught in the riot and took refuge in my shop. I'm seeing her home."

"All right then, but don't dawdle."

"You know those men?" Bonjute asked him as they walked away.

"I served with them for a bit, at the end of the siege."

"Why do they call you Brocky?"

Fauston shrugged. "Soldier's nickname."

"I hope Jehan is all right," Bonjute said grimly. "Because if she is, I'm going to use her skin to make a new saddle."

They reached the earl's palace and stopped. "Will I see you again?" Fauston asked her.

She seemed surprised. "Do you want to?"

"Yes."

"Why?" She waved an arm, as though remembering the sex they'd had. "Apart from *that*, of course."

Fauston smiled. "Because I think we could be friends."

She stared at him for a long moment. At last she said, "I'll send word when I'm available."

He watched as she returned to her house.

Chapter 54

THE TWO PARTIES met a few miles north of Acre, on a wide stretch of beach. Guy of Lusignan watched as King Richard and Conrad detached themselves from their respective groups and rode forward, Richard with his reddish gold hair and crimson surcoat, shaven-headed Conrad wearing his usual yellow surcoat and black biretta.

As always when he saw Conrad, Guy's mind went back to that battle in the early days of the Acre siege. The battle had devolved into a meleé, both sides mixed up in the thick dust, blows given and taken, screams and shouts in many languages.

Guy had seen a Christian knight unhorsed by a spear. As the man lay stunned on his hands and knees, two mounted Saracens attacked him. Guy had intervened, beating the Saracens back and grievously wounding one. He retrieved the fallen knight's horse and guarded the man while he staggered to his feet and shook his head clear. As Guy held the knight's horse so he could mount, he realized with a start that it was Conrad of Montferrat. He pretended he had known who it was all along, though, giving Conrad an ironic salute before riding back into the battle.

Since that day Guy had asked himself many times if he would have saved the man's life had he known it was Conrad. He hoped he would, as a Christian, but knowing the endless grief Conrad had caused him, he would always wonder . . .

❧

Richard and Conrad approached each other, their horses' hooves throwing clumps of wet sand as the waves advanced and receded. Gulls cried overhead.

The two men halted opposite one another. Conrad bowed from the saddle, crisp, formal. "Sire."

"My lord Marquis," Richard acknowledged. "It is good of you to meet me."

Conrad nodded.

"Let us walk together," Richard said.

The two men dismounted. Their squires held their horses while the two men paced along the shore, just out of reach of the probing waves. They were of a type, huge men, with Richard a bit taller and more lithe, and Conrad bulkier. The main difference between them was that Richard had been born to a high state whereas Conrad, as a soldier of fortune, had carved himself a place at the top.

Richard wasted no time. He was determined to put the German in his place once and for all. "Why have you and the duke of Burgundy fomented a rebellion in Acre? Burgundy I can understand—he's King Philip's lackey, and trying to make trouble for me—but I did not think you would try to undermine the crusade this way."

Conrad was defiant. "If anyone is trying to undermine the crusade, it is you. You could have been in Jerusalem by now, but you sit at Ascalon and dither."

"It may be your opinion that I could be in the Holy City by now, but it is not mine. I have a reason for being in Ascalon, and I need you to join me there."

"I am flattered, but I have my own plans."

Despite himself, Richard felt his temper giving way. "Is that why you negotiate with Saladin behind my back?"

If Richard expected to get a rise out of Conrad with that revelation, he was disappointed. The German shrugged. "I can send representatives to anyone I chose. I don't need your permission."

Richard stopped in the wet sand. "I'm tired of your obfuscations, lord marquis. I'm tired of you trying to undermine me. We need to work together if we're to recover the Holy City, can't you get that through your head? Us being at cross purposes plays into Saladin's—"

"Work together?" Conrad said, and now anger lit his dark eyes. "I find that amusing coming from you, Richard. I have never gotten any support from you—none—so why should I give you any? You choose to thwart me and belittle me in favor of your cousin, that imbecile who lost the kingdom of Jerusalem."

"That was not Guy's—"

"Of course it was his fault, his and his alone. Were it not for his incompetence, none of us would even be here now. The Holy City would still be in God's hands. Tell me why we should recover Jerusalem and hand it over to that fool just so he can lose it again."

Richard tried to reply, but Conrad kept going. "You will depart this land ere long, but I will remain. Saladin knows this, that is why he negotiates with me. I am the one he will have to deal with in the long term. Once you are gone, I will have a free hand. Saladin is ill and his sons hate each other. I will negotiate for what I can get now, and when Saladin dies and his sons fight amongst themselves for his throne, I will take what I want."

"I can't wait that long," Richard said. "I need Jerusalem now."

"That is your concern, not mine. I am not going to sacrifice my plans in order to bolster your reputation. You may think you're the second coming of Charlemagne or Alexander the Great, but I don't. And even if you were, I wouldn't care."

Richard took a deep breath, trying to hold his temper. "You keep taking like you're in charge of the kingdom. Might I remind you that the succession has been decided. We have followed the rule of law, and Guy has been chosen—"

"Guy is nothing! His claim to the throne ended when his wife died without issue. He has no blood ties to this kingdom. I am married to the last king's surviving child. Not only that, the native barons support me. Everyone supports me but you. Once you're gone, Guy won't last a fortnight."

Richard drew himself up. "I'm tired of arguing with you. I demand that you stop interfering with the politics of the kingdom. I further demand that you come to Ascalon and assist me."

There was a pause, then the ghost of a smile appeared on Conrad's thick lips. Richard couldn't remember if he'd ever seen the fellow smile. "And under what authority do you make these demands?"

"By my right as duly elected leader of the army."

"And if I refuse?"

"All your lands will be forfeit."

Now Conrad actually did smile. "If you want my lands, come and get them. Saladin couldn't take them, let's see how far you get."

It had been a bad bluff, and Richard knew it, and that made him all the angrier. Richard had no way of taking Conrad's lands short of war, and the army would never support that. "So you will not join me in Ascalon?"

"I will not join you in anything until you acknowledge me as the rightful king of Jerusalem."

"Very well, we will take Jerusalem without you."

Richard pivoted in the sand and strode away, red-gold hair bouncing on his shoulders. Then his temper got the best of him. He turned back, and in a voice that could be heard by everyone on the beach he said, "You will never be king of Jerusalem, do you hear me? Never!"

Chapter 55

"**T**HE EMIR DESIRES your presence."

Again. The summons Ailith dreaded. The one that came every night.

"Inform the emir that I do not feel well."

The servant, an Arab boy dressed in white, bowed and left.

"How long can you keep this up?" Margaret asked Ailith.

"I don't know," Ailith replied.

In what seemed like no time, four armed soldiers appeared at the door to Ailith's quarters. "The emir wants you," said the first, a noble by the richness of his helmet and mail.

Ailith said, "I told the emir, I am indisposed."

"The emir does not care."

"But I—"

"You are to come with us or we will carry you." The soldier was impassive, but it was clear he would not be put off.

Ailith cast a despairing look at Margaret, then she rose from her divan and followed the soldiers. They led her across the darkened courtyard. She was aware of stares from dimly lit balconies, from Aysun and the rest. She felt their hatred. She managed a quick glance at the African girl, Lamiya, and thought she detected a look of sympathy.

The soldiers led her to Qaymaz's quarters, where they bowed and departed.

Qaymaz wore his usual robe of blue silk. His hair was swept back from his darkly handsome face, a face now clenched with anger. "Why have you refused to see me?"

Ailith kept her eyes down. "I have been indisposed, lord."

Qaymaz slapped her, knocking her back across the room. "Do not lie to me!"

She held a hand to her cheek. "It is not a lie! Ask Hassan—"

He slapped her again, dropping her to her knees. "It does not matter what Hassan says! I can see there is nothing wrong with you."

Ailith rose unsteadily. Her cheek stung; she felt it reddening.

Qaymaz moved closer. "You realize I can have you killed for disobeying my summons?"

"Yes, lord."

"Then why are you doing it?"

"I . . ." She did not know what to say, and her voice tailed off.

Qaymaz raised his hand again, but Ailith did not shrink from it. She lifted her jaw defiantly, as though welcoming the blow. She'd been beaten plenty of times by her father, and she'd stood up to him, as well.

Qaymaz seemed to think better of it and lowered his hand. "I leave to rejoin the army tomorrow, and by all that's holy you will not refuse me tonight."

Ailith said nothing.

Qaymaz stepped back and eyed her shrewdly. "Has Aysun had something to do with your reluctance to attend on me?"

Again Ailith said nothing.

"She threatened you?" His brow darkened. "She knows you are not to be hurt."

"She threatened my servant, Margaret." Best to get it out, Ailith thought.

"I see." Qaymaz flung open the ornately carved wooden door. "Summon Narcissus," he told a servant outside.

He paced back and forth impatiently on the carpeted floor until the big eunuch arrived. "Lord?" Narcissus said.

Qaymaz regarded him. "I leave for the army in the morning."

Narcissus looked puzzled. "Yes, lord, I am aware of -- "

"If anything happens to this woman *or* her servant— *anything*—while I am gone, I will have you skinned alive, then fed to wild pigs."

If it was possible for a black man to blanch, Narcissus did just that.

Qaymaz went on. "And you can tell your *friend* Aysun that I will kill her children in front of her, then put out her eyes and cast her into the street. The other women I will have whipped, then give as whores to the army."

Narcissus swallowed.

"Is that understood?" Qaymaz said.

"Yes, lord."

"Good. Now leave me."

Narcissus turned with as much dignity as he had left and departed. A servant closed the door.

Qaymaz faced Ailith. "Now," he said, "come here."

~

After another seemingly endless sexual encounter, they both lay on the bed, exhausted, Aililth as always fighting back tears of shame and humiliation for what she had become. After a while, Qaymaz rolled onto his side and stroked the inside of her thigh. His long hair hung alongside his face. "There is something I must tell you before I go back to the war. I've wanted to tell you before this, but I—I lacked the courage."

Ailith frowned, wondering what a man like this could possibly lack the courage for.

"I am in love with you," Qaymaz said. "Totally. You are all I think about."

Ailith stared. She hadn't expected this. She knew he desired her, of course, but she thought that was as far as it went.

Qaymaz went on. "I have given this much thought. When I return, it is my intention to make you the Preferred One."

Ailith sat up. "But . . . Aysun?"

"I will get rid of Aysun. I will get rid of them all. The ones with children will be given houses and incomes. The others I will give as presents to my brother emirs. Narcissus, as well. I will have no one in my bed but you, no one in my *harim* but you. I want you to have my children. You do not even have to convert to Islam, I don't care."

"I—I don't know what to say."

He placed a finger gently to her lips. "Say nothing. I will take care of everything."

"But your wife. Won't she—"

"Matters of the *harim* are not her concern." He kissed Ailith, kissed her breasts and swirled his tongue around her nipples. "It grows late, and I have much to do. I would take you to war with me were it not so dangerous. I could never forgive myself if something happened to you."

Ailith's head spun. She tried to take in what she had heard. Qaymaz was on his feet now, a long silk shirt covering him. He was saying something, seemed to be expecting an answer. "What?" Ailith said.

"I said, I was wondering. You are English. When you were in the infidel camp, did you hear of an English company called Heads of Death, or Death Heads, something like that?"

Ailith's heart caught. Was this a trap? Cautiously she replied, "Death's Heads. I heard of them; they were part of my—my former lord's troops. I don't know much about them, though. Why do you ask?"

It was not the first time that Qaymaz had unburdened himself to Ailith. He seemed to have convinced himself that she cared for him as much as he cared for her. And now that she was to be the Preferred One, he would share with her secrets that even his wife did not know. "I am in a dilemma. I hold the Death's Heads' commander as a slave. I wanted to kill him, but the sultan insisted that I take him alive. The sultan thinks the fellow is an honorable man. Should the sultan come to the Blue Fort—and he is bound to at some point—he will want to see this man. And, knowing how soft hearted the sultan can be at times, I am afraid he will look for an excuse to free him." With his fingers he smoothed his long hair back into place. "I need the man to meet with a plausible accident, and soon. The sultan won't like it, but those Death's Heads have killed too many of my people to let him go free. Plus Mahmoud says he stirs up the other slaves. Do you agree with my decision, or should I let the man live?"

Did he somehow know that she was friends with Roger? But he couldn't. She tried to sound unconcerned. She rose and kissed Qaymaz on the cheek. "Whatever my lord desires."

Qaymaz talked on, but Ailith heard no more. She was in a daze from that moment until she returned to her own quarters, the dawn just breaking.

Everything had changed. Ailith would be safe, exalted even. Margaret would be safe.

But Roger . . .

Margaret rubbed sleep from her eyes as Ailith entered their quarters. "Margaret, find Hassan. Tell him I must speak with him. Right away."

Chapter 56

WHILE WAITING FOR Hassan to arrive, Ailith carefully slit the hem of her best robe and removed the fifteen marks that were sewn inside. The money was her share of the loot that she, Roger and Fauston had taken from that fat priest in Dunham Wood.

Roger and Fauston had long since exhausted their shares, but Ailith had never spent a penny of hers. She had vowed that she never would, though she was not sure why. It meant something to her to keep the sum intact. It had become a symbol—though again she was not sure why. Amazingly, the money had not been discovered when the Saracens captured and searched her. Even Margaret didn't know she had it.

Now it was time to break her vow and put the money to use.

From the courtyard came the clop of hooves, the low talk of men, the creak of leather, the distinctive bell-like jingle of Turkish bridle harness and accoutrements.

Ailith peered out. It was just going dawn, the eastern sky grey and pink, the morning air fragrant with hibiscus and orange blossoms, birds twittering in the aviary. Qaymaz was in the courtyard, wearing light mail, the blue sash around his helmet. He was waiting for his escort to form up. Only his personal guard stayed with him at the Blue Fort. He would meet the rest of his division on the road. He stood beside his black war horse, talking to the slave overseer, Mahmoud, in low tones.

Was he giving orders for Roger's "accident"?

Qaymaz's wife and children came to see him off. Ailith knew nothing about them, didn't even know their names. She had only seen the wife once before, and that from a distance. The wife was veiled, so Ailith couldn't get a good look at her, and her shapeless robe gave no hint as to her build. She and Qayamz folded hands and bowed to one another formally. Then Qaymaz cuffed his son manfully on the shoulder and lifted and hugged his two daughters.

Qaymaz's concubines were shadows on their balconies. Qaymaz looked around, as though taking attendance, as though he didn't care otherwise. When his eyes reached Ailith, though, they lingered. Ailith forced herself to nod slightly in return.

Why does he love me? What have I done to deserve such a fate?

Then Qaymaz was mounted and clattering out the gate, followed by his bodyguard, and Ailith withdrew from her balcony.

Soon after Qaymaz's departure, Margaret arrived with Hassan. Margaret limped more noticeably than ever after the beating from Aysun. Her face was red from climbing the steps.

Ailith got right to the point. "Margaret and I need to escape this place as soon as we can," she told Hassan.

"Sooner, if you ask me," Margaret muttered.

Ailith told Hassan what Qaymaz had planned for Roger. Hassan shook his head. "You are certain he means to have Roger killed?"

"He told me so."

Hassan wiped a pudgy hand across his mouth. "An escape will require money for horses and supplies."

Ailith showed him the fifteen marks, and his eyes widened. So did Margaret's. "God save us," she said, "where'd you come by that?"

"It's a long story. I'll explain later."

"We will need a plan," Hassan said. "Roger cannot just stroll out of the slave compound."

"Can we bribe the guards?" Margaret said.

"Not Mahmoud, the head guard," Hassan said. "He is as fanatical as one of your Templars."

"One of the others then?"

"I do not think so. Yasir is not a brute like Mahmoud, but he is honest. Besides, he would know that were he to be caught, he would be subject to unimaginable torture, and it might not be worth the risk to him. Any of the others we approach will probably feel the same way." To Ailith he said, "Will you and the Lady Margaret be leaving with Roger?"

"If we can," Ailith said, "but either way, we're leaving. I can't stand to be with that monster Qaymaz another second. Anyway, when Roger is gone, Qaymaz will know who must have been behind it, and he'll have me and Margaret killed."

"The men in Roger's hut, will he be taking them too?"

Ailith grimaced. "I hadn't thought about that. He'll probably want to."

Hassan raised his brows. "That will mean more horses. It will also make it more difficult to keep the preparations secret. The plan must come together quickly."

Ailith understood. "What about you?" she asked Hassan. "Will you come with us? If Qaymaz learns that you helped us . . ."

"God willing, I will stay here and take my chances. Qaymaz can be cruel—"

Margaret barked a laugh.

"—but he gave me a position when no one else would. I am obligated to him. Besides, I have experience with your infidel cousins. I cannot always count on Roger being there to save my life when the feringhees decide to make an example of me."

Ailith thought of something. "What will happen to the other women of the *harim*?"

Margaret said, "Maybe we'll get lucky and Qaymaz will have them roasted alive."

Hassan was less sanguine. "I expect their lives will go on much as before." He thought for a moment. "We could use another person for this enterprise, one who has intimate knowledge of the palace. Can you think of anyone?"

That morning, in the bath, Ailith approached Lamiya.

"Would you like to go home?"

Chapter 57

𝕵AUSTON AND BONJUTE met several days later, as soon as she could get away safely, Bonjute veiled so she wouldn't be recognized in the crowded streets as she made her way to Fauston's quarters.

Bonjute was ready to tear into him again, the way she had the first time, but he stopped her. He took her in his arms and kissed her tenderly. She reacted almost in panic, as though she didn't know what to do, and Fauston thought in amazement, *She's never been kissed like this before.* Gradually she grew less tense, let Fauston fold her close to him, returned his long kisses as best she could, at first awkwardly, then with feeling, then with passion and enjoyment.

Unlike the first time, Fauston took their lovemaking slow. She let him take the lead, fell into the rhythm of it, kissing, caressing, exploring cavities and crevices, and when the end came she cried out in a scream that was primal but also somehow magical, as though she had gone somewhere she had not known existed.

Later, he leaned over and kissed her sweaty stomach. "Friends?" he said.

She smiled. The hard planes of her face had disappeared, as if they had only been put there for show. "Friends."

She turned onto her side and held him close. "I've never had a friend before."

He gave her a skeptical look, and she explained. "Oh, maybe when I was little, playing with the servants' children, but even then I think they were wary of my position. My mother died when I was very young, and I was forced to become lady of the household. Because I was so young, I took the job seriously, enforcing discipline, punishing miscreants—including some of those girls I had played with not long before. I got carried away with myself so that people would see I was in earnest, and I got the reputation for being a tyrant."

She paused. "My father married again, but for whatever reason he wanted me to continue running the household— maybe because he found my harsh style entertaining for one so young, maybe because I did the job so well, or maybe because his new wife wasn't interested.

"Then I was married to Geoffrey, but by then my reputation preceded me. People—even Geoffrey—expected me to behave in a certain way, and since it was the only way I had ever behaved, it was not difficult to do."

Fauston frowned. "You have no friends even among the other noblewomen?"

Bonjute's laugh was charming, as opposed to the arrogant bark she presented to the rest of the world. "Hardly. There is too much plotting and backbiting and intrigue among the noblewomen. It is like warfare with good manners."

She raised her head and kissed him. "No, I'm afraid you're it." Then she looked at him with something like alarm on her face. "You are my friend, aren't you? Truly? This isn't just some casual seduction on your part?"

He took her hands in his. "I will be as true a friend to you as it is possible to be. I swear it."

"You won't betray me?"

"Never, though my life depended on it."

She smiled and lay against him contentedly. "So, tell me something of yourself."

"There is little enough to tell," Fauston replied. "I was born a poor farmer's son in Trentshire. I ran away from home because there was not enough food to go round and took up a life of outlawry in the forest."

She raised herself to one elbow. "Really? I would never have guessed. Did you ever encounter that outlaw—the famous one—the one called . . ." she ransacked her memory, "Brock something? Brock the Badger?"

Before he could answer, her eyes widened and she sat up. "Wait—that fellow in the street the other night called you 'Brocky.' " Her eyes widened further. "Oh, my God, you're him, aren't you? You're Brock the Badger!"

Fauston thought about denying it, but he could not lie to her. He never wanted to lie to her. He nodded, knowing he might be destroying whatever there was between them. "I am. Are you going to report me to the authorities?"

"No, of course not."

"You don't find it horrible?"

A glint came into her eye and she put her lips to his. "Actually, I find it kind of exciting."

They made love again, and long before they were done, Fauston knew, as he had known the first time he had held her in his arms, that he no longer had any desire to leave Acre.

Chapter 58

𝕴T WAS COLD for April. The wind blew off the sea, bringing bands of rain. They were in the great hall of Ascalon—King Richard, Alart and Andrew of Chauvigny. The hall had been rebuilt hastily, and it showed, but a proper job would have to wait until the fortifications were complete.

For all the time he had spent here, Richard didn't like Ascalon. It was cold and forbidding, a place made only for war. There was no town or city nearby where he and his friends might go in disguise and sample the pleasures of life or try out new songs. It was the kind of soulless structure the Templars or Hospitallers might have built, and he guessed one of those orders would garrison it when the crusade ended.

Alart interrupted his thoughts. "From what I've been told, many of the barons consider Saladin's new peace terms reasonable. Especially the men who have been here since the beginning. They think it's the best deal we'll get."

"Do they now?" Richard replied. The new proposal had been brought by Humphrey of Toron and Saladin's brother, al-Adil, yesterday. Al-Adil still expressed interest in marrying Richard's sister Joanna, and Joannna had warmed to the idea as well—she had gotten to like the Holy Land and its climate—but Richard no longer had any faith that the proposed union could be brought to fruition. He no longer had faith in anything but himself.

"Yes," said young Andrew of Chauvigny. Andrew was devoted to Richard, but his father was ill, and Andrew longed to go home before the old man died. "The Holy Cross will be returned to us, and we get to keep everything we've captured. We can even have Beirut."

Richard's jaw clenched. "Have you forgotten what brought us here, Andrew? What about Jerusalem?"

Andrew spread his hands. "Well . . . we won't get to occupy Jerusalem, but Christians will be granted right of pilgrimage there. We'll have the right to keep our priests there as well. That sounds fair to me."

"It sounds fair to a lot of people," Alart warned.

"And how long do you think we'll keep those rights?" Richard snapped. "They say Saladin is ill. His successor may not feel bound by the treaty. He may deny us access to the Holy City, and we'll be right back where we started."

A gust of rain battered the hall's partly shuttered windows, and Richard went on. "We didn't come here to *visit* Jerusalem, we came to free it, as is our duty to God. And free it is what I intend to do. I know the men are tired and want to go home, but we have taken a sacred oath."

Alart was loyal to whatever Richard wanted. "Then you still plan to lure Saladin onto the plain of Ascalon and defeat him here?"

"Not defeat him." With a loud *crack*, Richard pounded a fist into the palm of his other hand. "Crush him."

"The barons don't—"

"The Devil with the barons. The barons are a bunch of sheep, always bleating about something."

On the battlements an urgent horn blew, followed by shouts.

"What manner of mischief is this?" Alart wondered.

The three men left the hall and mounted the battlements, where they saw a party of Christian knights riding hard for the castle. Chauvigny pulled the hood of his cloak over his head to keep the rain off his carefully brushed hair. "Whatever they want, it must be important if they come by land." Travel to Ascalon by road was hazardous because of Saracen patrols, and most visitors chose to arrive by sea, despite the lack of a proper port.

The party drew closer. The knights were Templars, and they were escorting a cleric. Richard, Alart and Chauvigny descended to the courtyard as the party rode through the main gate. The Templars' white robes were mud splattered, their horses lathered with sweat. They were all young men— most of the veteran Templars had died either at Hattin or at the battle of Cresson, two months before that.

Richard recognized the cleric. It was Robert, prior of Hereford. He was originally from Provence, and Richard remembered him from those days. He was young and vigorous, known for his prowess at hunting. Indeed, he had joined Richard on the chase more than once.

The prior was even more travel stained than his escort. Dark circles hung beneath his eyes. He dismounted and dipped a knee into the gravelly mud before Richard. "Sire."

With the crook of a finger, Richard bade him rise. "It is good to see you again, Prior Robert." Puzzled, he added, "But I thought you were in England."

"I was, sire," the prior said. "I am here at the behest of the bishop of Ely."

"Yes?" Richard's tone indicated that he knew the news, whatever it was, would not be good.

The prior swallowed. "It is about your brother, Prince John."

Richard let out his breath in resignation. "Come to the hall. There is a fire burning, and we can get out of the rain."

Inside the hall, the prior warmed his hands at the fire. "Now what's this about John?" Richard asked sharply.

The prior glanced at Alart and Chauvigny and said, "He amasses more power by the day, sire. He dispenses justice as he pleases, ignoring the law, and raises taxes as the whim strikes him. He confiscates estates that have been held for a hundred years and bestows them upon his friends. He treats the royal treasury like it is his own purse; he loots churches and abbeys and imprisons anyone who questions his acts. Your chancellor has fled to France in fear of his life."

He paused dramatically. "Bishop William instructed me to tell you that your bother has usurped so much power that if you do not return to England soon, you'll have no kingdom to return to, because John will be the king."

Richard's face betrayed no emotion, but he stood straighter, held his head higher. This news changed everything. Richard's destiny, his place in history, was intertwined with the success of the crusade, fate had decreed that. But . . . but he could not afford to lose England. England's wealth kept the Angevin empire going. It kept the crusade going. Without England, Richard was lost.

"Thank you for bringing me this news, Prior Robert," he said politely. "Lord Andrew will see that you and your escort are provided refreshment and suitable quarters."

As Chauvigny led the tired prior away, Richard turned to Alart. "John promised me that he would be on his good behavior when I gave him charge of England, but he has obviously reverted to his old ways. We must depart the Holy Land as soon as possible. Summon a grand council of the barons, to be held here a week from this day. They must decide who is to lead the crusade when we have gone."

Chapter 59

TATTERED AND WORN, the banners of the crusade's leaders decorated the walls of Ascalon—all save that of Conrad of Montferrat, who had as usual refused to come. From the castle's highest tower, the French *fleur-de-lis* hung beside the three lions of England. King Philip was not present, of course, but his representative, the duke of Burgundy, had against protocol claimed the right to display Philip's banner.

There was a time when Richard would have flung the *fleur-de-lis* from the walls, as he had done with the flag of Leopold of Austria. Given his mood, he might have flung the duke of Burgundy from the walls as well. Now he no longer cared. His mind was on England, and on his duplicitous brother, John. Richard liked John—they had always gotten on well together—but the fellow had no self-control. Richard had known that, yet he'd left John in charge of England anyway. The resultant situation was as much Richard's fault as it was John's, and that was what upset Richard most.

The council was held in the great hall. Men packed themselves in. The weather had turned warm, and even with the windows open to the sea breeze, it was sweltering inside. Precious fabrics were splotched with sweat stains; the air reeked with the perfumes men wore to cover their odor. Men were present from every county in Europe and every barony in Outremer. There were bishops and archbishops, dukes and counts and earls. There were men four years from their homes and men who had arrived in the Holy Land that week.

Richard sat on the dais. Sweat glistened on his broad forehead; it flattened his copper-colored hair to his neck and temples. With him were the Grand Masters of the Temple and Hospital, as well as Guy of Lusignan, with the ever-present gold circlet in his hair.

As Richard looked out on the crowd, one figure caught his eye. He bounded from the dais and pumped the man's hand. "Geoffrey!" he exclaimed with delight. "I did not think to see you here. I was told you were near death."

Geoffrey of Trent looked pale and drawn; he had lost a lot of weight. His once-red beard was completely grey now, and his hair half so. He said, "My wife purchased a relic for me. It has—it has seemed to help. I have recovered some of my strength. As one of your senior commanders, I did not think I should miss this council."

"Well, I'm glad you came. It's good to see you up and about. Maybe I should get your wife to purchase a relic for me. God knows I could use one the way things are going."

He gripped the earl's shoulder companionably and ascended the dais once more. He gave a signal and trumpets blew, bringing the noisy room to silence. The packed crowd knelt while Richard's chaplain blessed them, then Richard rose and faced the assemblage. "My lords, I regret to inform you that urgent business requires my return to England."

That set off a a buzz round the hall.

Richard had expected more noise, but he guessed that the news must have leaked out. He raised a hand for quiet, and the hall gradually fell silent.

Richard went on. "I have called you here so that you may decide who will now lead the army."

There was whispering and talking, but it was conducted calmly, as if all this had somehow been discussed beforehand.

Richard raised his voice above the noise and continued. "We must end the arguing that has divided us for so long. For the sake of unity, I propose that Guy of Lusignan be formally crowned king of Jerusalem and named commander of the army."

Sitting in his chair nearby, Guy preened as much as he could while still trying to seem modest.

Another buzz ran round the room. Then, as if it had been rehearsed, spade-bearded Balian of Ibelin, most influential of the native barons, stepped forward. "Sire, you say that Lusignan should be our king, but that is not your choice to make. It is a choice for the barons of this kingdom, and the barons of the kingdom will have no one for their king but the marquis of Montferrat."

Before Richard could reply, the grizzled duke of Burgundy stepped forward as well. "And the army will have no one but the marquis for its commander."

Guy leaped to his feet. "Traitors!"

One-eyed Henry the Lion, lord of Deraa, eyed Guy balefully. " 'Twere best you leave the country, Lusignan. You are no longer welcome here."

Guy snorted. "You'll have to kill me first."

Henry smiled. "As you wish."

Guy flared with anger but was wise enough to make no further comment.

Richard was caught off guard; he had not expected this. All of the barons, save for his own vassals, seemed to be in predetermined accord. This rebellion, for that was what it was, must have been in the works for some time, probably under Conrad's direction, with Ibelin's assistance. Richard's imminent departure had precipitated it into the open.

Burgundy went on, "We are tired of dithering, Richard. We wish to march on Jerusalem, then go home."

The bishop of Beauvais added, "Whether you leave or stay, sire, the army desires a new commander. We should have been in Jerusalem by now. Instead we fortify Ascalon, to what purpose no one can say, save as a waste of time and money." This statement was a huge blow to Richard, as Beauvais had always been one of Richard's staunchest supporters.

Richard would have defended his Ascalon stratagem, but he never got the chance, as noble after noble—Raynard of Sidon, the counts of Dreux, Chalons and Holland, the archbishops of Ravenna and Mainz, even the Papal legate, the bishop of Verona—stepped forward to announce their support for Conrad and their discontent with Richard's handling of the crusade.

Richard endured it stoically, at least on the outside. When all was done, he turned to the one great noble who had yet to speak. "And you, Earl Geoffrey? What say you?"

Geoffrey of Trent drew himself up as best he could, given his weakened condition. "I am sorry, sire, but it is my belief that, with your departure, the crusade would be best served by making Marquis Conrad king of Jerusalem and commander of the army."

There were cries of approval from Trent's friends. Even the earl of Leicester, Richard's most loyal vassal, showed a thin smile of admiration at Trent's courage in going against his king.

Guy was open mouthed. "Are you going to let them do this?" he demanded of Richard. "This is defiance of my authority—of your authority. As king, it is my right to lead the crusade. You must—"

Richard silenced him with a wave of the hand. Guy was Richard's kinsman and Richard had assisted him as best he could. Ultimately, it was not enough, and nothing was going to change that.

Richard drew himself up and addressed the audience. "I will have King Guy renounce his claim to the crown—"

Guy protested. "You have no right to—"

Again Richard silenced him. "I will have Guy renounce the crown on one condition—that this council cede to him governance of Cyprus." Maybe Cyprus's wealth would assuage Guy's hurt feelings.

Philip of France was Cyprus's co-owner, and his representative, the duke of Burgundy, promptly said, "You may consider that done, sire."

"Very well," Richard said. Guy puffed himself up like he was about to protest again, but before he could, Richard turned to the count of Champagne. "Nephew, make all haste to the Marquis Conrad and inform him of this council's decision. Let Conrad's coronation be held in ten days' time in the city of Acre."

The hall erupted in cheering. Only Richard's most loyal supporters failed to join in, as did Geoffrey of Trent and the bishop of Beauvais, both of whom looked sad. To the jeers and catcalls of the native barons, Guy of Lusignan stalked from the hall without a word, still wearing his crown.

Richard stood stone faced amidst the shouting. Had ever a man fallen so far, and so quickly, as he had?

When he had arrived in the Holy Land, he had been treated as a conquering hero. After Arsuf, he was a demi-god. Now he was no longer wanted. In a few short months he had gone from being the next Alexander to being discarded.

How had it all gone so wrong?

Chapter 60

THE LITTLE PARTY crept through Qaymaz's palace. They had waited till after *isha*, the nighttime call to prayer, when the building would be as quiet as it was ever going to get.

Qaymaz's palace, which occupied more than half of the Blue Fort, was a maze of cleverly designed corridors with frequent turns, easy to get lost in. Ailith had never been in Bedford Castle at home, but she'd seen it from the outside, and compared with the Blue Fort, it looked like something a child had put together.

Ailith had been hoping that Lamiya knew a passage that would get them to the garden gate unobserved, and Lamiya had not disappointed. The plan was to exit the palace into the *harim* garden, then use a waiting ladder to go over the wall at the back of the garden and into the new gardens beyond. "There will be horses waiting in the new garden," Hassan had told Ailith and Margaret, "tied to a fig tree near the head of the irrigation ditch the slaves are building. Roger will meet you there. Do not wait too long for him, however. If he does not appear, save yourselves and ride east. Hide by day, when Qaymaz's men will be looking for you, and travel by night. May Allah look favorably upon your endeavors."

Ailith had given Lamiya what remained of her fifteen marks. "This is enough to buy your passage south," Ailith had told her. "After that, it's a matter of luck. A lot depends on the shipmaster or caravan leader you attach yourself to." She paused. "Are you sure you want to do this, Lamiya? An unscrupulous ship's captain might sell you into slavery again, under much worse circumstances than you face now."

"I am willing to take the risk," the African girl had replied with determination.

Now the three women moved along, their way lit by flickering shadows from an occasional torch. Lamiya went first, followed by Ailith and Margaret. Lamiya and Ailith had to keep stopping and wait for Margaret to catch up. The one-time washerwoman was limping badly, a pained grimace on her face.

At last they reached a plain wooden doorway that opened onto the *harim* garden. As they did, Lamiya stepped back and shouted into the darkness. "Here they are!"

Chapter 61

𝔄S IF BY magic, torches blossomed into light around them. From out of the glare appeared Aysun, along with the chief eunuch Narcissus, and a quartet of armed guards.

Aysun gazed lazily at Ailith. "Going somewhere?"

Ailith said nothing.

Aysun tisked. "Caught in the act of escaping. Even Qaymaz could not defend you from this. I suppose you thought you were going to return to return to your pagan friends?"

Again Ailith said nothing.

"Obviously your show of fealty to our master was a sham," Aysun continued, then let out an exaggerated sigh. "Qaymaz will be *so* disappointed." She smiled. "But of course you will be a dim memory ere he returns, so that will soften the blow."

She turned to Lamiya. "Impressive work, Lamiya. You have our thanks."

Lamiya bowed. "It was my pleasure, Preferred One."

Ailith looked to Lamiya, her cheeks burning from betrayal. "How could you? All that talk about hating it here. You tricked me."

Lamiya shrugged. "It was the price of being accepted in the *harim*." She laughed scornfully. "Anyway, you tricked yourself. What kind of fool thinks I would want to go back and live in a hut made of sticks?"

Aysun addressed Ailith once more. "So what are we to do with you? Something slow, I should think. Don't you agree, Narcissus?"

The big eunuch smiled with anticipation, but before he could say anything, Ailith grabbed Margaret's arm and shouted, "Run!"

Ailith jerked open the door—thank God it was unlocked—and the two women dashed into the darkened garden with a surprised Narcissus and the guards steps behind, Aysun and Lamiya trailing them.

Ailith cut to the right, trying to throw the pursuing guards off track. She and Margaret ran through the garden— or as fast as they could run with Margaret lagging behind the way she was—then they slowed. The noise of their running would tell their pursuers where they were. There was no moon, so they were totally unseen. The guards' torches cast cones of light into the darkness as they searched, but they illuminated little of the garden.

Stealthily, Ailith made her way toward the garden wall. She waited for Margaret to catch up. "The ladder is supposed to be at the northeast corner of the wall," Ailith whispered.

Margaret replied with a shake of the head, her big chest heaving. "I'm played out, my lady. That last bit o' runnin' done for me. I'm finished. You go on, I'll hold 'em off."

"No," said Ailith, shocked. "There's no way I'll —"

"Go on, my lady, or I'll curse you for a Trentshire peasant."

"But—"

Margaret shoved her. "Go!"

Ailith hesitated, then started for the wall.

❧

Margaret buried herself in the inky blackness behind the elaborately sculpted hedges near the fountain. Her ankle was on fire; she could barely put any weight on it—Christ knew what that bitch Aysun had done to it. She would have been a fatal drag on Ailith even had they reached the horses, so she had stayed behind, determined both to slow the pursuit and to extract some measure of revenge for what had been done to the two of them. She would have liked to have a go at Qaymaz, but that was not to be. God willing, someone else would do for him.

The entire palace was in an uproar now. More men poured into the garden. Margaret held her breath as two guards trotted past the fountain, wavering forms in the reflected light of their torches off the shimmering water.

She saw movement to her right. It was Aysun and a single guard. The guard carried a torch in one hand and his spear in the other. He held the spear lightly, not expecting trouble back here.

Another figure trailed them.

Lamiya.

Margaret waited until the guard was level with her. Quietly and with a quickness belying her size and the agony in her ankle, she stepped from the shadow and wrenched the spear from the startled man's hands.

Aysun sensed the movement and turned. "What—?"

That was all she got to say because Margaret plunged the spear into her chest, just below the breastbone. She jerked the spear free, turned and thrust it into the startled Lamiya's throat. She freed it once more and was looking to hurl it at the guard, but the guard's curved sword cleaved into her skull first . . . .

∾

The guards were just steps behind Ailith and gaining. She heard their footsteps. She would never make it, but she had to keep going.

She reached the far end of the garden, nearly running into the wall in the dark. Suddenly there was an anguished cry. Then another. The pursuing guards dropped away amid shouting and confusion, mixed with loud wailing. Margaret must have been successful. Ailith took advantage of the reprieve to move along the wall, using her hands to guide her, until she found what must be the northeast corner.

There was no ladder.

No time to think why, or to look for it. Behind her the torches were coming on again, anger in the guards' voices now. Whatever Margaret had done, it had enraged them.

The wall was higher than Ailith was tall. She backed up, took a few steps and jumped. Her fingers caught the top of the wall, but she couldn't hang on and fell off.

The torches were closer, the shouting confused. They hadn't seen her yet, but that would change in a few seconds.

She jumped again. Again her fingers caught, and this time she held on long enough to get a foothold on the stone wall. She hauled herself to the top, scraping the insides of her arms raw, than half fell, half threw herself over. She hit the ground hard, knocking the air out of her, lucky she hadn't broken anything. On the other side of the wall the shouts and torchlight were close. They had seen her go over.

Now she had to find the head of the irrigation ditch and the fig tree nearby. She smelled horses and headed in that direction. Behind her at least one torch was coming over the wall. She reached the fig tree, and there were the horses, three of them, saddled, with panniers of provisions and water on the saddles.

"Roger!" she called in a loud whisper.

Roger wasn't there.

The torches were close now. Ailith mounted one of the horses, considered leaving the other two but realized she might need them. Hassan had told her to save herself if Roger wasn't there. She swore and decided to do the one thing she wasn't supposed to do.

Leading the other two horses, she started for the slave quarters.

Chapter 62

"YOU SPEND TOO much time with the feringhees," Mahmoud scoffed at Hassan. "They are not worth it."

"Perhaps our master is tired of having to buy new slaves after you kill the old ones," the plump physician retorted.

"He gets most of his slaves for free," Mahmoud said.

"Then perhaps he's tired of always having to get more. I don't know the answer, I just do as I am told, and I have been told to take care of the slaves."

It was after supper. Hassan was making the rounds of the men in Hut Three, giving them medicine to reduce fever and diarrhea, patching wounds left by Mahmoud's staff. He came to Roger. "Don't waste your time with that one," Mahmound told him. "He won't be around long."

"What do you mean?" Hassan said.

Mahmoud smiled knowingly. "Call it a guess."

Hassan ignored him. Roger sat on his filthy straw pallet, fresh welts showing through what remained of his shirt. Hassan put salve on them, then he parted Roger's beard and examined the scar on his cheek. "It's a miracle that hasn't festered."

Roger wondered why Hassan was going on about the wound on his cheek; the scar had long since healed. Suddenly Hassan slipped an object from his sleeve into Roger's sleeve. Roger felt cold metal against his skin—the object was a knife.

"There are two horses in the *wadi* beyond the compound," Hassan murmured, still looking at the scar. "They were all I could obtain. The Lady Ailith will be waiting near the head of your irrigation ditch."

Roger sat straighter. "Ailith?"

"S-h-h," Hassan said.

Roger stared at him, then whispered, "You're a good friend, Hassan."

"I am happy to do it," Hassan explained. "I owe you my life."

Hassan finished making his rounds of the prisoners and left the hut. When he did, Mahmoud and the other guard, Yasir, left as well, bolting the door behind them. Roger considered how to escape the hut, then he smiled, because the first part of the plan he came up with would be both enjoyable and long overdue.

He rose and crossed the hut to where the dark-haired man-at-arms Borchard coversed with the sailor Tillo.

"*Monsieur* Borchard," Roger smiled, "Might I have a word?"

Borchard looked up at him with ill-concealed disdain.

"Please?" Roger said.

"Is that one of your knightly orders?"

"Call it a request," Roger said politely.

Swearing, Borchard rose. "What is—?"

Roger punched him in the jaw as hard as he could and sent him sprawling.

There was stunned silence in the hut, then Tillo tackled Roger, hitting him in the midriff, and both men went to the dirt floor. Tillo's intervention prompted Pentecost, Hillaire and Yves to join in, and the inside of the hut turned into a noisy brawl.

The hut door slammed open and the two guards ran in. Mahmoud laid about him with his staff. "Stop! Stop!" Yasir joined in halfheartedly.

The fighting ceased. The combatants separated. Mahmoud lashed the staff across Roger's face. "What is the cause of this disturbance?"

Roger took the blow without flinching. He slipped the knife from his sleeve and smiled. "I am."

With his left hand, Roger grabbed Mahmoud's arm, pulling Mahmoud toward him, driving the knife blade into Mahmoud's chest as he did and twisting it. "I only wish your death could have lasted longer," he said into Mahmoud's ear.

There was a startled expression on Mahmoud's bearded face. Then his eyes dimmed and he toppled into Roger, who shoved him to the floor.

The other guard, Yasir, tried to run, but Pentecost and the farmer Yves grabbed him and held him tightly, holding his mouth closed and pinning his arms. "Throw me that knife," Yves told Roger.

Yasir's face filled with terror.

"No," Roger said.

Yves said, "Why—?"

"Because he's treated us fairly. Gag him and tie him up."

Yves and Pentecost gagged and tied Yasir with strips torn from his own tunic. As they did, Roger turned and smiled at Borchard, who had risen to his knees. "Sorry, Borchy, but it was the only way I could think of to get those two in here." He addressed the other men in the hut. "Right, lads, I told you I was going to escape. Now, who's coming with me?"

Pentecost, Yves, Ahmed and Zoltan stepped up. Roger tossed Mahmoud's sword to Yves, while Pentecost took Yasir's weapon. "How did you get that knife?" Yves asked Roger.

"Don't worry about that now," Roger said. "Who else is going?"

The ancient priest Lambert sighed, shaking his head. "Thirty years ago I would have joined you, but I am too old now." He made the sign of the cross. "God grant you good fortune."

Borchard was on his feet now. "I'll join no party led by you," he sneered at Roger. The side of his face was red where Roger had hit him. "I'll wait to be rescued by our army."

"I'm staying as well," said the footman Hillaire. "I'll take my chances on a prisoner exchange."

"As will I," said the flabby merchant Alberic.

"I'll go," said Tillo. He noted the surprise on Borchard's face and added, "I'll do anything to get out of this shit hole."

Borchard said, "If you're going, so am I."

"Thought you wouldn't join a group with me," Roger said.

"Changed my mind," Borchard told him. He kicked Mahmoud's body as if that made him feel better somehow. "Now are we going or not?"

To those who were staying, Roger said, "Good luck, my friends. God be with you."

They left the hut one at a time, Roger leading. They moved quietly across the compound, keeping to the shadows. They made it to the wall unseen and headed for the gate.

"Now what?" whispered Yves when they were close to the gate.

Roger took a deep breath, then he left the shadows and ran up to the two guards at the gate. "Please," he pleaded breathlessly, gesturing at Hut Three, "there's a fight and the guards can't control it. I think one of them is dead."

Involuntarily, the guards looked to where he was pointing. As they did, Roger seized one from behind and slashed his throat with the knife, while Pentecost rushed forward and dispatched the other with Mahmoud's sword.

That gave them two more weapons—the dead guards' swords going to Tillo and Borchard.

"There are two horses waiting for us in the *wadi*," Roger told the men.

"Only two?" Borchard said.

"Better than none," Pentecost told him.

Roger unbarred the gate and the six men ran for the brush-filled *wadi*. They slid down the *wadi's* rocky side. The *wadi* was long and twisting. They were familiar with the it because they used it as a latrine during the day. "Where are these horses?" Borchard said skeptically.

"Stop yapping and look for them," Roger snapped.

Behind them horns were blowing; there was the distant cry of voices, of orders being issued. "They already know we're gone," Roger said. "I was hoping it would take them longer. Hurry—we don't have much time."

The men spread up and down the *wadi*, cutting themselves on thorns in the thick brush. Roger was in the center of the line, Borchard and Tillo ahead of him. There was movement around one of the *wadi's* many bends, muffled voices, the snort of a horse. "Did you find them?" Roger asked in a loud whisper.

No answer. He moved toward the sound, and as he did, two horses scrambled out of the *wadi* and galloped off into the night.

Roger left the *wadi* and chased them a few steps before giving up. "It's Tillo and Borchard," he told the others as they came up.

"Bastards," Pentecost said. "No more'n I'd expect of them."

Roger noticed something else. "Where's Ahmed?"

There was no sign of the young Arab. "I have not seen him since we left the compound," Zoran said. "I think he decided to make his own way home."

More horns were blowing. Horses approached the *wadi*.

Roger said, "We have to meet Ailith by the irrigation ditch behind the palace."

"Who's Ailith?" said Yves.

"The person who made this escape possible."

"Going up by the palace is too dangerous," Yves protested.

"Anyone who doesn't want to come with me is free to go his own way."

No one wanted to strike out on their own. The little party made its way toward the Blue Fort, while behind them the pursuing horses had reached the *wadi*. "They've picked up our trail," Yves said, looking back.

From the palace, horns blew, and now the sound of horses came from that direction, as well. There was no time to scatter and flee. The horses were almost upon them.

They formed a tight group and drew their weapons. As they did, the horses from the palace appeared out of the darkness. There were three of them, two without riders, and they were led by a woman, who had to swerve abruptly to avoid running down the men in the road.

"Ailith," Roger breathed. He and Ailith stared at each other for a moment, ignoring the stamping horses, then Roger said, "We thought you were Saracens."

"Close enough," Ailith told him. "They're right behind me."

"We'll have to ride double," Roger told the others. "Zoran, you're behind me. Yves and Pentecost, ride together."

The men mounted and they started off, heading east.

Chapter 63

THEY RODE THROUGH the darkness, with the drumming hooves of Qaymaz's men behind them. They had to go at less than a full gallop lest their horses injure themselves on the rough ground and so that they wouldn't tire out the two animals that were being ridden double.

"There's no way we can outrun them," Roger shouted to the others. "We need to lay up somewhere and hope they pass us by."

Soon a hill loomed to their right, its mass blocking out the stars. Roger pointed, "Up there."

They went up the hill, letting the horses pick their way in the dark, walking them at the end where it was steep. At the top was a fortress-like jumble of rocks, where they waited.

Their pursuers came closer. Hooves beat the earth, reached a crescendo, then passed by the hill and kept going. After a while they could no longer be heard.

Roger and his companions breathed a sigh of relief. "We'd better stay here tonight," Roger said. "We don't want to ride up their backsides in the dark, or run into them on their way back to Qaymaz's castle. We'll find another way off this hill tomorrow."

Roger realized he had forgotten something. "Gentlemen," he said formally, indicating Ailith, "this is Ailith, the lady responsible for our escape. We knew each other in England before all this started."

Zoran and Pentecost introduced themselves to Ailith, but Yves was suspicious. "Why does she dress like one o' them?" he asked.

Roger was about to reply, but Ailith beat him to it. "Because I was a slave," she said, "part of Qaymaz's *harim*."

There was a pause, Pentecost and Zoran digesting this information, Yves muttering something, then they settled in, making themselves as comfortable as they could. There was a coil of rope on one of the saddles, and they unsaddled the horses and hobbled them. There was no grazing for the animals up here, no water either. All of the men were in bad shape; their clothes were so ragged it was as if they had no clothes at all. They wrapped horse blankets around themselves against the night chill. The sweat they had worked up during the escape made them shiver as it dried.

Roger took a place beside Ailith, and almost immediately regretted it. A rush of old feelings flooded through him, feelings he had tried to suppress and that he wasn't sure he wanted to remember now.

"I need to thank you for what you did for us," he said awkwardly.

"There's nothing to thank me for. Thank Hassan if you want to thank someone."

"Still . . ."

"You would have done the same for me."

Ailith propped herself against her saddle and held out her horse blanket for Roger to share.

Roger hesitated.

"Come on," she said. "It's not like we haven't done this before."

Roger was still reluctant. It didn't seem right somehow, not after he'd revealed his feelings for her at Acre and she had spurned him for the earl of Trent.

"Oh, for Heaven's sake," she said. She slid close to Roger and wrapped her blanket and his around the both of them, molding her body to his for warmth. "This is like being in England again, when we were on the run from Gregorius and Auberie." Her voice softened. "It was a shock, seeing you at the Blue Fort."

"I was just as shocked seeing you. How did you end up there?"

"Your friend Dirk captured me during the attack on our camp. He carried me off and sold me to Qaymaz. Margaret, too."

"Where is Margaret?" Roger said.

"Dead." Ailith lowered her head. "She died so that I could escape."

She paused, as if she could not find words to express her feelings for Margaret. Then she said, "When did they capture you? Was it at the big battle?"

"Yes."

"They say we were beaten."

"No, we won. Saladin's army was routed. I saw Dirk with Qaymaz's men and left our formation to go after him."

Her voice went cold. "Did you . . ?"

Roger nodded slowly. "Yes."

"I'm glad. God help me, but I am."

Roger went on. "I was deep in the Saracen lines by then, and that's when I was captured. Qaymaz was there and he was about to kill me, when old Sidesaddle himself rode up and made him stop. Said he wanted me to live. Something about me and King Richard—I couldn't understand all they were saying."

"So Qaymaz made you a slave?"

"Yes."

"It must have been an ordeal. I've seen how the slaves get treated."

Roger shrugged.

"Qaymaz hates you," she said, "I don't know why. He told me he was still going to have you killed. It would be an 'accident,' he said. He's afraid Saladin is going to set you free or exchange you for a prisoner."

Roger didn't know why Qaymaz hated him either. Maybe he knew that Roger was the son of his worst enemy. "And what has your life been like?"

"Physically, not as bad as yours, as you can tell from my clothes. Mentally, it's been a nightmare. I've been a sex slave, forced to give myself to a man I loathe." She shuddered. "I feel so violated, so *unclean*. The worst part is, Qaymaz has treated me well. I'd rather he'd beaten me. Before he went back to the war, he told me that he loved me, that he wanted to make me his Preferred One, to bear his children. If I hadn't escaped, I think I would have killed myself."

She bit back a sob, and Roger took her hand. The hand felt cool. Despite her recent high status, her palm and fingers were callused from a lifetime of hard work. "It's all right now," he told her.

She sniffed. "Don't fool yourself. Just because we've escaped, doesn't mean we're safe. They'll come after us.

Narcissus' life is forfeit if he loses me, and he'll spare no effort in getting me back. I expect it's the same with you."

"Probably," Roger admitted.

He was suddenly very tired. For the first time, he relaxed against her, letting her warmth spread through him. She clung to him more tightly, as though for safety, and almost immediately they fell asleep.

Chapter 64

ZORAN LEFT THE group before dawn, while they were watering the horses from the bags provided on the saddles. "You are traveling east," he told them. "I go the opposite way, to Damascus. It is not a crime to be a Kurd in Damascus, I think."

"You're not worried about Qaymaz's men catching you?" Pentecost asked him.

"I do not think they are much interested in me," Zoran replied. "Or in you, my friend. It is Roger and the lady Ailith they want."

There was silence while that sank in, then Roger said, "Take one of the horses."

Smiling, Zoran shook his head. "I will walk. I have always walked. Anyway, you need the horses more than I do."

Roger took his hand. "Good luck to you, Zoran."

"And to you, my brother," Zoran said. "You will need it." He took the hands of Pentecost and Yves, as well, then put his hand over his heart and bowed to Ailith. "Lady."

Ailith returned his bow. Zoran turned and was lost in the predawn darkness.

As the sky lightened, they searched the eastern horizon. There was no sign of pursuing Saracens.

"Don't think they gave up, do you?" Pentecost said.

"No," Roger said. "Narcissus will be organizing a proper expedition to come after us. They'll pick up our tracks soon enough, and they'll have plenty of food and water and extra horses so they can ride us into the ground."

Pentecost and Yves exchanged glances.

Roger went on. "I know we shouldn't ride by day, but we need to put some distance between them and us. Get the horses saddled."

Zoran's departure left three horses for four people. Despite Ailith's protestations, Roger and Pentecost would not permit her to ride double with anyone. "Why not?" Yves said. "She's Qaymaz's doxy, let her ride double like the rest of us. Better yet, leave her here."

Roger drew himself up, and there was a warning note in his voice. "That's not going to happen."

Yves started to reply, but Roger cut him off. "Why are you so against Ailith?"

" 'Cause I don't trust her, that's why." Yves balled his fists and started toward Ailith. "Look at her, she's not one of us. She don't deserve to—"

Roger grabbed him. "Calm down! What's the matter with you? She didn't ask to be a slave. If she's caught, her fate will be far worse than ours. She wears those clothes because Qaymaz makes her do it."

Yves wrenched away from him. His eyes were alight; spittle flew from his lips. "It's different for you, you didn't lose everything to the Goat Fuckers. You didn't watch your wife raped to death. You didn't watch your children beaten and taken away where you'll never see them again. I'd kill every single one of them bastards if I could—men, women and children. I'd wipe them and their so-called religion from the face of the earth, and it still wouldn't be enough."

There was a taut silence, then Ailith spoke calmly, soothingly. "I'll change into something else if these clothes bother you so much."

Yves took a deep breath. The red in his tanned cheeks faded; his crazed eyes returned to something like normal. "No, you're all right. Forget what I said, I didn't mean nothing by it. It's just that I . . ." His voice tailed off.

"I understand," Ailith told him. "I'd probably feel the same way."

Embarrassed, Yves attempted to diffuse the situation with humor. "Besides, what are you going to change into? You didn't bring a wardrobe with you."

Ailith smiled. "I was hoping you wouldn't take me up on my offer."

They left the hill, going down the opposite side from the one they came up, doing their best to hide their tracks. The ground was level at the bottom, and they headed west, the sun at their backs. They rode all that day and all night, as well, and as dawn lit the eastern sky on the second day, they got off the path they had been following and camped in the lee of a small hill to the north. It wasn't a great spot—it wasn't even a good spot—but because the ground was so level here, it was the best spot they could find. They watered the horses and kept guard, taking turns lying at the top of the hill and watching their back trail.

Their legs and backsides ached from riding, the skin rubbed raw. There was no shade. The sun burned down. Their throats were dry and caked with dust. Save for a swallow, they saved all the water for the horses.

"I cursed the rain when we were back at camp, but I wish we had some now," said Yves, who was just above them on guard. Looking down the hill, he added, "Sorry what I said about you, Lady Ailith."

"It's forgotten," Ailith told him. "And don't call me 'lady.' I'm just Ailith."

Yves returned to guard, while Roger, Ailith and Pentecost lay against the side of the hill. Ailith studied Roger's bearded cheek. "Nice scar."

"I got it the day before Acre fell," Roger said.

"That's what you get for playing soldier."

Roger pretended to be put out. "People tell me it makes me look distinguished."

"They lie."

Next to them, Pentecost lay with his eyes half closed against the heat and the brightness of the sun. "What are you going to do when we get out of this?"

For Roger the answer was obvious. "I'll go back to the Death's Heads. If any of them are still alive, or if they haven't left for home." They'd heard no news about the crusade; it might be over for all they knew. "What about you?" he asked Pentecost.

"Reckon I'll go back to the army as well. Not like I got any other choice."

"The Hospitallers?" Roger said.

"Dunno. Everybody I knew in the Hospitallers is dead or a slave."

From above, Yves said, "I can't be a farmer again, my land is gone. Guess I'll join the army, too. Maybe get some of my own back."

Pentecost looked at Roger. "Would you take us in your Death's Heads?"

"Be happy to," Roger said. "We've no crossbowmen, though. We're spearmen and axe men, with a few archers."

"Any o' them's all right with me."

"Me, too," said Yves.

Pentecost turned to Ailith. "What about you, miss? What are you going to do when we get back?"

Ailith sighed. "I haven't thought about it. I've been learning music, maybe I'll be a troubadour." They grinned, then she grew fatalistic. "I can always be a washerwoman again, I suppose. It's not like there's no need for them."

Suddenly Yves exclaimed, "Look!"

The others crawled to the top of the hill, peeking their heads over, shading their eyes from the sun. In the distance, they saw a column of mounted men, headed east, Saracens by the way they rode.

"I'll bet it's Qaymaz's men," Ailith said. "The ones who were chasing us last night. They're returning to the Blue Fort."

They waited and watched, the sun beating down. Eventually the column resolved itself into a troop of Saracen cavalry. In the middle of the column rode two bare-headed men, one dark haired, one short and burly. They were tied up and bloodied.

"Poor bastards," Pentecost said. Then he stiffened. "Say, that first one looks like Borchard. Hard to tell, he's beat up so bad."

Yves said, "The other one is Tillo—by Christ, I can barely recognize him. Serves 'em right, stealing our horses and running out on us like they done."

"Don't envy what's going to happen to 'em, though," Pentecost said. "No one deserves that. They must have kept going on the same road we was on, and the Goat Fuck—beg your pardon, ma'am—and the Saracens followed their tracks and caught up with 'em."

Left unspoken was the thought that Borchard and Tillo's impending fates might easily have been their own.

Late in the day, they were all back up the hill, watching again, because a dust cloud, made golden by the setting sun, had appeared in the east.

"That'll be Narcissus," Roger said, "hunting us. I think it's time for us to go."

Chapter 65

THAT NIGHT THEY entered a belt of forest not unlike the one in which Roger had been captured—rough ground and boulders and clean-scented pine trees. There was no talking. Because of the trees and the broken ground, Roger and Ailith became separated from Pentecost and Yves, whose turn it was to ride double. As the sound of their companions' horse receded to the right, Roger wanted to call out to them, but he couldn't because there was no way of knowing if Saracens were around. After a while they couldn't hear the other horse at all.

Later they came upon a shallow stream. Despite the April rains, this was the first fresh water they'd encountered since their escape. Roger and Ailith let their thirsty horses drink, then refilled the water bags and drank themselves. The water was cold and refreshing after a day in the scorching sun. They drank their fill, waited, then drank again.

Still no sign of Pentecost and Yves.

"Where do you think they went?" Ailith said.

Roger shrugged. "I don't know, but we can't wait here for them. They'll have to catch up."

Not long before dawn, the trees thinned. The land leveled out and became arid again, the thin grass already turning sere. They would have liked to follow the stream, but that was the obvious route for them to take, the one their pursuers would probably use to follow them, so they covered their tracks by entering the stream, then exiting further down in a *wadi*. The *wadi*'s bottom had dried to mud, which was ideal for leaving tracks, but it was also extremely rocky, and Roger hoped that would make their trail hard to spot. They stayed in the *wadi*, which ran north of east. As light returned to the land, they unsaddled and tethered the horses. They climbed the *wadi*'s side and looked in all directions, but the two missing men were nowhere to be seen.

"Maybe they've already laid up for the day," Roger said, "or maybe they got disoriented in that forest and went the wrong way."

"Or maybe they decided they were safer not being with us," Ailith said pointedly.

Neither mentioned the possibility that the two men had been caught.

The sun rose higher and the dust of their pursuers became visible. It was decidedly closer than it had been yesterday.

Ailith's face fell. "We're not going to make it. They'll catch us before we reach the coast."

She gripped Roger's arm. "Promise me something—you won't let them take me alive."

Roger stared at her.

"I'm serious. Qaymaz will want revenge for my escape and for my helping you to escape. And that revenge is likely to be extremely unpleasant."

This unexpected request set Roger's mind racing. Killing Ailith was something he could not contemplate. "What if Qaymaz doesn't take revenge? What if he's willing to take you back? You said that he loves you."

"No. I'd rather be dead." She grabbed his sleeve again. "Promise me."

Roger attempted to humor her. "All right, I promise."

"I mean it, Roger. I want you to swear an oath to the Virgin Mary."

Roger caught his breath. An oath was unbreakable.

"Do it," she pressed. "Swear on the blood on the Virgin."

"I—"

"Do it!"

Roger took a deep breath. Solemnly he said, "I swear on the blood of the Virgin that I will not let Qaymaz—"

"Not just Qaymaz—any Saracen."

"That I will not let the Saracens take you alive."

That seemed to make her feel better, and she lay down in the mottled shade of some brush.

What have I done? Roger thought. Deeply troubled, he climbed the *wadi* and studied their back trail once more. Their pursuers, course seemed a bit different than their own, more easterly.

"They're following the stream," Roger told Ailith, "heading away from us. They must not have seen our tracks. If they keep to the course they're on, there's a good chance they'll miss us."

Ailith joined him and watched. "Please God they do."

That night they started off again. As they grew nearer to the sea, there were orange and lemon groves, along with scattered villages. They decided to risk being seen and push on past dawn, to reach a rocky ridgeline that promised a better hiding place than the flat ground they were on now.

As the sky lightened, a bell tinkled, and suddenly, as though conjured from the ground, there was a boy tending a herd of goats.

The boy stared at them. He looked somewhere between nine and eleven years of age. He wore a *dishdasha*, the long Arab shirt, a skullcap and sandals. Acting as though it was perfectly natural for a filthy man in tattered Western clothing and a blonde woman wearing expensive clothes meant for indoor use to be out here, Roger raised a hand in greeting and smiled at the boy.

The boy did not respond. He stared at them.

Roger and Ailith kept going, heading for the rocky ridge. Ailith glanced back. The boy was still staring at them.

"We should have killed him," Ailith said.

"I know," Roger said.

"The stream's not that far. He could tell Qaymaz's men where we are."

"I know! I couldn't kill a boy, though. I couldn't."

Quite unexpectedly, Ailith smiled. "I'm glad. You did the right thing."

"And if we're taken because of it?"

"As someone I know always says—it's God's plan."

They reached the red-orange rock of the ridge, went part way up it and looked back.

The dust cloud had changed course. It was headed directly at them.

Ailith sighed. "I wish God's plan worked in our favor for once."

Roger agreed. "I know He's testing us, but I get tired of being tested."

The pursuers were coming on fast. Before long, Roger and Ailith could make out individuals in the dust, spread like dots in a line across the plain. To the rear, two awkward-looking beasts that must be camels carried supplies, and there was a string of spare horses. A large black dot rode in front of the group.

"That's Narcissus," Ailith said.

There was a distant yell. One of the dots seemed to be gesticulating at something on the ground.

"They found our tracks," Roger said.

Ailith licked her sun-cracked lips. She didn't say anything. She didn't have to.

"They'll be on us soon," Roger said. He peered up the slope. "We'll have to let the horses go and try to lose ourselves in the rocks."

"But without the horses . . ."

"If we run for it, those men will catch us. Our horses are too big for us to hide them in these rocks. Without them, we might be able to find a bolt hole where the Saracens will miss us. It's our only chance." *And a damned small one*, he thought.

They unsaddled the horses and drank as much as they could from the water bags. The animals remained where they were for the moment, but it wouldn't be long before they wandered in search of forage. The Saracens would find them and care for them, so at least something good would come of this. Roger took Ailith's hand and the two of them started up the ridge, picking their way through the rocks.

Higher and higher they climbed. Roger's heart was racing from exertion, his breathing grew labored. He had lost a lot of his endurance in his months as a slave. Ailith kept up with him, though not without difficulty. She'd gotten little exercise in the *harim*. Her silk bodice and dress were filthy and torn; her fair hair had come loose from its braid. Her thin slippers were cut to shreds, and her feet left smears of blood on the rocks. Hurriedly Roger wrapped strips from what was left of his shirt around her feet.

Below, they heard voices. "The Saracens found the horses." Roger said. "Probably picked up our tracks as well. Hard to hide that blood."

They kept climbing, silently as possible, careful to place their feet on rock where they could, so as not to disturb the soil. Roger's foot slipped on a rock, dislodging it. The rock tumbled down the hill in a little shower of stones, eliciting excited shouts from below.

Roger swore. He readjusted his grip on Ailith's hand and they kept going.

"How come whenever I'm with you we're being chased by somebody who's trying to kill us?" Ailith puffed.

"It was just the one time," Roger told her.

"Are you sure? It seems like a lot more."

Narcissus's men were gaining ground on them; the noise they made kept getting louder. Roger and Ailith were tired and thirsty. They half stumbled, half tripped down an incline into a jumbled maze of boulders, looking for someplace— any place—to hide. One side of the depression was a multi-planed slab of rock, and between two of the planes Roger saw a crevice. The crevice seemed just wide enough for a man to squeeze into. There was nowhere else to run, no other hope, and even this hope was for a miracle.

"Come on," he told Ailith.

Ailith was doubtful. "What happens if we get stuck in there?"

"The same thing that happens if we don't try. Now come on."

He wedged into the crevice and pushed himself along, the orange rock alternating with swirly layers of grey. The crevice narrowed until he was barely able to move, scraping his knees and elbows raw on the harsh rock as he tried to get through.

Ailith was right behind him. "How are you doing?" he asked her.

"How do you think I'm doing? It's easy for you, you're all skinny from starving yourself the last six months. I been eating regular."

Abruptly the crevice widened and they found themselves in a sort of cavern. The cavern was not very deep. There was a narrow opening in its high ceiling, but the sun did not reach the bottom at this time of the day—if it ever reached the bottom at all—leaving the cavern in semi-darkness. It was damp and moldy, and the rock floor was slick.

Like a grave, Roger thought.

"Do you think they'll search in here?" Ailith asked.

Yes. "I hope not."

Ailith pulled Roger's knife from his waist and handed it to him. "Remember," she reminded him. They pressed themselves against the cavern's far wall, where the shadows were deepest, and awaited the inevitable.

There were footsteps on the hillside above them. Men speaking in low voices. A higher-pitched voice giving orders—that must be the eunuch, Narcissus. Roger gripped the knife and wondered if he would be able to kill Ailith when the time came, because the time would surely come in a matter of moments.

He'd taken a sacred oath to kill her, and he couldn't break that oath on pain of Hell, but he was bound for Hell already for killing Auberie, so what was the difference? Would Ailith really be better off dead than recaptured? And why had God made that a question for Roger to decide?

A clatter of stones. Someone sliding down the incline near their hiding place. Roger readied the knife. He would slit Ailith's throat, then go for the Saracen. At least he could take one of the bastards with him. Ailith braced herself against the cavern wall.

Cautious footsteps beside the crevice. Would the Saracen think Roger and Ailith could have wedged themselves through it?

The footsteps stopped. Roger and Ailith held their breaths. From above, someone called to the Saracen and he replied. His friends knew where he was now, and they'd come looking for him if he failed to return. There was no longer any chance of hiding from them.

The Saracen entered the crevice, grunting, cursing, struggling to force his way through the narrow opening.

"There's something I have to tell you," Ailith said, and there was urgency in her voice.

"Sh-h-h!"

"But—"

"Later," Roger said, though there would be no later.

Roger raised the knife to Ailith's throat, the blade against her sweat-streaked skin. He prayed and prayed that the Saracen would turn back, but the man kept coming.

The knife at Ailith's throat wobbled.

He couldn't kill her.

But he had taken an oath.

He had taken an oath, and he had to do it.

With a last heave, the Saracen plunged through the crevice into the cavern, his curved dagger ready to strike. Roger started the knife into Ailith's throat, realized at the last second he couldn't go through with it, pulled the knife back and sprang at the Saracen.

The two men stopped.

The Saracen was Yasir, the guard from Hut Three whom Roger had left bound and gagged.

Roger and Yasir stared at each other, neither man willing to strike the first blow. Ailith, who was unaware that Roger knew the Saracen, looked from one to the other in puzzlement.

After a long second, Yasir hesitantly lowered his dagger. Roger did the same with his knife.

Yasir placed a finger to his lips, motioning upward. Then he inched back out of the crevice, and they heard him climbing the incline.

Roger and Ailith did not relax. What if Yasir had merely backed off to save his own life? What if he was going to bring Narcissus and the whole pack of them down on their hiding place?

They heard Yasir say something to the men above him. They couldn't understand his words, but the tone was obvious: "There's no one there."

Narcissus swore, and the Saracens moved on up the hill. After a while, they came back down, muttering, wondering how the feringhees could have gotten away. Narcissus berated his men, and his voice was tinged with desperation, presumably because he knew his fate if Ailith and Roger weren't found.

Ailith turned to Roger, eyes wide. "Why did he do that?" she whispered.

Roger shook his head in amazement. "God's plan."

"Thanks for killing me, by the way."

"Sorry. I'll make it up to you later."

Roger and Ailith remained where they were the rest of the day. "Stay quiet as you can," Roger told her. "If I was Narcissus, I'd leave men behind to see if we emerge from a hiding place."

Sure enough, toward dusk, they heard the footsteps of what sounded like a pair of men above them, retreating down the hill.

Not long after, Roger and Ailith pushed through the crevice. Ailith knelt and made the sign of the Cross, her eyes closed. "What now?" she said as she stood.

"Now we walk," Roger said.

They edged down the hill and started across the rocky plain. It was full dark now, with only a carpet of stars overhead to light their way. They walked for what seemed like forever. They were so tired and hungry, thirsty and footsore that they could barely remain upright. They half-closed their eyes and let their heads droop, as though to get some sleep at the same time as they moved.

After what seemed forever, Roger stopped, holding Ailith back with his arm. "There—do you smell it?"

Swaying on her feet, Ailith lifted her head. Then she realized what it was. "The sea."

There were no whoops of joy; they were too tired for that. But the realization that they were near the coast gave them renewed energy. Their footsteps were lighter now, their heads higher.

They topped a rise and saw a bright glow in the distance.

"A city," Roger breathed. "Acre—it has to be."

They stood there, staring at the distant light, spellbound by it, smelling the salt air. Roger could almost hear waves caressing the beach.

"We made it," Ailith said in a tone that said she could scarcely believe it.

Roger turned to her. "Now what was it you wanted to tell me so badly back there?"

She took a deep breath and started to reply, but he went on. "Here we're about to be killed, and of all the times to pick, you—"

"Would you let me get a word in edgewise!" she said.

Roger stopped.

She went on. "I wanted to tell you that I love you."

Roger's eyes widened in surprise, and she stared into them. "I've always loved you, even when I said I didn't. I'm sorry things worked out the way they did between us. I was such a—"

Roger pulled her to him and kissed her. It was her turn to be taken by surprise, then she kissed him back, eagerly, her eyes wet with hot tears.

The kiss lasted a long time. When it was done, Roger held Ailith close and ran his fingers through her hair. She closed her eyes and rested her head against his chest. "I lied when I said that kiss back in England didn't mean anything to me. The truth is, I've never forgotten it."

Roger took her by the shoulders and looked into her eyes. "I never should have left you that day."

She smiled up at him. "I never should have let you go."

They kissed again.

EPILOGUE

"YOUR WIFE'S STILL getting dressed, sire. Swears she won't be but a minute."

"Well, there's a surprise," Conrad remarked drily. Isabelle was always late, and to her a "minute" could mean the half-turn of an hourglass. But Conrad was fond of the little minx and he couldn't be angry with her. The archbishop's dinner probably wouldn't start on time, anyway—he was as bad as she was.

"You going to wait here, sire? Want me to bring you some refreshment?"

"No thank you, Otto. I think I'll go outside and stretch my legs."

"Very well, sire." Conrad was not officially crowned yet, but people were already calling him 'sire.' "I'll assemble an escort."

"That won't be necessary," Conrad said. "I'll just take Guerin and Aleaume." He nodded toward two big men in the corner.

"Is that wise, sire?"

Conrad laughed. Otto had been a man-at-arms, a good one, and a favorite of Conrad's. He'd been severely wounded at the battle of Camerino, years ago, and couldn't fight after that, so Conrad had made him his steward. Otto was fiercely loyal to Conrad, and Conrad feared he was becoming over protective. "Don't be such an old hen, Otto. I'm just going for a walk up the street, nothing will happen to me. I'll be back

377

in a bit to fetch Isabelle. You may assemble a full escort then."

The hatchet-faced steward frowned; he plainly didn't like this. "Are you—"

"Yes, Otto, I'm sure."

Otto acquiesced and bowed. "As you will, sire."

Conrad rose from the window seat, from which vantage point he had been observing the teeming street below—a different view than the one from his castles at home, where he'd been accustomed to living on isolated cliff tops and mountainsides. He adjusted the black biretta on his shaven head and smoothed the yellow silk robe that showed off his massive chest. Since Conrad had been selected for the kingship, the biretta had become increasingly popular in Tyre—and in Acre, as well, if rumor was to be believed. The shaven head made Conrad look appropriately fearsome, but he mainly did it because long hair made his scalp itch.

There were many preparations still to be made for the coronation, which was in two days' time. Conrad and Isabelle would sail for Acre tomorrow, and Archbishop Josicus was hosting a farewell dinner tonight for those nobles of Tyre unable to accompany the royal party.

"Royal party"—the phrase had a nice ring to it. Conrad had begun as a simple crusader, arriving with a small retinue on a ship from Genoa, and he had already achieved far more than he had ever dreamed possible. Lordship of a wealthy city, a beautiful young wife whom he plowed whenever he wanted—and he wanted it a lot—and now a crown.

Soon he would be a major power in the Levant; the two obstacles to that happening had finally been removed. First, that idiot Lusignan had been sent packing to Cyprus. Conrad was honest enough to admit a certain kinship between himself and Lusignan—they were both adventurers. The difference between them was that Lusignan's talents lay in seducing women and flattering rich men, whereas Conrad had actual military, diplomatic and administrative skills. Conrad would make the kingdom of Jerusalem important again, more important than it had ever been, and that was something Lusignan never could have done.

The second obstacle had been Richard of England. For all his prowess as a warrior, the crusade would have been better off had Richard never come. All he had accomplished in his time here was to keep Conrad from the throne.

Conrad cracked a rare smile as he descended the wide interior steps of his palace. Once he was king, he would consolidate his power and wait for Saladin's failing health to run its course. After that, there would be civil war among Saladin's sons—and perhaps his brother—for the succession. Conrad would be patient, chipping away at the edges of Saladin's empire, more of an annoyance than a serious threat to anyone, and then, when the Saracens were at their most disorganized, he would strike. A lightning campaign would take back Jerusalem and the rest of the kingdom that had been lost—and maybe a lot more.

The crusaders from the west wouldn't like the delay, of course. They wanted Conrad to march on the Holy City right away—it was one of the reasons they had supported him to be king. But the truth was, he had played them false to get that support. He could accomplish what he wanted without them. They had a timeline, and he didn't. He wasn't going home like they were—this was his home. Besides, there would always be a steady stream of young men from the west, eager to fight infidels, from whom he could build up his forces.

He left the palace and entered the crowded street. Guerin and Aleaume struggled to stay close to him in the mob. Conrad had made Tyre a cosmopolitan city. There were men from every county in Christendom, Muslims from every principality in the East, along with Africans, Greeks and an occasional mustachioed fellow from far-off India. There were soldiers, merchants, whores, men hawking goods and foodstuffs of every variety. There were horses and camels and men playing flutes. Men laughing, men shouting, men singing bawdy songs, women with lithe figures and veiled faces. There was even a snake charmer, and Conrad paused beneath a colorful awning to watch him.

He started off again, and again his bodyguards got separated from him in the press. People recognized him and edged away in respect, even as they cried, "Good day, sire!"

Conrad responded with a good-natured wave; he could afford to be good natured on this day. In a moment he would return to his house. Maybe there would be time for a quick coupling with Isabelle. She would fuss about her expensive clothes getting rumpled before the big dinner, but he didn't care.

He reached the cathedral and was about to turn for home, when he spied the young priest in training, Michael, crossing the street toward him, hands stuffed in his bell-like sleeves. Michael, who was attached to his household, was studious, and Conrad enjoyed sitting with him of a rainy day debating obscure bits of theology.

"Michael, my young friend!" Conrad exclaimed. "How are you?"

Michael bowed low and smiled, unusual for one so serious. "Greetings, sire. Shouldn't you be at the archbishop's house for dinner?"

"I'm waiting for my wife to get dressed," Conrad said. He let out a mock sigh. "You religious fellows don't know how good you have it."

Serious again, Michael said, "If you have a moment, sire, I'm curious about a point you made when last we met."

Abu Flath, once called Tarik, couldn't believe his luck. He had finally been given the order to carry out his mission, and at the same moment, his target had become nearly impossible to get close to. In frustration, abu Flath had already booked passage to Acre, in hopes that he would have better luck there, but now, by the grace of Allah, here was his target in front of him, trailed by two clumping bodyguards who were too far behind to be of any assistance.

Abu Flath said, "If you have a moment, sire, I'm curious about a point you made when last we met."

Conrad creased his heavy brow, as if trying to remember. "Which point was that?"

"This sharp one."

Abu Flath pulled the expensive dagger that Sinan had given him from his sleeve and thrust it at Conrad's chest. He aimed at the German's heart, intending to stab him again and again in a series of rapid strokes, but Conrad was incredibly fast for a man of his size, and he turned just enough so that the knife went into his side, instead. Abu Flath felt the blade go through Conrad's yellow robe and shirt, through skin and gristle, felt it slide across a rib.

Conrad grunted and tried to steady himself, ironically using abu Flath's shoulder for support. Abu Flath drew the blade from Conrad's side and stabbed again, again trying to get at Conrad's heart, but the angle was bad and the blade merely scraped Conrad's chest. By this time Conrad was falling and people were crowding around, trying to see what was going on, blocking abu Flath from another attempt.

"He's fainted!"

"Get him water!"

"He ain't fainted, he's been stabbed. Look at that blood!"

"Did you see who did it?"

"Goat Fucker—had to be."

Incredibly, no one seemed to realize that the young priest standing there was the one who had attacked Conrad. Abu Flath tried to force his way closer to his victim and finish the job, but he was cut off by the growing mob of people.

Then the two bodyguards were there, beating people away with curses and the backs of their swords. A whistle sounded. Abu Flath knew he would not be able to complete his mission, not now, so he backed away, losing himself in the crowd, and withdrew to contemplate what he must do next.

The street was in an uproar; Abu Flath saw a Muslim merchant on the ground, being stomped by the mob. He slipped into the nearest building, the cathedral, where he might gather his thoughts.

It was dark and cool in the cathedral. Empty, too, since everyone had left to see what the commotion in the street was about. The noise from outside was muted here. Abu Flath pondered his next step. He had been expected to die on this mission, so there was no question of his returning to the Eagle's Nest. Sinan would make him jump off the mountain if he came back a failure, so he had to devise a new plan. It might take him months to get near Conrad again, because Conrad was sure to be guarded closely after this. Abu Flath would have to change his appearance, as well. A soldier, perhaps..?

Loud voices. Footsteps on stone.

"Make way, you fool, make way. Get him out of the sun."

"How is he?"

"He'll be all right, God be praised. It's not a bad wound, but it's too far to carry him to his house. Put him there and summon the physicians."

"Put a guard on the doors, too—and find some water."

They were bringing Conrad into the cathedral. They laid him on the stone floor, making a pillow with someone's cloak, stemming Conrad's wound with strips torn from the hem of his yellow robe.

"Move back, there! Move back! Give him air!"

Abu Flath stared from the shadows, scarcely believing his good fortune. Truly Allah was great. Abu Flath stuffed his hands in his sleeves and started for the group.

"Where's that damned doctor?"

"Here he comes—the priest!"

"Out of the way, give him room."

As abu Flath grew closer, Conrad raised his head and saw him. "That's no doctor!" he cried. "That's the man who stabbed me."

"What!" men said, disbelieving. But before they had a chance to stop him, abu Flath raised both hands and plunged the razor-sharp dagger into Conrad's heart. Blood sprayed abu Flath even as the feringhees were pulling him away from the dying man.

Somebody held abu Flath by the collar. Blows rained down. His nose shattered, his face was wet, an eye seemed to explode, teeth were dislodged.

Then it stopped.

"Why did you do this? Who paid you?" said a garlic-and-wine-scented voice that he did not recognize. He was pounded in the jaw. "Who paid you!"

Sinan had ordered abu Flath to resist their questions as long as he could, in order to make his answer seem more plausible, but he thought of what was in store for him from the barbarian feringhees—eyes gouged out with red-hot pokers, fingernails pulled, bones smashed with hammers— and he was no longer a fierce killer. He just wanted to get it over with. Allah save him, he did not want to undergo their torture. He wanted to be back home with his mother and sister. He wanted to enter Paradise.

"King Richard did it!" he cried through broken teeth. "It was King Richard who paid me!"

Author's Note

Richard the Lionheart's name sometimes appears on lists of history's great generals, which seems odd because his military reputation rests almost entirely upon the battle of Arsuf. In the same fashion, Arsuf occasionally appears on lists of the world's great battles. The battle itself was indecisive, so perhaps the fascination with it endures because it featured the two foremost commanders of the age—Richard and Saladin.

As with anything concerning the Middle Ages, it is difficult to discover the true facts of the battle, but in general they are as I have presented them. It seems to have been a near-run thing, with a possible Saracen victory spoiled by the crusaders' counterattack. There are two eyewitness accounts. Beha ad-Din, Saladin's chronicler, says the counterattack was a well-coordinated move involving Richard's entire army; while Ambroise, a Norman minstrel in Richard's employ, claims in his *Histoire* that Richard would have destroyed Saladin's army had the rear guard not attacked prematurely. He blames the attack on the Hospitaller's marshal, William Borrel. Richard later claimed the same thing. Interestingly, Ambroise also hints that the rear guard was in more or less desperate straits and in danger of being overrun when the counterattack occurred.

Richard's massacre of the Acre prisoners tends to be glossed over by a number of his biographers, as though they do not wish to tarnish his reputation. Their general consensus is that it was unfortunate but a military necessity. I leave the reader to decide.

The killing of Conrad of Montferrat was almost certainly carried out by the Assassins, but who ordered—or paid--for it is in doubt. At the time, it was widely believed that King Richard was responsible for the murder, though this seems out of keeping with his character. The consensus now seems to be that it was ordered by the Old Man of the Mountain, Sinan, in retaliation for a shipload of goods that Conrad had stolen from him. This is possible, but it is curious that the man who had the most to benefit from Conrad's death—Saladin—is rarely considered as being responsible for it. Perhaps this is because Saladin's PR department, if I may use the term, is as strong now as it was in the 12th century. People simply refuse to believe that the sultan could have done anything unchivalrous. He is regarded as the Muslim version of "the perfect Christian knight," which is possibly why the contest between him and Richard continues to fascinate.

As in *Death's Head*, I have simplified the facts of the story. The peace negotiations were incredibly complex and, beyond the bare facts, likely of little interest to the reader. And, yes, Richard did offer his sister in marriage to al-Adil, though historians are mixed on how serious he was. I have once again narrowed the cast of characters, because to include all the personages involved with the crusade would make the story needlessly confusing.

Richard did throw Leopold of Austria's banner into the ditch at Acre. Leopold, however, had the last laugh. On the way home from the crusade, Richard was shipwrecked, and, in disguise, attempted to make his way overland to friendly territory. He was captured by none other than Leopold, who, after holding him prisoner for some months, turned him over to the Holy Roman Emperor. The emperor, in turn, held Richard for a ransom that is estimated to have totaled two to three times the annual income for the entire country of England. Despite the enthusiasm with which obtaining the funds for this ransom is depicted in Robin Hood movies, it is difficult to imagine that the average Englishman was thrilled about paying it.

Lastly, all the relics mentioned in this narrative actually existed.

As always, any historical inaccuracies in this story are entirely my fault. Roger of Huntley's story will continue with the next volume of this series, *Death and Glory*.

About the Author

Robert Broomall is the author of a number of published novels. Besides writing, his chief interests are travel and history, especially military history, the Old West, and the Middle Ages. He also likes to cook, much to the dismay of those who have to eat what he prepares.

Amazon author page: https://www.amazon.com/author/robertbroomall

Facebook:
https://www.facebook.com/RobertBroomall.author

Connect with Bob: robertbroomall@gmail.com

14574285R00221

Made in the USA
Lexington, KY
08 November 2018